"...we're crazy."

"I'm beginning to wonder about us myself." Justin grinned. "I can't remember the last time I had a paint fight."

"Me, either." Allison chuckled.

"But I liked the result." His gaze suggestively returned to her lips.

"Justin!"

His roguish grin was unapologetic. "I can't help it. When I get close to you, I almost forget that I'm a thirty-three-year-old father. It's like I'm back in school."

"And you have a crush on your English teacher."

His expression grew serious. "Allison Greene, I never had a teacher like you. And the things I feel and think when I'm with you have absolutely nothing to do with elementary education." He added, "On the other hand, I've been out of circulation for a long time. Maybe you *could* teach me a thing or two...."

ABOUT THE AUTHOR

After writing the dramatic "Angel" series, Kathy
Clark wanted to work on something lighter in
tone. She had a lot of fun writing *Good Morning,
Miss Greene*. Anyone who has ever had a child or
been manipulated by one will surely understand
Allison and Justin's dilemma. Kathy is extremely
proud to report that #366 *Angel of Mercy* was
awarded the *Romantic Times* Reviewer's Choice
Award as the best Harlequin American Romance
of 1990.

Books by Kathy Clark

HARLEQUIN AMERICAN ROMANCE

224–SWEET ANTICIPATION
282–KISSED BY AN ANGEL
333–SIGHT UNSEEN
348–PHANTOM ANGEL
366–ANGEL OF MERCY
383–STARTING OVER

KATHY CLARK

GOOD MORNING, MISS GREENE

Harlequin Books

TORONTO • NEW YORK • LONDON
AMSTERDAM • PARIS • SYDNEY • HAMBURG
STOCKHOLM • ATHENS • TOKYO • MILAN

This book is dedicated to all the unsung heroes of our society—our schoolteachers. You are the single greatest influence on all our tomorrows.

A special thanks to my sons' kindergarten teachers, Bonnie Gilas, Juniel Worthington and Pam Bubendorf. You gave my boys a gentle shove toward success when, sometimes, you should have given them a swift kick! You are appreciated. Keep up the good work.

And thanks to the Pachecos for the use of their family!

Published February 1992

ISBN 0-373-16428-9

GOOD MORNING, MISS GREENE

Chapter One

"Daddy, let's go. I don't want to be late."

Justin Sloane looked up from the box of colorful school supplies in his hands. His daughter, Whitney, was handling the occasion of starting kindergarten with much more composure than he was. He had tossed and turned all night, dreading the morning—the day his little girl would take her first major step to growing up.

Justin watched as Whitney carried her cereal bowl and his coffee cup to the kitchen. In many ways she was very mature for her five years, yet he cherished the innocence he still saw in her young eyes. All too soon that innocence would disappear as she met with outside influences.

He could remember when she had been able to walk under the countertop without bumping her head. He'd had to put childproof latches on all the lower cabinet doors and be careful not to leave things too close to the edge of the drain board in case her inquisitive little fingers should pull something off.

He had treasured each milestone of her childhood, overwhelmed with fatherly pride as she learned to walk at nine months, speak in complete sentences at one year of age and sing "The Alphabet Song" when she was three. He read dozens of books to her, delighted when she began to recognize the simple words, and he was equally pleased that she loved to bring her coloring books into his office and sit quietly while he worked.

But even though he had personally witnessed her growth, he hadn't, until the first day of school approached, realized that by growing up, she would be growing away from him. Yesterday her world had revolved around him—and his around her. Today she would be expanding that world to include other children and adults.

It was selfish, he knew, but since his wife's death four and a half years ago, Whitney had been his whole life. He wanted her to have a happy, normal childhood, but he would do anything to protect her from whatever pain the outside world would bring.

"Daddy..." This time the exasperation was clear in her voice as she dragged out the word into two long syllables.

Justin forced his lips into a cheerful smile. "Let me get my keys." He walked into his bedroom and retrieved them from his dresser, then returned to the hall. "Don't forget your lunch."

"I already put it in my book bag."

"And a roll of paper towels."

"I've got them, too."

"And the box of tissues..."

Whitney's sigh was patient. "Daddy, don't worry. I've got everything."

He reached out and tugged her long, dark ponytail. Earlier that morning she hadn't been able to sit still while he brushed her hair and secured it with an elastic band and a big bow. It had taken him months to learn how to tie bows so both loops and the trailing ribbons were about the same length. His big fingers still fumbled with the tiny buttons at the back of her dresses and the buckles on her dress shoes.

Raising a little girl was quite an experience, but he felt he was doing a good job.

Dressed in a crisp cotton blouse and a bright red jumper, she looked adorable. His heart swelled with the love he felt for his little girl. This was the first day of the rest of her life. Never had the saying seemed more profound.

"Well, if you're ready to go, what are we waiting for?" he teased.

It was a short drive from their condo in Georgetown to the small school in Empire. Nestled deep in the Rocky Mountains, the elementary school drew students from several sparsely populated towns in the area. On that particular morning, almost-empty school buses were lined outside the doors while a continuous line of cars pulled into the parking lot. It seemed that many other parents had, like Justin, chosen to accompany their children to class on the first day.

Whitney lost much of her bravado as she stood next to her father in the doorway of her classroom. Her hand found its way into the warm protection of his much larger one as father and daughter hesitated, waiting to see if there was any organization to the chaos they were witnessing.

Some children had already found their places and were sitting, watching the proceedings with wide-eyed bewilderment. Other students were clinging to their parents in a last-minute spurt of terror.

A smiling woman who Justin assumed was the teacher circulated among them. She knelt until she was eye level with each frightened youngster, then she would talk earnestly to the child until the tiny fingers transferred their death grip from the parent's to the woman's waiting hand. She would lead the child to one of the tables that were clustered in front of her desk and smoothly draw his or her attention until the parents were able to slip away.

Gradually she made her way to Whitney. With a friendly but distracted glance at Justin, she turned her attention immediately to the child.

"My name is Miss Greene, and I'm your teacher. What is your name?"

Whitney's response was shy and barely audible, but Miss Greene must have heard it, because she reached out and took the little girl's free hand.

"I'm very glad to meet you, Whitney. I've got a place all ready for you over by the rabbit cage. I'll bet you'll like sitting by Mr. Wiggly Nose and Snow White. Would you come with me so I can introduce you to them?"

Whitney glanced up at her father, waiting for his approval, but before he could speak, he felt her hand withdrawing from his.

"You go on, angel," he encouraged, not because he wanted to, but because he knew it was what was expected of him. "I'll be back this afternoon to pick you up."

Whitney took a step forward, a movement Justin measured in miles rather than inches. He wanted to sweep her into his arms and carry her back home with him where she would be safe. There were so many dangers, both known and unknown, that could take her from him. And Justin wasn't sure he could bear another loss.

As if she sensed his pain, Whitney stopped and turned back to him. Reaching out, she patted his arm and looked up at him with solemn blue eyes. "Don't worry, Daddy. You won't be by yourself for very long. And as soon as I learn how to read, I can help you with your work."

Along with the affection his daughter's concern generated came a wave of guilt. She should be worrying about how her own day would be rather than about her father's welfare.

He squatted down with one knee resting on the floor as he met her gaze.

"From now on, Whitney, you have your own job, and that's learning everything you can in school. It's going to be lonely at home without you there to help me, but I've got plenty to do to keep busy." He looked up at Miss Greene, and she immediately picked up on his cue.

"We're going to be so busy here that you'll have lots of things to share with your dad every evening. And he can come back and visit us or eat lunch with you whenever he wants."

Whitney's gaze moved from her new teacher to her parent. Justin nodded his agreement and stood.

"I'll be back at two-thirty," he reassured her. "Have fun and show Miss Greene what a good girl you are."

A new wave of parents arriving with their children swept around him, separating him from his daughter. He watched as Whitney waved goodbye, then walked with her teacher across the room. On the tables in front of each tiny chair were colorfully decorated name tags with heavy yarn loops tied to them. Whitney examined hers, even managing a genuine smile before she slipped the yarn around her neck. Miss Greene and Whitney exchanged a few more words and, although he couldn't hear the conversation, he knew by the reverent look in his daughter's eyes that Miss Greene had the situation under control.

Justin's gaze followed the teacher as she approached the new group of people. Except for a spray of bangs across her forehead and a few curly tendrils at her temples, her shoulder-length light brown hair was held back by a headband. She was petite, probably not more than one or two inches over five feet. Not really pretty in the conventional sense of the word, there was something about her that held his attention.

As she bent over to talk to a frightened little boy, Justin noted how quickly she gained the boy's trust and realized it wasn't her rather plain features that made her interesting, but the strength and warmth of her personality.

She made him remember Mrs. Kirkmeier, his own kindergarten teacher. Not that Miss Greene acted or looked like Mrs. Kirkmeier. Heaven forbid. He wouldn't wish Mrs. Kirkmeier on his worst enemy. Even though he had been big for his age, he remembered how much her towering height and no-nonsense attitude had intimidated him.

Instead, Miss Greene's diminutive height and gentle spirit were the polar opposite of Mrs. Kirkmeier. He was glad that Whitney's education initiation would be with someone like this teacher.

Miss Greene, he repeated to himself. That meant that unless she had kept her maiden name, there was no *Mr.* Greene. Not that he was interested, because he wasn't. Of all the things Justin didn't want in his life right now, a romantic relationship was tops on the list. Even though it had been almost five years since Caroline's death, he still had no interest in finding another wife. He and Whitney were getting along just fine as they were.

A parent bumped into him and Justin was reminded that it was time to leave. He allowed himself one last glance in Whitney's direction. She was still obediently sitting at her table. Her attention was focused on the two miniature lop-eared rabbits who hopped around in their separate cages and stared back at the children with what appeared to be equal fascination. Only the tight grip Whitney had on her backpack as she hugged it to her chest revealed she was more unnerved by the situation than she pretended to be.

Justin had to fight an almost overwhelming urge to rush over and take her away from all the noise and confusion. She was only five, *barely* five, actually, since her birthday was on the first of June. The school district wouldn't object if she waited until she was six to start school. In fact, Justin had recently read an article in the newspaper about the advantages of children waiting until they were older and more mature before they started school.

But Justin hesitated. It was for those two reasons that he knew he couldn't possibly take Whitney out of school now. She was already mature beyond her years. Besides being able to say the alphabet, count to a thousand, and recognize all of her shapes and colors, she could add single-digit numbers and read many short, simple words. If she waited another year, she would be so far beyond her classmates that she would be bored to tears.

No, as much as he'd like to keep her young forever, he knew it was time to let go. As painful as it might be for both of them, he had to let her grow up.

Justin turned and slipped out of the room before Whitney looked in his direction again. In his haste, he bumped into a woman who had stopped just outside the doorway and was leaning against the wall. A tear trickled out of the corner of her eye and raced down her face.

"I'm sorry. I didn't mean to..."

"Oh, no, you didn't hurt me," she rushed to explain. "It's just that..." Another tear escaped. "I didn't want Danny to see me cry. He's confused enough as it is...with the first day of school and all." She glanced down at Justin's hands. "Could I have one of those?"

He looked at the box of tissues he had completely forgotten he was holding. After ripping the paper strip off the top, he held the box out to the woman.

She gratefully took a tissue and dabbed at her eyes. "I know it sounds silly, but I feel like I've lost my baby."

Justin nodded. He knew exactly what she meant.

"At least they're in good hands," he said in a valiant attempt to reassure her . . . and himself. "Miss Greene seems nice enough and she has a way with the kids."

"Yes, you're right." She wadded the damp tissue into a soggy ball and stuffed it into her pocket, then reached for a dry one. "Now I know why they told us to bring a box of tissues." She sniffed. "They're not for the children, but for us parents."

"It hasn't gotten any easier through the years, has it?" Justin mused. "The first day of school is hell."

MISS GREENE SHUT the door after the last parent had left, then turned to face the children. Whitney reluctantly tore her attention from the rabbits and stared at her teacher.

"Hello, boys and girls. I'm very glad to have you in my class. We're going to learn many things, but we're also going to have a lot of fun. Why don't we begin with an exploration of our classroom?"

Whitney looked around, her gaze taking in the walls that were covered with pictures, the shelves lined with toys, and the huge chalkboard behind Miss Greene's desk. Compared to her neat little bedroom with its one framed picture of Cinderella dancing with Prince Charming, the colorful clutter of the classroom was a visual delight.

Miss Greene led the way as they traveled around the room, pausing to investigate the play kitchen, the bean bin, the birthday tree, dozens of colored plastic trays holding blocks and other small toys. Whitney became even more convinced that she was going to like school.

It wasn't that she didn't have any toys of her own at home. Her closet and shelves were full of books, dolls and games. But she didn't have anyone to play with. Oh, sure, her daddy tried. He tried to look interested when they played Candyland. He even sipped pretend tea out of her tiny china cups and talked to her dolls as if they were really visiting guests. But Whitney suspected he wasn't having as much fun as she was.

But here, at school, there were lots of kids to play with. Maybe Whitney would even be able to make friends with some of them and then they could come to her home to play. She shivered again, but this time it was with excitement instead of fear. Daddy was fun and Whitney knew he needed her. But it would be so nice to have a friend her own age.

Of course, that would mean Daddy would be lonely.

"And here is the rest room. Whenever you need to use it, please raise your hand and I'll give you permission. Just remember to wash your hands and turn out the light every time when you're finished," Miss Greene said as she completed the tour.

Whitney barely glanced into the small single-unit bathroom that was solely for the use of the kindergarten students. Instead, her attention was once again centered on her teacher. Whitney couldn't remember ever seeing anyone more beautiful than Miss Greene. She was very nice, just like Whitney's daddy. Maybe Miss Greene would like to come over to Whitney's house sometime, too, and keep Daddy company while Whitney played with her new friends.

Whitney smiled. That would work out great. She would have someone to play with and so would her daddy. Whitney had been worried about him spending all day alone while she was at school. But now she could see that it was going to be even better than before.

Yes, this kindergarten thing was going to turn out okay.

Chapter Two

"So, Ali, how did it go?"

Allison Greene turned her attention from the last car pulling out of the school's drive-through lane. "Oh, hi, Chris." The frozen welcome-to-class-and-I-promise-not-to-bite smile slid away to be replaced by a weak grin that was closer to a grimace. "Not too bad, really. I had only three criers and two of them were parents. How about you?"

Chris laughed. "With second-graders I don't get all the weepy farewells you do with kindergartners. My students may be antsy, but at least they know what to expect. I don't see how you can stand having to deal with kids who don't know anything about classroom behavior, as well as trying to teach them the basics."

One by one, the images of her new students flickered through Allison's thoughts. There was Sean, a deceptively angelic looking, blond-haired boy who showed promise of being the class brat, and Meagan, bright and spoiled, who had quickly appointed herself the leader. But for every Sean and Meagan, there were children for whom school was an awesome experience, such as Rosa, a quiet, gentle-spirited little girl. She was so anxious to learn that she hung on Allison's every word. And Matthew, who was very immature for his age and didn't have a clue what was expected of him.

Then there was Whitney, who watched Allison with huge, hungry eyes. Allison wasn't quite sure what it was that had so captured the little girl's attention, because Whitney was obviously well-mannered and months ahead of her fellow students in the academics department.

"I love children at that age. They're so eager and impressionable. If their first educational experience is positive they will have a solid foundation for the rest of their lives." Allison shrugged and continued without a hint of boastfulness, "I think I can make a difference."

"Well, you have my admiration and my sympathy."

"Thanks. I can use both." Allison glanced at her watch. "I've got a zillion things to do before I go home today. And tomorrow I'll have a new class and another first day of school."

Chris shook her head. "That's another reason I wouldn't trade places with you for anything in the world. Kindergarten is the only grade in this school district with two classes that meet on alternate days." With a sarcastic twinkle, she added, "Double your pleasure, double your fun..."

"Double your work load," Allison admitted.

"Double your headaches."

"Speaking of which, I could use a couple Tylenols right now. Even though I've been teaching for seven years, I keep hoping that first days will get easier."

The two women leaned against the bicycle rack and welcomed the warmth of the afternoon sun and the freshness of the mountain breeze that washed over them.

Her friend shook her head with cheerful resignation. "Some are better than others. But as long as kids are kids they're going to resist giving up the freedom of summer for the regimentation of school."

Allison pulled off her headband and shook her hair until it fluffed around her face. "I know how they feel. I could've

used a couple more weeks of freedom myself. I was hoping
to finish painting the house before the first snowfall.''

"What took you so long? I thought you started on that
at the beginning of summer.''

"I did. But it was sort of like opening Pandora's box.''
Allison's sigh was tinged with melancholy. "I don't think
Aunt Millie did any upkeep on the outside of the house for
the last ten years. The old paint was peeling off in strips, so
I knew I would have to scrape the wood first. When I started
doing that I discovered some rotten and broken boards that
had to be replaced. Then I noticed that the wood holding in
the panes of glass in the windows was in horrible condition, so I had to have new windows installed. And, of
course, there was the roof....''

Chris covered her ears. "Enough. Enough. That's why I
live in a condo. I don't want to have to deal with all that
mechanical stuff. What I don't understand is why you insisted on doing it yourself instead of hiring out the whole
job.''

"On my salary? You've got to be kidding!'' Allison
snorted. "I'd rather eat regular meals and pay my heating
bills all winter than pay a handyman fifteen dollars an hour
plus materials. Besides, I didn't think it would become a
lifelong project. I've handled a paintbrush before. I expected to zip through the job in a week.''

"Well, you should have counted on Murphy's Law. I always allow at least twice the time and three times the ex-
pense for any project my husband decides to take on.'' Chris
slid Allison a sly smile. "Husbands can be pretty handy to
have around, especially when you own an old house like
yours.''

"Why, that's a terrific idea,'' Allison responded with
wide-eyed enthusiasm. "Tell Jared I'll have the coffee hot

and the paint stirred on Saturday morning at seven o'clock.''

"I didn't mean *my* husband, although I'm sure he'd be *delighted* to help," Chris sputtered in exasperation. "I meant . . ."

Allison couldn't hold back a satisfied chuckle. More determined matchmakers than Chris had been trying to find a suitable husband for Allison for years—all without success. It wasn't that Allison was anxious to conform to the old-maid schoolteacher stereotype; it was just that she wanted her Mr. Right to arrive in his own good time and of his own free will. "I know what you meant. And even though I'm sure your husband would give up his Saturday, please don't ask him to. I was just joking about that."

"But he really wouldn't mind."

"I'm sure that's what he'd say because he's a nice guy. But I know how important Saturdays are when you work all week. There's not that much left to do, honestly."

Chris laughed. "Well, you skirted the *real* issue once again. However, that nasty word *work* keeps pushing its way into our conversation. As much as I hate to go back inside, I'd better bite the bullet. My kids kept me jumping all day long so I haven't had time to finish my first-day chores."

"Neither have I," Allison agreed. "There's something explosive about kindergartners and construction paper. A pair of scissors in their hands turns one colored sheet of paper into an almost unidentifiable autumn leaf and a thousand tiny snips of confetti. I always try to clean up the worst of the mess before the janitors see it."

"And I'll bet you'd clean your house *before* the maid arrived, wouldn't you?"

Allison laughed along with Chris as they walked down the hallway to their respective classrooms. Luckily Chris didn't seem to notice the nervous ring to Allison's laughter.

Chris's teasing comment had struck remarkably close to home. The truth was she had always tidied the house before the maid arrived, because she was ashamed her mother never lifted a finger to keep the house clean. Allison was always intentionally evasive about her background. It wasn't because she was ashamed or because her childhood had been unpleasant. It was just that Allison wasn't sure how her new friends in this less-than-affluent area would accept the fact that Allison's family was incredibly wealthy.

They might not understand why Allison had gone against the wishes, even the threats, of her parents when she chose to be a teacher. As the baby of the family, Allison had been expected to marry and settle down in a house near her parents, with her only responsibilities to be a good hostess for her husband and to produce children for her parents to show off to their friends. Any urges she might have for outside activities could have been resolved with her volunteering for charities like her mother did.

When Allison had changed her major in college from art to education her parents had thought it was a passing phase. After all, they had been able to talk her older brother into going to medical school. They had planned for him to join her father's practice. Unfortunately the Vietnam War had changed those plans.

With ten years difference in their ages, Allison had been pretty young when Craig began his tour of duty. But she had been old enough to recognize the difference in the easygoing, laughing young man who left and the melancholy adult who returned. He still teased her mercilessly and he could tell a joke better than anyone she knew. But beneath the surface, Allison had sensed a pain that went beyond the serious leg wounds that had earned him a Purple Heart and a medical discharge.

Craig had tried to pick up his life where he left off. He even brought home a wife, a nurse in the EVAC hospital where he had been taken after he was shot. Allison liked Angela right away and, for a while, it looked as if Craig would get well, both physically and mentally. When he committed suicide several years later everyone had been shocked . . . and everyone's life had changed.

Through it all Allison persisted in becoming a teacher and had no trouble finding a job in Boston. Even though she had moved into an apartment of her own after her graduation, her parents still held hope that she would come to her senses and were equally persistent in trying to find a wealthy society husband for her. When her favorite aunt died and left Allison a small house nestled in the quaint community of Georgetown, Colorado, Allison immediately applied for a teaching position at every school district within commuting distance. It had taken another two years before there was an opening for a kindergarten teacher, but it had offered her a perfect way to finally cut the apron strings and try to be totally self-reliant.

It would be very easy for her to admit that she couldn't make it on a teacher's salary, but Allison was determined to try. She knew her parents would help her financially, but the conditions would pull her back to the nest. As her thirtieth birthday inched closer and closer, Allison knew it was better to struggle on her own than to smother beneath her parents' overprotective possessiveness.

She sat at her desk and surveyed the disaster area of her classroom. Only hours earlier, the floors had been spotless, the tables sparkling clean and everything in its proper place. Now, even though Allison had helped each student transfer his or her supplies into individual plastic bins and instructed them all on how to push their chairs under the tables and clean up their work space, the room was a mess.

Allison picked up the metal garbage can and circled the tables, picking up as many colorful pieces of construction paper as possible. With a wet rag, she wiped the glue off the tabletops and, in some cases, the seats of the chairs. She then fed and watered Mr. Wiggly Nose and Snow White. Within the next week, after things had settled down, she would let the children take over that particular task.

Another hour was spent labeling all the plastic bins and school supplies that the children's parents had failed to mark. Finally, as the sun was beginning to slip behind the jagged mountain peaks, Allison put the name tags of her next day's class on the tables just as she had that morning. Tomorrow would bring another group of terrified kindergartners and teary-eyed parents . . . and another first day of school.

THE FLUFFY CALICO CAT twined around her legs, greeting her with very vocal pleasure. Allison wasn't certain whether the cat was glad to see her or if the cat knew mealtime was near.

When she was growing up, Allison hadn't had a pet of her own. Her mother was allergic to animal fur and her father was too busy to care. For her first teaching job in one of the rougher districts of Boston, she had discovered that a baby rabbit was a guaranteed icebreaker. The second rabbit had been an Easter gift from one of her students and had proved equally helpful in reaching shy students and teaching everyone responsibility.

The cat had appeared on her doorstep several days after Allison moved to Georgetown, and when no one responded to the Found ads, Curiosity had become a permanent part of Allison's expanding family.

"Did you take good care of the house today while I was gone, Curiosity?" Allison dumped the contents of the can of cat food into a dish. "Since I don't have a dog, you have to be my guard cat, you know."

Actually Allison felt relatively safe in the small town. With about eight hundred residents, there wasn't much crime to worry about, especially when compared to Boston. She appreciated Curiosity more for the companionship than for any intimidation the friendly cat might offer to man or mouse.

Allison opened a can of soup and fixed a salad for her own supper. She was too tired to consider anything more complicated. After a long, hot bath, she snuggled under the covers and drifted off to sleep with a smile on her face. There were certain advantages to teaching two classes. At least she didn't have to spend every evening preparing the next day's lesson.

"I'M READY FOR SCHOOL, Daddy."

Justin opened his eyes and automatically glanced at the clock before struggling to focus on the small figure that was perched on the end of his bed. "Whitney, what are you doing up so early? You know you don't have school today."

"But why not? I want to go."

He sat up, pushing the pillows behind him as he leaned against the headboard. He had stayed up late the previous night, working out the bugs in a new computer program, and had planned on sleeping an extra hour or so this morning. He hadn't counted on Whitney getting up at dawn and dressing for school. Hopefully he would be able to convince her to change back into her nightgown and return to her bed for a while longer. He always tried to take time for a father-to-daughter talk whenever Whitney wanted . . . but six o'clock was not his wisest and finest hour.

"Whitney, I explained to you that because there aren't many people living in this area, there is only one kindergarten teacher and she has two classes. Instead of each class going a half day every day, your class goes on Mondays and Wednesdays, and every other Friday, and the other class goes on Tuesdays, Thursdays and on the Fridays you have off."

She considered that explanation for a minute before adding brightly, "But if I were to go to school *every* day, I'd be *twice* as smart by the end of the year. I don't think Miss Greene would mind having me in both of her classes."

Justin raked the thick dark hair off his forehead, grimacing as he pulled his fingers through the tangles. He had a feeling this conversation was going to take longer than he'd anticipated. It wasn't clear why Whitney was so anxious to go to school, especially after yesterday's hesitation. But he could see that, for whatever reason, it mattered very much to her.

"I'm sure Miss Greene would love to have you in her class every day. But, you see, she has planned her lessons so that no one in either class will miss anything. With two groups, she just repeats the lessons, so you'd be hearing the same thing twice. You're so smart you'll learn it all the first time, so if you had to hear it again, you'd be bored."

"It would be *fun* to go to school every day," she persisted.

"I'm glad you like school so much."

Whitney's blue eyes sparkled and she crawled over the covers until she could snuggle into the curve of her father's arm. "I really, really do, Daddy. There are puzzles and games we can play with when we finish our work. There's even a playlike kitchen with pots and dishes. Our room has its own bathroom. And there are some computers just for us to use. Of course, they're not like your computer. Miss Greene's going to show us how to use them next week."

Justin smiled down at her. He was genuinely pleased by her enthusiasm. But still it puzzled him. Whitney's closet was full of toys and games. She had been helping him make meals in a real kitchen for years, and she even had her own educational "talking" computer that had helped her with her math and word recognition. None of the things she was so fascinated with at school were new to her. Whitney had everything she could possibly want at home.

He squeezed her tiny shoulders in an affectionate hug. "Do you want to know a secret?"

Eagerly she nodded. "Yes, please tell me. I love secrets."

"My secret is that I'm glad you get to stay home two or three extra days each week. It's so quiet here without you that yesterday I turned the television on *Sesame Street* while you were gone. Next year when you're in first grade, you *will* be at school all day every day, so I think it's good that you go to school only every other day now because we'll both have time to get used to our new schedules."

Whitney yawned and rubbed the back of her hands across her eyes. "But I still would like to see Miss Greene every day. She's *real* nice, Daddy. And pretty, too." She yawned again. "I hope I grow up to be just like her."

Pretty? Just like Miss Greene? Justin chuckled at the thought. Kids had so much imagination.

He looked down at his daughter. Now that he was wide-awake, she had fallen back to sleep. Gently he eased her down on his pillow, then he slid out of bed and folded the comforter over to cover her.

Well, Miss Greene had certainly made a terrific first impression with Whitney, he thought as he let the warm water in the shower beat against his skin. Whitney didn't usually take to strangers so quickly. But, he supposed, it was natural for a child to develop a form of hero worship for her teacher. Soon enough Whitney would realize that Miss

Greene was no more special than anyone else. And Justin decided he would do nothing to extinguish those stars that twinkled in his daughter's eyes. Life had a way of doing that on its own.

"GOOD MORNING, CLASS." Allison greeted them with a warm smile.

"Good morning, Miss Greene," the children replied in loud, shrill voices. After three weeks of school, they spoke with a self-confidence and a familiarity that increased with each passing day.

Allison called the children to the alphabet circle. "Okay, today when you answer the roll call, please tell me what you ate for breakfast this morning. Jennifer Adams..."

"Uh...I can't remember." The little girl fidgeted, her fingers twisting in her short, bouncy curls.

Allison didn't ask for their personal information because she really wanted to know, but rather to encourage the children to use their memories and to think through their responses.

"Please try to remember, Jennifer. Was it cereal or eggs and bacon," Allison prompted.

"Oh, yeah, now I remember," Jennifer answered proudly. "I had Rice Krispies. I wanted Lucky Charms, but my brother ate them."

"That's good, Jennifer. Meagan Anderson..."

"A cheese omelet."

Allison continued down the list, checking each name as the child responded to the question. Then she drew a name out of the helper cup. "Today's helper's name begins with an *M*. Who could that be?" The children began shouting names until they correctly guessed Matthew.

Shyly at first, the boy stood and walked toward Allison. She held out the child-size United States flag and he took it from her, concentrating with an intensity he hadn't shown before as he carefully kept it from touching the ground while everyone said the Pledge of Allegiance.

"'...under God...indivisible...with liberty...and justice...for all.'" Allison paused and let the children stumble over the words as they tried to follow along. From experience she knew it would take most of them months and some of them all year before they would be able to recite even half the words correctly. Sometimes it took all her willpower not to laugh at the creative interpretations of the pledge's words the kids came up with.

"Today we're going to learn about the United States flag. Matthew, would you carry the flag around our circle so we can all count the stars and stripes. Does anyone know how many stars there are?"

They spent a few minutes talking about the flag, then Allison let all the children design their own. She enjoyed seeing what they liked and felt was important. As they worked, she walked around each table, stopping to help and to discuss the pictures.

Of those she could recognize without asking the daunting "what is that?" question, most of the boys' flags had simplistic cars, airplanes or motorcycles on them and most of the girls' had flowers or houses. Allison commented on each, encouraging the children to be colorful and creative, and not particularly surprised by anything she saw until she reached Whitney.

On a background of pale pink, Whitney had drawn a black horse rearing against a cloudy sky. The details and intricacies of the animal were incredibly accurate for an elementary-age child, but especially from a five-year-old.

"Whitney, this is very good," Allison complimented. Allison could see the child had a real talent that should be encouraged.

Whitney glowed from the words of approval. "Thank you, Miss Greene. I really love horses."

"Do you have a horse?"

"No, we don't have room for one. But Daddy says he will take me riding someday."

"Where did you learn how to draw horses so well?"

"From my color books. And I watch them on television," the girl replied. "Last Christmas Santa Claus brought me a little stable with a whole herd of horses. It's made out of real wood. My daddy had to put it together."

Whitney's passion for horses was evident, but Allison noted the little girl spoke of her father in that same awed voice. What about her mother? Allison couldn't remember ever hearing the other parent mentioned in any conversation, or seeing a woman pick the child up after school. But now was not the time or place to ask that question. Allison decided to check Whitney's file in the office. It always helped to know the situation at home when she tried to communicate with a child.

She continued moving around the room until everyone had finished their flags.

"Next Wednesday we'll be having an open house," she informed them while they were cleaning up their areas. "I'm going to display all of your flags on that wall." She indicated a wall that was covered with red, white and blue paper. "Before you leave today I'll give you an invitation that you will give to your parents. I hope they all can come so they can see how hard you've been working, and so I can have a chance to talk to them."

"What about my mama's boyfriend?" came a boisterous voice.

"Sean, remember to raise your hand if you wish to speak," Allison gently reminded him.

His hand immediately stretched upward and she gave him permission.

"Is it okay for my mama's boyfriend to come to open house?" he asked. "She's been dating him since my daddy moved out."

"Of course. Your mother may bring whomever she wants. Now it's time for us to line up for lunch. Matthew, you're today's helper, so you can be the leader." Allison picked up the basket of lunch boxes and watched as the children jostled and wiggled into a relatively straight line.

After lunch Allison sat on a bench and watched her students enjoy their afternoon recess. Because children that age had so much energy, Allison liked to take them outside several times a day whenever the weather was good. In the classroom they were in constant motion, even when sitting quietly in their seats. Allison accepted it as a fact of kindergarten life, because the kids truly seemed incapable of being absolutely still.

And, she had to admit, she enjoyed getting out of the classroom and being in the September sunshine as much as the children. Soon enough their trips outdoors would be limited by heavy snow and frigid temperatures.

"If this is Monday, then this must be Class A."

"Chris," Allison reprimanded good-naturedly. "You know we don't call the classes A or B or even One or Two. We wouldn't want the kids to think they're second-best."

Chris settled on the bench next to Allison. "Then what *do* you call them?"

"The Buffaloes and the Rams. I think the kids would rather identify with a wild animal than just a letter of the alphabet."

"Well, whatever you call them, I still think it's difficult to keep up with two classes. I have enough trouble with thirty-one kids. How do you handle forty?"

"At first they blend together," Allison admitted. "But after I get to know each child better, I don't have any trouble separating the classes. And I'm looking forward to open house so I can match parents to kids."

"Yes, I like to do that, too. If they realized how much the kids talk about them—and what they talk about—the parents would be shocked."

Allison chuckled her agreement. "You wouldn't believe what one of my students brought to show-and-tell last week."

"What? Tell me," Chris prompted.

"Polaroid pictures of his parents in bed. And they weren't sleeping!"

"No!"

"Yes. I got calls from six parents complaining that their children had seen pornographic pictures." Allison didn't tell her friend about the rather harrowing interview with Mr. Gibson, the school's principal, who had taken a dim view of the entire incident.

"How would a five-year-old get his hands on something like that?" Chris asked, shaking her head incredulously.

"I have no idea. I'm not sure if the boy knew just what he was showing off to everyone."

"You have to wonder who took the pictures."

Allison sighed. "Nowadays, children know so much more about sex than I did at that age. I can't believe some of the dirty words they write on the bathroom walls here at school."

"I know what you mean," Chris agreed. "I didn't hear some of them until I was in college."

They were both silent for a few minutes as they watched their students run and play with wild abandon. With all the configurations of families and stepfamilies the kids had to deal with and with the changes and pressures of modern society, Allison couldn't help but think they were being forced to grow up too quickly. Children shouldn't have to handle adult situations. They should be having fun, laughing and thinking childish thoughts rather than being expected to be little adults.

Chris's chuckle brought Allison's attention back to her friend. "You're probably going to get to meet these photogenic parents at the open house."

"Oh, no," Allison gasped. "How will I ever be able to look them in the face when I talk to them?"

"You might as well look them in the face. You've seen everything else." Chris's chuckle turned into a full-fledged laugh.

Allison gave her a withering glare. "You're really getting a kick out of this, aren't you?"

"You bet. It's little things like this that make open house so much fun."

Suddenly Allison wasn't looking forward to it as much as she had been moments before. There were some personal things about the parents she would rather not know. And to think she would get to meet Sean's mother's boyfriend and find out about Whitney's missing mother. Maybe it would be better if she didn't dig too deeply.

Chapter Three

Allison had staggered the times on the invitations so that the parents of the students in her Rams class were scheduled between five-thirty and seven in the evening and the parents of the Buffaloes were scheduled between seven-thirty and nine. The thirty-minute breather would give her time to pick up the papers of those Rams whose parents hadn't been able to attend and pass out the papers of the Buffaloes before their parents arrived.

But several Rams parents stayed late, and she barely had time to distribute the papers and check her hair before the next wave of arrivals began.

It was easy to see where Meagan got her superiority complex. Both of her parents were successful doctors. Punctual to the minute, their examination of Meagan's papers was crisp and businesslike and their conversation with Allison equally brisk. Even though they seemed a bit distracted, there was no doubt they doted on their only child. As they left, Allison overheard them promising Meagan a new television as a reward for her good work. Their attitude confirmed Allison's suspicion that Meagan was very spoiled. But Allison also knew that the combination of Meagan's natural abilities and her parents' devoted support of the lit-

le girl would give her the self-confidence to succeed at
whatever she tried.

Sean's mother did, indeed, arrive with her boyfriend. The
attractive thirtyish woman could barely tear her gaze away
from the years-younger man long enough to glance at her
son's papers even though Sean became increasingly loud and
obnoxious. Allison's heart went out to the little boy, who
had apparently learned to be bad because it was the only
way he could get any attention. She vowed to try to be more
patient with him and go out of her way to show her approval when his behavior was good and his work acceptable. She knew she couldn't single-handedly change his
behavior patterns, but perhaps she could help him see that
he could get much more positive attention by being good. If
only she could transfer just a tad of Meagan's self-
confidence to Sean. Unfortunately, she was a teacher, not a
magician.

When Matthew's parents arrived, Allison took them aside
for a private talk. She learned that he had turned five only
a week before school started, which explained why he was
so far behind the other children in the class in both mental
and motor skills. At that age every month counted when it
came to measuring maturity, especially for boys, who ma-
tured much more slowly than girls. Matthew was a perfect
example of a child who should have waited another year
before beginning school. But since he had already started,
to drop out after almost a month might make him feel he
had failed.

As a compromise, Allison recommended extra attention
at home so Matthew could practice using scissors, writing
and focusing on his assignments, and his mother agreed she
would work with him. She even volunteered to come to the
school every Monday and act as an aide to help work with
the slower children on a one-to-one basis.

Allison greeted Rosa's mother warmly, anxious to tell the woman how hard her daughter was working. But when she tried to talk to her, Allison discovered Rosa's mother didn't speak any English.

More and more parents were filtering into the room and Allison knew she needed to spend time with each. Yet she was determined to find a way to communicate with the small, black-haired woman who was admiring Rosa's flower-covered flag. Rosa looked on with her usual bright-eyed silence. She reminded Allison of a little bird, hearing everything yet too shy to jump into the middle of the action.

Allison listened to Rosa's mother's melodic voice chatter to her daughter and Rosa's soft tones responding. Even though Allison couldn't understand a word, it was evident the woman was very proud of the girl.

"Rosa, would you tell your mother something for me?" Allison asked.

Slowly, shyly, the child nodded.

"Tell her I said you are an excellent student and I'm very pleased with your progress."

Rosa hesitated, her huge brown velvet eyes searching Allison's as if trying to assure herself her teacher was sincere. When a tentative smile played across her lips, she seemed to grow stronger beneath the unexpected praise. After she spoke to her mother, the older woman turned to Allison with a smile that broke the language barrier.

"*Gracias, señorita. Muchas gracias,*" she said, and clutched Rosa's folder of papers to her chest as if they were the most valuable treasure in the world.

Reluctantly Allison turned away. There were now dozens of parents mingling in the room and less than an hour left. She would have liked to say more to Mrs. Torres, but speaking through an interpreter slowed down the process considerably. She surveyed the crowd, pleased with the turnout and hoping they would be patient. Almost every student was represented by at least one parent. Allison's gaze stopped on Whitney...and her father. There was no sign of her mother.

She had checked the girl's file earlier in the week, but it hadn't made any mention of a Mrs. Sloane. It showed that Mr. Sloane was self-employed and that his parents, who were listed as an emergency contact, also lived in George- town. But even under the "remarks" section there was no notation of where Mrs. Sloane fit into Whitney's life. Alli- son returned the file to the cabinet without knowing very much more about the little girl than she had before.

Justin followed Whitney, her hand tugging him along on a tour of the room that followed the same course as she had taken on the first day of school. After stops at all the places she considered highlights, they ended up in front of the rabbit cages.

"Aren't they cute, Daddy? Miss Greene said they have babies once a year and that some of us can take one home if it's okay with our parents. Can I have one, Daddy? *Please?*"

Justin's mouth opened to voice an automatically nega- tive response. But staring down into the pleading eyes of his daughter he knew it wouldn't do any good to point out that they lived in a town house with only a small concrete patio and that she was too young to take on the responsibility of a pet. Instead he dodged the issue with the standard paren- tal phrase, "We'll see."

"I would take good care of it. I got to feed them once when I was the helper. If we get all our work done and we're quiet, we get to let one of them out. I like Mr. Wiggly Nose the best. He likes me, too. I save him some lettuce from my sandwich and he eats it all."

She unlatched the rabbit's door and reached inside. Mr. Wiggly Nose amiably hopped over and sniffed her outstretched fingers.

"Are you supposed to open the cage?" Justin asked.

"Miss Greene lets us. But one of her *Big* Rules is that we don't ever, *ever* let Mr. Wiggly Nose and Snow White out at the same time. She said if they get together they'll make babies."

Justin bit back a grin.

"How do they do that?" Whitney looked up at him, waiting for an explanation.

"Do what?"

"Make babies? How do they do that?"

"Uh..." Justin stalled, his mind whirling as he tried to think of an answer that would satisfy her curiosity without going into details that were too graphic for her. He knew he would have to have "the talk" sooner or later. Heck, he thought dryly, it had been so long since he had experienced it, he might not remember how to explain it.

"You know how I told you that mommies and daddies fall in love and get married. That's sort of what Mr. Wiggly Nose and Snow White would do."

Whitney was silent for a moment as she stroked the rabbit's soft black-and-white fur and considered her father's explanation. "Why don't I have a mommy?"

"Whitney, you know that your mommy died when you were a little baby."

"I know that Mommy died. But why don't you get me *another* mommy? Some of the kids in my class have two or three mommies."

"It's not that easy, sweetheart." Justin frowned. Trying to make a five-year-old understand about true love and the difficulty of replacing a lost love was even more impossible than explaining the physical act of making babies. "It would take someone very special to take your mommy's place in my heart and our lives. I haven't found anyone I want to love and marry.''

He didn't understand the smug smile that tugged at the corners of her mouth. But he breathed a sigh of relief that she didn't pursue the matter any further.

"So what is a Big Rule?" he asked as she shut and latched the cage door.

''A Big Rule is something that is *very* important, like finishing our work and putting up our colors and scissors.'' She led the way to a corner of the room where two large beanbags had been casually arranged next to a bookcase. ''A Regular Rule is something sort of important, like standing in a straight line when it's time to go to recess or to lunch. And then there are *Giant* Rules,'' she explained with a dramatic spread of her hands.

''Like brushing your teeth?''

''Oh, no, that's a Big Rule,'' Whitney replied solemnly. ''A Giant Rule is not to talk to strangers or go any place with them. Another Giant Rule is to always wear our seat belts.''

Justin lifted his gaze to the sea of people flowing in slow circles around the room, until he could see Miss Greene through a gap in the crowd. His daughter talked about the woman endlessly, Miss Greene did this and Miss Greene said that. It had gotten to the point that he dreaded hearing that name in a conversation.

But, he had to admit, she must be doing something right. The children were listening to her. He couldn't count how many times he had talked to Whitney about why she had to wear a seat belt, but still he had had to remind her every time they drove somewhere. Until the past two weeks. It wasn't until this moment that he realized she was automatically putting her belt on as soon as she got into the car. She had even caught him a couple of times, practically ordering him to fasten his seat belt. And it was all because of the often-quoted Miss Greene.

Now that he thought about it, Whitney was also brushing her teeth without being told and turning off the television and the lights when she left the room. Justin suspected those were some of Miss Greene's "Rules," too.

Justin's curiosity was piqued. How could she make such an impression on the kids? He watched as the boys and girls jockeyed for position so they would be standing next to her, touching her, drawing her attention. It was obvious they adored her.

Another feeling, suspiciously close to jealousy, inched into Justin's consciousness. He was accustomed to being the center of Whitney's world, the first person she turned to with a problem and the main influence on her thoughts and actions. It wasn't something of which he was proud, but he was forced to admit that he didn't particularly want to share his space on her pedestal. Especially not with Miss Greene.

"Come on, Whitney." He rested his hand on her shoulder, gently propelling her toward the door. "We'd better leave now. It's already past your bedtime."

Whitney stopped so suddenly Justin had to leap sideways to keep from stepping on her.

"We can't leave *yet*," she exclaimed, her eyes wide with horror at the suggestion. "You haven't said *anything* to Miss Greene."

"She's busy. I can talk to her some other time." Justin gave Whitney a gentle tug, expecting her to obediently move along.

"No! You *have* to talk to her *now!*" Whitney stated emphatically. She dug her heels into the carpet and stiffened her body so it was impossible to move her without making a scene. "I won't leave until you do."

Justin had never seen his daughter act like that. Of course, there was an occasional display of naughtiness, but rarely did she absolutely defy him.

"Whitney...!" His voice was low and edged with an implied threat of a reprimand.

She looked around, first at her teacher, then back at her father. Slowly her eyes filled with tears. "But, Daddy, I *really* want you to talk to Miss Greene. And she wants to meet you. It's *important.*"

He had no idea why, but he could see it was, indeed, very important to Whitney that he speak with her teacher. Perhaps she expected Miss Greene to brag about how good Whitney had been doing in class. Or maybe one of Miss Greene's Rules was that she speak to each parent on openhouse night. Whatever the reason, Justin decided that if it meant that much to his daughter, he could stay a little while longer.

"Okay, Whitney. We'll stick around for a few more minutes. But if we do get to talk to Miss Greene, it's going to have to be brief. I have work to do tonight and even though you don't have to go to school tomorrow, you need to get to bed soon."

Whitney looked up at him with a wisdom beyond her tender years. "We'll see," she whispered in a voice so low Justin wasn't sure he'd heard her correctly.

The crowd began to disperse quickly as parents gathered up their children's take-home papers and moved toward the door. Justin had almost been hoping there would be no break in people vying for the teacher's attention, then he could legitimately tell Whitney he'd tried but simply couldn't wait any longer. He had nothing to say to Miss Greene, and he didn't need her to tell him how wonderful and intelligent his daughter was.

However, within five minutes, the room was empty except for Justin, Whitney…and Miss Greene. Grabbing one of her father's large hands in both of her small ones, Whitney practically pulled him across the room until he was standing directly in front of the teacher.

She was leaning over her desk, replacing a file in the drawer when Whitney announced with unnecessary pomp and circumstance, "Daddy, *this* is Miss Greene."

The teacher turned, greeted Whitney with a genuine smile and a gentle brush of her hand across the top of the little girl's dark hair. "Hello, Whitney." She then let her steady gaze move up until it met Justin's, and she extended her hand toward him. "Hello, Mr. Sloane. I'm glad you were able to make it tonight. I was hoping we would have a chance to talk."

Stifling a resigned sigh, he stared down at her. Politely his hand reached out and grasped hers in what was supposed to be a brief, disinterested shake. Instead, he felt his fingers tighten as an unexpected warmth rushed through him. Her eyes, a clear summer green sprinkled with flecks of sparkling gold, held his gaze as she studied him with open interest.

For a second, a brief unnerving second, he felt a flutter in his chest and a stirring deep in the pit of his stomach. Both were sensations he hadn't experienced in so long that he was struck speechless. Equally startling was the fact that the infamous Miss Greene had triggered those long-dormant feelings.

She was even smaller than he had guessed, standing almost a foot shorter than his six-foot height. Her body was slender and perfectly proportioned, and her hand, still cradled in his, felt almost as delicate as Whitney's. Her hair, pulled back into a neatly plaited French braid, was a light brown. It looked soft, almost irresistibly soft.

The outline of her face was not quite oval, but not quite square as strong jaws met in a firm chin that had a hint of a feminine cleft in its center. Her high, rounded cheekbones were splashed with a pale pink, and her intelligent forehead was almost hidden beneath a light layer of bangs.

But it was the rosy curve of her lips, slightly parted as if she were drawing in a surprised breath, that drew his attention. Justin swallowed as he surprised himself with an almost undeniable urge to feel the fullness of those lips...first beneath his fingertips, then beneath his own lips.

Abruptly Justin pulled his hand away and thrust both it and its possibly traitorous mate into his pants pockets. Miss Greene—he felt silly thinking of her so formally after he had just been tempted to kiss her—was having almost as powerful an effect on him as she apparently had on her students.

Good Lord, Justin, he chided himself, *has it been so long since you've had a woman that you're tempted by the first one you touch?* He didn't usually react so quickly and indiscriminately to a female, and he couldn't explain what had just happened.

"Mr. Sloane...are you all right?" The woman's concerned voice broke through the mists of his musings.

"Uh...I'm fine." Embarrassment replaced the improbable urges to touch this woman whose first name he didn't even know, and added to his unfamiliar confusion. His mind raced for an explanation that would satisfy her curiosity. Somehow he sensed that she wasn't a person who would be easily fooled.

"Sorry," he stated at last, somehow managing a convincing chuckle. "I guess you caught me daydreaming. Put me in a classroom and there goes my concentration. Old habits die hard, I suppose."

Her features relaxed into a grin. "What is it about little—and big—boys and school? The same child who can play Nintendo for five hours without a break can't sit still long enough to sing 'The Alphabet Song.'"

"Ah, 'The Alphabet Song.' I'd almost forgotten about that."

As if on cue, they burst into song, running from *A* through *Z* as if it were something they sang together often. Justin noticed that Whitney was watching them with the incredulous yet indulgent look children have when witnessing adults doing something silly.

"That ages us, you know." Allison laughed, a light, friendly sound that immediately drew his attention back to her. "The modern approach to teaching is that children shouldn't learn 'The Alphabet Song' because they won't be able to remember their letters unless they sing through it."

"That's ridiculous. Generations of kids have learned their alphabet with that song. Why do they always try to fix something that isn't broken?"

The teacher shook her head. "I have no idea. Children need the basics and they need teachers who care. Anything else just slows down the process."

"That must be why Whitney is doing so well," he commented with a sincerity that shocked him.

For several long moments, the two adults stared at each other in comfortable silence. Justin forgot his predisposed dislike of the woman and his eagerness to leave. In fact, he forgot the reason he was there in the first place.

"Daddy," Whitney interrupted, tugging none too gently on his pants leg, reminding him of her presence. "I'm hungry. Would you get me an ice-cream cone?"

Justin blinked, then glanced down at the little girl. "It's too late for ice cream."

"Please, Daddy. On our way home we could go to that good place."

"Whenever we want an ice-cream cone we go to the burger place down the road," he explained to the teacher. "They have the best twisty cones anywhere."

"Yes, I know," Miss Greene admitted. "I go there all the time. They have good hamburgers, too."

"Miss Greene can go with us, can't she, Daddy?" Whitney's high voice piped in.

"Miss Greene probably has plenty of better things to do than to go with us," Justin stated.

"Can you go with us, Miss Greene?" Whitney asked her teacher, circumventing the protocol of going through her father. "You can have rainbow sprinkles on your ice cream."

The teacher looked from Whitney to her father, apparently measuring the sincerity and advisability of the invitation. "Actually, I would like to talk to you about your daughter."

Justin was pleased . . . and suddenly as nervous as a sixteen-year-old on his first date. "Whitney and I would love to have you join us."

The classroom door suddenly swung open and the janitor, pushing a vacuum cleaner, stepped inside then stopped.

"Oh, I'm sorry. I thought everyone had left," he said, and began to back out of the room.

"I guess that decides it," Miss Greene said. "You can stay and clean the room, Larry. We're leaving right now."

It took her a few more minutes to gather some papers and clear her desk. A quick check of the rabbits and she was ready to go.

Justin escorted them down the long, lonely hallway of the deserted school building. As he held the door of Miss

Greene's car open for her, he said, "Oh, by the way, my name is Justin."

She smiled up at him and replied, "Nice to meet you Justin. You can call me Allison."

"We'll meet you at the restaurant, Allison," he replied, enjoying the feel of her name on his tongue.

He and Whitney got into their car in record time. He was so deep in thought about the woman in the car ahead of him that he barely noticed that Whitney snapped on her belt. And he didn't see her lean back in her seat, a satisfied smile on her face.

Chapter Four

"What on earth do you think you're doing? Have you lost your mind completely?" Allison asked aloud even though she was all alone in her car. The glare of headlights in the rearview mirror was her only answer.

Yes, she legitimately wanted to talk to Mr. Sloane about his daughter. The little girl was sweet, intelligent and very mature for her age...almost *too* mature. From the way Whitney interacted with the other children, Allison guessed the girl hadn't had many playmates. Perhaps she spent most of her time around adults. There were many positive aspects to that, but there were also some negative ones. Being treated as an adult could boost her composure and challenge her mind. But it could also cause her to skip an important step in the developmental process. Just possibly Whitney had never had the opportunity to be a child.

Allison also wanted to see if Mr. Sloane was aware of the girl's artistic talent. It should be encouraged and developed through lessons if Whitney was interested in pursuing it, which Allison suspected she would be.

And it was important that she find out about Whitney's mother. Since so many lesson plans revolved around the home and family, Allison always liked to know about the children's domestic status. She didn't want to accidentally stumble upon an awkward or painful situation that would embarrass the child.

It didn't take long to reach the restaurant since it was only about a block from the school. Allison pulled into one of the empty parking spaces and got out of her car. Already the fall nights were cool, and she shivered as she stood next to the vehicle, waiting for Whitney and her father to park and get out.

The misty glow of the streetlights bathed the man's face, highlighting the strong, masculine angles of his jawline and cheekbones and making his dark hair look almost black. She couldn't see his eyes, but she had barely been able to tear her gaze away from them earlier. Allison, who felt her own hazel eyes were such an ordinary, indecisive color, had always wished they were blue, especially the brilliant, sapphire shade Whitney and Justin shared.

Justin. She knew she should try to continue to think of him as Mr. Sloane, father of one of her students. But from the moment their hands touched and their eyes locked, Allison knew they had crossed an invisible line. From then on it would be difficult, if not impossible, to keep a formal distance between them, if only in her thoughts.

Allison knew it wouldn't be wise for her to get involved with a parent. She knew she shouldn't be going out to a public place with him and his daughter. But somehow her usual caution had slipped away.

"I want a chocolate-and-white twisty cone and some French fries," Whitney stated as she slipped one hand into Justin's and the other into Allison's. "What kind of ice cream do you like, Miss Greene?"

Allison smiled down at the little girl and pretended to consider the question as if it were of great importance. "It used to be chocolate chip, but now I think it's Cookies and Cream."

Justin held the door open and waited for them to enter.

"Daddy's favorite is 'nilla." Whitney shook her head in exasperation. "Can you imagine anyone whose *favorite* is 'nilla?"

"As a matter of fact, my brother's favorite was vanilla," Allison commented.

"You have a brother?"

Allison nodded, but she didn't go on to explain that he had died several years earlier.

As she heaved a wistful sigh, Whitney didn't notice the suddenly sad look on her teacher's face. "I wish I had a brother or a sister. It would be fun to have someone to play with all the time."

"He was a lot older than I, so we didn't play together."

"Okay, you two," Justin interrupted. "You need to tell me what you want to eat."

"You go ahead. I'll order mine separately," Allison protested. She certainly hadn't intended that he pay for her meal. It would make it seem too much like a date.

Justin opened his mouth to protest but must have seen the determined gleam in her eye, because he promptly turned to the waiting proprietor and ordered French fries and two ice-cream cones for Whitney and himself.

Allison should have felt the thrill of independence. Instead she felt a little silly as she ordered an ice-cream cone and a cola. Justin's offer had been polite rather than presumptuous. It was only a two-dollar snack, not a seven-course meal—hardly worth the mental dilemma she was having. But she had been insisting on paying her own way for too long.

They took their food to one of the four tables in the small dining area.

"You know, it's really too late to be eating this," she felt compelled to remark as they devoured the delicious junk food.

"What are you talking about?" A teasing glint flashed in Justin's clear blue eyes. "There are at least half of the four basic food groups represented here." He picked up a French fry and dipped it into ketchup. "See, this is a double vegetable." He took a generous lick of his plain vanilla ice cream. "And this is a milk product. A real stretch of the imagination might even include the cone as a grain."

Allison gave him her best teacher's stare, a direct look that had withered the best—and the worst—of students and parents. But the sight of his pink tongue against the whiteness of the ice cream was surprisingly erotic and a powerful opponent to her primness, even though it had all been in jest. For just an instant, a dangerous flash of a second, Allison could imagine how his tongue would feel touching her lips. Its coldness against the chill of her mouth would quickly warm. A shiver raced through her that had nothing to do with the temperature of the ice cream in her hand.

As if reading her thoughts, he reached toward her until his index finger came in contact with the curve of her bottom lip. She didn't move; she didn't even breathe as he rubbed his fingertip lightly over her tender flesh. Then, abruptly his hand drew away.

"You had ice cream on your lip," he explained, wiping his finger on a napkin.

Allison felt a heated flush rush to her cheeks. How embarrassing! All the time she had been imagining he was irresistibly caressing her lip, he had merely been cleaning up after her messiness just as he would have wiped his daughter's mouth. At the moment, Allison felt about as young as Whitney... and a hundred times as foolish.

She stood up so suddenly her chair skittered backward and almost overturned. "I'd better be going," she said, hating herself for the breathlessness of her voice.

Justin stood, too. "So soon? You haven't even finished your cone."

Uncharacteristically awkward, she busied herself by cleaning the already spotless part of her table and reaching for her purse. Anything to keep from meeting his gaze. She hoped he hadn't guessed how wildly improbable her thoughts had been, and she dared not give him a chance to read it in her eyes.

"I have a class tomorrow," she mumbled, and turned to leave.

She felt his fingers again, but this time they gently wrapped around her forearm, effectively halting her escape.

"But we didn't get to talk about Whitney," he reminded her.

"It's probably just as well. I'd rather she didn't hear it all, anyway. Maybe you can stop by the classroom later this week."

Still he didn't release her.

"I have a better idea. Since it was our fault that you stayed out so late tonight, Whitney and I will cook dinner for you tomorrow night."

Startled at the offer, Allison's head snapped up. She knew as soon as she looked into his fathomless blue eyes that she was lost. But, valiantly, she tried to gather her wits.

"Oh, no, I couldn't do that. It would be better if we met at school. Besides, Whitney will be at your place and we wouldn't have a chance to discuss what I wanted . . ."

"Whitney could go to her grandparents as soon as we finished the meal," he cut in. "They live in the same town house complex that we do."

"Uh . . . I just don't think it would be a good idea."

"Is there some sort of policy against meeting with parents outside of class?" he asked, his calm persistence even more unnerving than his words.

"Well, no . . . not exactly," she admitted warily.

"It would be a perfect opportunity to talk about Whitney. No other parents or kids will be around and the janitor won't pop in and disturb us." His broad shoulders lifted in a guileless shrug. "And you could leave as early as you want since it's a school night."

Like refusing his offer to buy her ice-cream cone, Allison was beginning to feel silly about turning down so innocent an invitation. Obviously this man had no personal interest in her. He just wanted what was best for his daughter. To refuse to meet with him when she truly did want to talk to him about Whitney would sort of be shirking her duties as the little girl's teacher.

Allison felt a much smaller hand touch her arm and she glanced down at Whitney, who had risen and was adding her pleas. "Daddy is a good cook, Miss Greene. And he lets me help. Please come over to my house."

It was more than Allison could resist. "Yes, I suppose I could stop by for a little while."

"Great. About six-thirty?"

Allison nodded and took the business card he handed her after he quickly sketched a map to his town house. "I've noticed this complex. It's by the lake, isn't it?"

"Yes, we have a terrific view from our back balcony."

"What can I bring?" Allison asked. "French bread? Ice?"

"Just yourself and your appetite," Justin answered with a jaunty grin. "Whitney and I will take care of everything."

Allison couldn't imagine a man handling an entire meal. Her father and brother had rarely stepped foot in a kitchen except to order a specific food be served. To be fair, her mother hadn't spent that much time in there either and had never understood Allison's interest in developing culinary skills. As it turned out, Allison had learned a lot at the elbow of the friendly cook who'd been with the family for years.

Her expectations of the kind of meal Justin would prepare weren't high, but she reasoned it wasn't the food but the chance to have a parental conference that triggered her acceptance.

Justin and Whitney walked with her to the cars. It wasn't until she was driving down the narrow mountain highway that led to the interstate that would take her to Georgetown that Allison began to breathe normally again. Once out of the magnetic field generated by Justin's blue eyes and sexy grin, her logic returned full force.

What had happened this evening? She couldn't remember ever being so attracted to a man that she entirely forgot her good ol' New England common sense. Especially when that man was the parent of one of her students.

In only a few months she would celebrate—a loose interpretation of the word—her thirtieth birthday. Was the stereotypical old-maid schoolteacher syndrome finally catching up with her? Was some sort of subconscious biological panic setting it so that she would be irresistibly drawn to the first eligible man she met?

Oh, Lord, she thought. She didn't even know if Justin was truly eligible. No mention had been made of his wife. However, that didn't mean there wasn't one somewhere. Obviously Whitney hadn't been found in a cabbage patch or dropped down his chimney by a stork.

Allison wasn't a foolish woman. Nor did she usually put herself in a position where she was almost guaranteed to get hurt. Why then had she agreed to go to Justin's house for dinner?

In an unusual display of temperament, she slapped the heel of her hand against the steering wheel. "What on earth are you doing? Have you lost your mind completely?" she asked herself one more time.

All day Thursday she continued her internal argument. She knew she should call Justin and tell him she couldn't make it. But she also knew that she wouldn't. It was those sorts of contradictory thoughts that were driving her crazy.

She considered asking Chris for her opinion that afternoon as they sat outside during recess. But since Allison hesitated to call either the ice-cream meeting or the dinner a *date,* she wasn't sure how to phrase her question. She couldn't exactly ask if Chris thought it was okay to meet with a parent away from the school if the intent was discussing the student, because, of course, Chris's answer would be positive. And to explain Allison's fear that the evening might be more social than she expected would expose her own preoccupation with the possibility.

Instead, she kept the conversation safely away from personal topics.

"Did you have a good turnout last night?" she asked as they watched the playground coach try to organize group activities.

"Not really," Chris replied. "The higher the grade level, the less the parental participation. That's the one good thing about kindergarten—most of the parents usually show up."

"Yes, they did. Out of thirty-seven students in both classes, thirty-one of them showed up with their parents."

"That's great. I have thirty-one kids in my class and only fourteen parents had an hour to spare." Chris shook her head with exasperation. "And then the others wonder why their kids lose interest in their schoolwork."

The bell marking the end of the period rang, and Allison and Chris reluctantly stood up.

"When my baby gets old enough to go to school, you can bet I'm going to be at every parent-teacher meeting," Chris added casually.

"*Your* baby?" Allison echoed, giving her friend a questioning look. "Since when do you have a baby?"

"Since about seven months from now," Chris announced, then laughed at Allison's shocked expression.

"Why didn't you tell me?"

"I just did. Actually, I only found out this morning. I had a doctor's appointment before lunch."

Allison grabbed her friend in a smothering hug. "Congratulations. I'll bet Jared is excited."

"You bet he is. We've been married for four years and had just about given up hope that we'd ever get pregnant."

The arrival of the playground coach with all of the students organized into ragged lines effectively ended the discussion of Chris's impending motherhood. But it stuck in Allison's mind for the rest of the afternoon. One more tick of the clock. One more reminder that life was passing her by.

SHE CHANGED CLOTHES three times before finally deciding on a white jumpsuit, belted with a string of silver conches studded with turquoise. A matching necklace and earrings given to her by her sister-in-law Angela completed the outfit, and Allison felt she looked as good as she could look. Perversely she considered changing into something more casual, but she decided she needed all the self-confidence she could get.

The sun had barely dropped behind the western Rockies, lighting the sky with a crimson glow as she parked in front of a row of town houses marked on Justin's map. His was on the end of a unit of four. Modern and obviously expensive, their rough cedar-and-stone design blended well with the countryside.

Whitney answered the door and greeted Allison with a delighted, "Hi, Miss Greene. Me and Daddy have been working all afternoon on dinner. We have pascetti and chocolate cake. Daddy wanted to make 'nilla, but I talked him into chocolate."

"Spaghetti," Justin interpreted as he stepped into the entry hall. "It's my specialty and Whitney's favorite. We make the sauce from scratch."

Allison followed Whitney into the den. The big room looked even larger with its vaulted ceiling and the open floor plan that made the den flow into a dining area and the kitchen. "Is there anything I can do to help?" she offered.

"No, thanks. Everything's under control in here. I was just about to put it on the table." He stood at the stove, stirring the contents of a huge pot. "Let Whitney show you the view while I drain the spaghetti."

Normally Allison would have insisted on pitching in. But when her heart skittered inside her chest at the very sight of Justin looking incredibly handsome in spite of the fact that he was wearing an apron and had a smudge of flour across one cheek, she knew better than to get any closer. She found the whole picture of a man knowing his way around a kitchen endearing . . . and absolutely fascinating.

Almost stumbling over her own feet in her haste, she followed Whitney through the French doors and onto the balcony. The brisk air off the lake cooled her hot cheeks and swirled her hair around her face.

"Do you go ice-skating, Miss Greene?"

"I used to when I lived in Boston," she answered, forcing herself to focus on the little girl who was trying so hard to be the hostess of the family. "But I haven't ice-skated in years."

"Me and Daddy ice-skate on the lake when it gets frozen. And we watch the cars with big spikes in their tires race on it, too. You can come watch them with us this winter."

It was more of a statement than an invitation, so Allison didn't bother to tell Whitney that there was little possibility of that happening. Instead, she changed to a subject every girl liked to discuss.

"You look very pretty tonight, Whitney. Is that a new dress?"

The child smoothed the full emerald-green velvet skirt and preened under her teacher's compliments. A wide strip of lace trimmed the hemline and collar, frilling like butterfly wings over the tops of puffed sleeves. "It's my Sunday school dress. I save it for *special* things . . . like having you come for a visit." She clapped her hands together and twirled in a circle, obviously enjoying the way the dress flared around her small body. "I can't wait to tell *everyone* at school that Miss Greene ate dinner at *my* house."

Allison sat down on one of the redwood chairs and held out her hands toward Whitney. "Come here, Whitney. I think we should talk about that."

The child moved closer until she was standing directly in front of Allison.

"I don't want you to tell anyone about me being here tonight," Allison stated. "I'm afraid if the other children hear about it, they might expect me to come to their houses for dinner and I don't have time to go to everyone's."

Whitney appeared to be considering the consequences with great reluctance. Obviously she had been looking forward to having unlimited bragging rights about the evening.

"I wouldn't want them to be disappointed or to have their feelings hurt, would you?"

"No, but..."

"It will be our special secret, just between you and me and your daddy. It's okay if you think about it, but I'd really like it if you wouldn't talk about it with anyone other than your daddy and me. Won't that be fun, for you and me to have a secret?"

The little girl's expression brightened and she giggled. "I *love* secrets."

"Then you won't tell anyone?"

"Oh, no, Miss Greene. I don't *never* tell secrets. I didn't tell Grandma that Daddy bought her a new sewing machine for her birthday."

"What's this about secrets?"

Allison jumped. She hadn't heard the door open and had no idea when Justin had joined them.

Whitney put her index finger against her lips and shushed him. "Me and you and Miss Greene have a *special* secret," she informed him in a loud whisper.

"About what?"

"Miss Greene doesn't want the other kids to know she had dinner with us. She says it will hurt their feelings."

Justin's gaze met Allison's. "She's probably right," he agreed, still talking to Whitney even though he was looking at Allison. "You and I are very lucky to have your teacher here tonight."

Allison's heart did a little tap dance again even though she wasn't sure how he meant his statement. Should she be so bold as to read into it that *he* was glad she had agreed to this meal? Or was he merely lumping himself with his daughter for emphasis?

"Dinner's ready," he continued, the tone of his voice warm—but not *too* warm—and friendly—but not *too* friendly. "May I escort you two ladies into the dining room?"

He took Whitney's hand in his and bent his other elbow and held it out so Allison could loop her arm through his. Hesitantly Allison complied, hoping he didn't feel the moistness of her palms through the sleeve of his sweater.

Justin held out their chairs with a flourish. Whitney tried to mimic Allison's demure acceptance of the chivalrous deed, but the little girl couldn't keep from giggling.

"Oh, Daddy. You have flour on your face."

Pretending to be horrified, he leaned toward her. "Please wipe it off for me. I certainly don't want to make a bad impression on Miss Greene."

Whitney used her napkin to rub the flour off his cheek. "All gone."

Justin gave Allison a conspiratorial wink, then passed her the salad bowl before he sat down. "I don't know what I'd do without Whitney around to take care of me."

As the meal progressed, Allison began to relax. Justin was an amusing host and Whitney such a well-behaved child that Allison realized most of their conversation was about topics much more adult than usual when children were included. It was obvious that, whatever the reason behind this single-parent household, the little girl was handling the situation remarkably well.

Allison expected Whitney to put up an argument when it was time for her to go to her grandparents' town house, which was in another unit across a small lawn. Instead, the child picked up her suitcase, which she explained held her nightgown and school clothes for the next day, and cheerfully walked to the front door.

"I'll be right back," Justin told Allison. "I just want to walk her over. Make yourself at home."

Allison nodded and took advantage of the time to freshen her lipstick and smooth her hair. She then returned to the den and strolled around the room, stopping to look at the books filling the shelves. She knew it was the teacher in her soul, but she was always impressed with the evidence that someone in the house did a lot of reading and loved books.

Pictures of Whitney were everywhere, both framed snapshots and professional, posed portraits. From the moment she was born, the child had been beautiful. And the older she got, the more promise she showed of becoming a real charmer. Allison had no doubt that Justin would have to beat the boys away from the door in a few years.

Allison continued her circle, hoping Justin wouldn't think she was snooping. But this was all part of Whitney's background, Allison reasoned, and Whitney was the purpose for this evening's meeting.

She stopped when she came upon a large photograph that had been strategically placed on the center of the mantel. Allison picked it up and drew it closer so she could more clearly see the very attractive blonde portrayed. The woman was smiling, not a wide, warm smile, but the smile of someone who was pleased with herself and her life. Allison recognized the poise and self-confidence that revealed, even more than the expensive fur draping her shoulders, that the lady came from a wealthy background.

''That's Whitney's mother,'' Justin spoke quietly, again surprising Allison by his presence behind her.

''She's very pretty.''

''She was beautiful,'' he corrected, his tone reverent.

Allison noted the undisguised adoration in the way his gaze caressed the picture as she replaced it on the mantel, and she knew without asking that Whitney's mother was dead. No woman in her right mind would leave a man who loved her the way he obviously still did.

"That was part of what I wanted to talk to you about." Allison forced herself to begin the conversation. Only moments ago she had been enjoying herself so much she had been in no hurry to go home. Now she couldn't wait to leave. "It's helpful when dealing with the students if I know their parental situation. And, when I checked the files, there was no reference to your wife. I didn't know if you were divorced or if she had..."

Her voice trailed off, hesitant to actually say the word. She still had no idea how fresh the wound.

Justin, apparently sensing her awkwardness, answered her unspoken question. "Caroline died when Whitney was seven months old. We were college sweethearts, but we waited until we graduated before we got married." He indicated that Allison should have a seat on the couch, and she silently complied as he went on with his story.

"Then we waited another six years before having a child. I had started working for a major computer company in Denver after graduation." Unable or unwilling to join Allison on the couch, he paced as if his reminiscences were too painful for him to remain still. "I suppose I wasn't a very good husband during that time. I thought I could spend all my time and energy focusing on developing my career until I became successful, and then I could settle back and enjoy my family.

"Unfortunately, life doesn't always happen according to our plans." His sigh was heavy with melancholy. "I traveled a lot, visiting other companies, setting up their systems, programming their computers and training their personnel. The money was excellent and the experience invaluable. Caroline said she didn't mind, so I kept my schedule full. Even when Whitney was born I was home only two weeks, long enough for Caroline to get out of the hospital, then I was gone again.

"We had big ideas, she and I. I wanted to start a business of my own eventually. Caroline kept busy volunteering with charities even after the baby was born. I'm not sure how she came down with it, but she developed some sort of viral pneumonia. We didn't think it was too serious, so I went out of town on a business trip as usual. I had barely arrived and checked into my hotel when Caroline's mother called and told me..." He paused and raked his fingers through his neatly combed hair. "Caroline was gone. It was just that fast. One minute she was here, the next she was gone forever."

"So Whitney never knew her mother?" Allison asked, more to break the silence that stretched between them than to hear the answer. It was obvious that a seven-month-old baby wouldn't remember anything.

"No," he stated flatly. "Unfortunately, I'm the only parent Whitney has ever known."

Allison could almost feel the hurt, the loneliness and, yes, the guilt that was torturing him. Instinctively she stood and went to him, reaching out to rest her hand on his arm in a gesture of support and compassion. "You've done a fine job. Whitney is a very bright, well-adjusted, happy little girl. Her mother would be proud of her."

As he looked at her, Allison saw the desperate need to believe that. He'd been carrying the weight of responsibility alone for years. Of course, his parents and probably Caroline's had been supportive. But he apparently needed some reassurance from an outside, impartial person.

"She's doing really well in school," she added. "She's months ahead of most of the other students, but she listens carefully and stays on task when there's an assignment."

Relief and appreciation pushed aside his frown of apprehension. "She loves going to school. If she could go every day, she would," he admitted, then smiled. "Actually, I think it's you she loves. You should hear all the nice things she says about *Miss Greene*. I hear almost every word you say repeated over and over."

Allison grimaced. "I suppose that's pretty boring for a grown-up."

"I'll admit I was more than a little aggravated that I could so easily be shoved aside in her affections."

His tone was light, but Allison suspected he was only partially joking.

"Have the two of you lived in Georgetown long?" she asked.

"When Caroline died, I quit my job, started my own business, and moved from the big city to a quiet, peaceful, small town where I could help my daughter see the beauty of life. And while it's quite a challenge raising a little girl alone, I can't say I've missed the corporate world at all. I drive into Denver about once a week to deliver or pick up new jobs. Sometimes Whitney rides along with me and visits Caroline's parents and sometimes she stays here with my parents."

"But what about her friends? Does Whitney have many playmates?"

He shook his head. "There aren't any other kids her age around here. But she has me and her grandparents to play with."

Allison wanted to tell him that as well-intentioned as that might be, it simply wasn't the same thing as Whitney having a friend her own age. But she sensed Justin was too vulnerable. His fathering skills wouldn't stand anything he might interpret as criticism.

"I'm sorry," he exclaimed. "I seem to have forgotten my hosting responsibilities. There's a cheesecake in the refrigerator . . . I'll confess that I bought it from that great bakery downtown—and a chocolate cake. The cake is for

Whitney, but I prefer cheesecake with Italian food," he explained. "I think there's some coffee left or I could make a fresh pot."

"No, I'd better pass on dessert." Allison's hand dropped off his arm and she stepped away, looking around for her purse. "Dinner was delicious. I'm truly impressed that you and Whitney are such good cooks."

"I didn't have a choice. I learned through trial and error, but now I think I'd make a passable chef... as long as it's not too fancy." He chuckled. "I can even decorate birthday cakes."

"I'll remember that when it comes time for a parent to bring food to class for a party," Allison promised. She started walking toward the door.

"Are you sure you couldn't stay a little longer?"

His voice was so close that she felt the warmth of his breath against her hair. "Tomorrow's a school day," she answered with less conviction than she should.

"I've enjoyed this evening," he stated simply.

Allison turned, tempted by the huskiness of his tone. Her emotions were in a tangle and she would have liked to stay long enough to sort through the possibilities. But as she looked up at him, her gaze fixed on the portrait displayed so prominently on the mantel.

Whitney's mother. Justin's wife. Caroline was gone, but she was still very much alive in Justin's heart. Allison wouldn't have minded getting to know Justin a lot better. But she preferred that he be emotionally available. And, at the moment, she didn't believe he was.

"Thanks again for dinner," she said, rushing the words out breathlessly.

"Maybe we could see each other again—" he began, but Allison interrupted.

"No, I don't think it would be a good idea. I wouldn't want the other children to find out. You know how cruel they can be, and if they think Whitney is a teacher's pet, it would be her feelings that get hurt."

Justin looked doubtful, but she left him no choice but to go along with her decision.

As Allison was driving the short distance to her home, she realized she hadn't discussed half the things she had intended to with him. Perhaps she would have a chance later...at a parent-teacher conference at school. She had no intention of meeting him anywhere else.

Of all the things Allison didn't want to be, a substitute teacher...substitute mother...substitute wife were tops on her list.

Chapter Five

"Good morning, class."

"Good morning, Miss Greene." All the students' voices competed for attention in the friendly greeting.

"Today's helper is..." Allison picked up the cup and withdrew an ice-cream stick before announcing "...Rosa. Okay, students, let's line up while Rosa gets the flag."

The children left their chairs and gathered around the alphabet circle. Whitney walked past Miss Greene, hoping the teacher would give her a special smile. But Miss Greene was distracted by a disturbance on the other side of the room and didn't even notice Whitney.

"Meagan, you're supposed to be in line," the teacher reminded the girl.

"But I was just helping Rosa with the flag."

"Rosa doesn't need your help with the flag, Meagan. It's her turn to be helper and it's your responsibility to be in line and ready to say the pledge with the other students," Miss Greene reprimanded sternly.

Meagan waited until Miss Greene turned her back, then the girl shoved Rosa, causing the smaller girl to stumble over a chair and fall down.

As usual, Miss Greene seemed to have eyes in the back of her head, because she whirled around in time to witness the entire scene.

"Meagan, that is not acceptable behavior." Although Miss Greene's voice was calm and low, her displeasure reverberated throughout the room. "As soon as we finish the pledge and the song, you will sit in the Time-Out Chair for thirty minutes. This is the third time this month that you've pushed someone, and I will not tolerate such roughness in my classroom or on the playground. I've tried to be patient, but I don't believe you're trying to get along with your classmates."

"But, Miss Greene, I want to be the leader." Meagan pouted, totally unrepentant. "I can carry the flag better than anyone."

Miss Greene took a deep breath before responding. "Everyone in this class carries the flag with great skill. You must learn to accept the fact that you cannot be the leader every day. And you must stop being a bully. I'm going to call your parents this evening so we can arrange a time for them to come in for a private conference. Now please join the others so we can continue with our lessons."

Whitney had been watching the interchange with wide-eyed interest. Wow, Miss Greene must really be mad if she was going to talk to Meagan's parents. Whitney was glad Miss Greene had never had to report misbehavior to Justin. There couldn't be anything worse than to have her father and Miss Greene think Whitney wasn't a good girl.

After they finished with their usual morning routine, Miss Greene introduced the day's lesson.

"We learned about dairy products such as milk and cheese on Monday. Today we're going to talk about fruits and vegetables. Can anyone tell me the name of a fruit?"

Several children raised their hands, and Miss Greene picked one to give the answer.

"Apples," Jennifer stated positively.

"Yes, that's right." Miss Greene took a picture of an apple and tacked it to a bulletin board beneath the heading "Fruits." "What are some others?"

As more answers were given, Whitney had trouble focusing while her teacher either added another picture to the board or she explained why the answer was wrong. They repeated the procedure with vegetables.

Whitney didn't raise her hand even though she knew the names of the fruits and vegetables mentioned. In fact, Whitney barely paid attention during the entire discussion. Instead, there was a frown on her face as she watched Miss Greene conduct the lesson.

It had been almost two weeks since Miss Greene had come to dinner at Whitney's house. Things hadn't progressed as Whitney had hoped. She'd expected her father and her teacher to fall madly in love the moment they were alone. Whitney had done everything in her power to help, even going to her grandparents for the evening when she had truly wanted to stay and spend more time with Miss Greene.

Her father seemed interested. He listened more attentively than before when she talked about Miss Greene. And Whitney mentioned her father as often as possible during conversations with Miss Greene. What Whitney couldn't understand was why Miss Greene hadn't come to their house again. Why weren't they all going out to movies and on picnics together as Whitney had imagined?

Whitney simply couldn't figure why grown-ups were so dumb. She had had it all worked out. Miss Greene could move into their house and they would all be a family. Whitney was even willing to share her room. It would be fun, like having a sister, and they could ride to and from school together. It would give her daddy someone to talk to and Whitney someone to play with. Why couldn't Miss Greene and her father see how easy it would be for them to be happy together?

She envied all the kids in her class who had real families. They had a father *and* a mother. And most of them even had at least one brother or sister. Whitney didn't understand why some of the kids had two or three families while she had only a father.

Oh, it wasn't that her father wasn't absolutely perfect, because he was. Whitney was incredibly proud of him. He was the smartest, most handsome man in the whole world. But there was a piece missing out of their lives.

More than anything else in the world, Whitney wanted a mother. And she was positive Miss Greene would make a perfect one. The problem was, how did a little girl convince two very dense adults that they should fall in love?

It was obvious that they needed to see each other again. Maybe that first evening they had both been too nervous. If only they could get together one more time, Whitney was positive they'd see what a terrific family they'd make.

"Whitney, you've been very quiet today. Aren't you feeling well?"

The little girl looked up and noticed, with surprise, that all the other students had gone to a pile of magazines, where they were choosing one for the day's assignment. Realizing she had Miss Greene's undivided attention, Whitney decided to get right to the point.

"Miss Greene, why haven't you eaten dinner with Daddy and me again?"

The teacher glanced around, quickly noting that no one had overheard Whitney's question.

"I haven't told nobody our secret," Whitney reassured her. "But I thought you'd be friends with my daddy. Why don't you like him?"

"Like him? Uh...of course, I like your daddy." Miss Greene looked very uncomfortable with the direction the conversation had taken. "He's a very nice man."

"Then why don't you come to our house? Didn't you have fun?"

"Yes, I had a good time. But, Whitney, you have to understand that I'm very busy. With two classes, I have to spend every evening getting ready for the next day's lessons."

"But don't you eat dinner?" Whitney asked with genuine concern.

Miss Greene was momentarily silent. Then, with one of those expressions grown-ups get when they're about to say something that has nothing to do with the issue, she answered, "Your father is a busy man, too, and I don't think he wants to have a guest for dinner every night. Besides, other than when there are school meetings, he and I have no reason to see each other."

"When is the next open house night?"

"We have only one of those a year," Miss Greene explained.

"You mean, Daddy isn't going to come to school ever again?" Whitney was horrified at the thought. How on earth would she get the two of them together if there were no more open houses?

"He can come visit you any time. And there's the Christmas program. I'm sure he wouldn't want to miss that."

Christmas! But that was months away. Whitney couldn't wait that long. She had already planned to ask Santa Claus for a baby sister, and she knew enough about families to know that her father would have to marry Miss Greene before her teacher could have a baby. Whitney wasn't quite sure how the process worked, but even Mr. Wiggly Nose and Snow White would have to get married before they had bunnies.

"Isn't there any other reason for Daddy to come talk to you?" she asked with growing desperation.

"I doubt it." Miss Greene smiled and reached out to tug affectionately on Whitney's long ponytail. "You're such a good girl that I won't ever have to call him in for a meeting like I have to for Meagan. Now I think you'd better go pick out a magazine. And don't forget your scissors and your glue stick. I've asked everyone to cut out pictures of fruits and vegetables and glue them on a paper plate. While you're getting your supplies, I'm going to pass out the plates."

Whitney obeyed, as usual, selecting a magazine and getting her plastic tray from the shelf before returning to her seat. She cut out pictures of cherries and lemons, then pasted them onto one side of the plate. She cut out pictures of corn and green beans and pasted them onto the other side, just as Miss Greene had instructed. After all, Whitney *always* followed the rules. She wanted her daddy to be proud of her so she stayed out of trouble.

It wasn't fair that Meagan, who was what Whitney's grandmother called a "spoiled brat," should get so much of Miss Greene's attention by being bad.

But Whitney had more pressing problems at the moment than to waste her time thinking about mean ol' Meagan. It looked as if Whitney couldn't trust her daddy and Miss Greene to handle the situation on their own, which meant that Whitney would have to think of some way to get them together again. Surely one more meeting would do it.

Whitney sighed. Grown-ups could be such a problem.

"HONEY, ARE YOU SICK?" Justin reached over and rested his open palm against her forehead. "You don't have any fever. Do you have a sore throat? An upset tummy?"

Whitney shook her head. What was wrong with adults anyway? Couldn't a kid sit around and think without someone asking if she was sick? "I'm okay."

Justin gave her another worried look before he turned back to his computer.

She was sitting at a small table next to his computer desk. He had set it up for her a couple years ago so she could bring her color books and puzzles into his office and play while he was working. Spread out on the table's surface were the large pieces of a puzzle that, when put together properly, would show a picture of a mare and colt galloping across a beautiful green meadow. Usually it would have taken Whitney only a few minutes to fit the pieces together, but tonight she was distracted.

"Daddy, Miss Greene and I talked about you today."

"Oh?" he asked absently, preoccupied by the numbers on the computer screen.

"She said she liked you." Whitney watched carefully for any response from her father. "She also said she had a very good time when she came to our house for dinner."

"Hmm. She did, did she?" Still he didn't look away from the monitor.

"Yes, she did. She doesn't eat much at lunch because she has to walk around and watch us."

"That's nice," he murmured.

Whitney was getting aggravated with him. He obviously wasn't taking this crisis seriously. "I was wondering if maybe we couldn't fix dinner for her again. Maybe tomorrow night—"

"Whitney," he interrupted, turning to her at last, "Miss Greene may have said she likes me, but she didn't mean she *likes* me. I don't think she wants to come back here for din-ner.''

"But, Daddy, of course she would. All you have to do is ask her."

"I already have."

Whitney's eyes widened. "You have? When?"

"A couple days after the dinner I called her and asked her to go out to dinner with me."

"You did?" Whitney was shocked. She didn't know her daddy had called Miss Greene. "When did you go?"

"We didn't. She turned me down."

"She turned you down?" Whitney echoed incredu-lously. Why would anyone refuse to have dinner with her daddy? "But why?"

He shrugged. "She said she was busy."

She had told Whitney the same thing. That didn't seem like such a bad reason. "Did you ask her again...when she wasn't busy?"

"No," he answered. "I figured it was just an excuse. She had already told me she didn't think we should see each other again outside of school. So, I guess I'm going to take the lady at her word and leave her alone." With that expla-nation, he returned his attention to his work.

Whitney was devastated. It wasn't that her idea to get them together was hopeless. It was just that they were try-ing so hard not to cooperate. And what could a little girl do to make two big people pay attention to her?

She twisted her ponytail around her finger into a tight curl. Daddy had said Miss Greene didn't want to see him *outside* school. But that didn't mean she couldn't see him *inside* school. If Whitney could just think of some way to get Miss Greene to call him in for a conference.

Meagan! Of course, that was the answer. Meagan got attention by doing bad things. Meagan's parents were going to be called in for a special conference with Miss Greene.

Whitney released her ponytail and it sprang free of her grip. All she had to do was create a little mischief. Then Miss Greene would call Whitney's daddy and they would get together and fall in love. She scraped the puzzle pieces back into the box, carried it into her bedroom and put it on the shelf where it belonged. Her daddy had taught her to take care of her toys. She always put them up when she was finished playing with them. But what if...

WHITNEY COULD BARELY wait to get to school on Wednesday. She had considered and rejected several plans of action. She knew she couldn't be mean like Meagan and actually hurt other kids, but even after a lot of thought, Whitney hadn't come up with a definite plan. She figured she'd sit back and wait until a perfect opportunity presented itself.

The class went through their daily routine, reciting the pledge, singing the National Anthem and answering the roll call by saying the name of their favorite cereal. Whitney waited impatiently, anxious to get some sort of inspiration.

Miss Greene explained about breads and cereals, which was the final food group, and read the class the big book of *The Little Red Hen*. Whitney fidgeted, unable to listen even though this was one of her favorite stories. She was beginning to get desperate. What could she do? She loved school and it went against her nature to be disruptive. But, she kept reminding herself, this was for the greater cause. It was a small sacrifice for her to get into trouble, because once her daddy and Miss Greene got together, they would all be so happy they would forgive her.

"I know you aren't supposed to play with your food," Miss Greene said, "but today we're going to bend that rule a little. I'm going to pass out pieces of yarn and some bowls of cereal. Sean, you're today's helper so please take this yarn and give everyone a piece."

While Sean distributed the yarn, Miss Greene placed a large bowl in the center of each table and poured Froot Loops into each of them. She demonstrated the threading process, then circled the room, watching, encouraging and helping tie a knot around one of the Froot Loops to keep the cereal from falling off the end of the string and then a final knot to join the yarn into a circle.

Whitney was enjoying the assignment so much that, for a moment, she forgot her plan. Sean walked up to Whitney and thrust his finished necklace in her face.

"I beat you, I beat you," he taunted. "And mine looks better than yours."

Without really thinking, Whitney grabbed his necklace, took a large bite out of the Froot Loops, then threw it onto the floor and stomped on it. The crispy fruit rings weren't constructed for such treatment and they immediately crumbled into a fine red, yellow and orange powder.

Sean's mouth dropped open as he stared at the devastated remains of his necklace. When he lifted his gaze to Whitney, his eyes were rounded in horror. "You broke it," he accused.

A hush had fallen over the room and his words echoed loudly, drawing Miss Greene's attention.

"What happened here?" the teacher asked as she surveyed the scene of the crime.

"She did it!" Sean exclaimed, pointing his shaking finger at Whitney. "She ate my necklace, then she stepped on it. Now it's ruined."

"Whitney did this?" Miss Greene was clearly surprised.

"Yes, Miss Greene," Rosa confirmed, as shocked as everyone else.

The teacher looked at Whitney and asked, "Why would you do that to Sean's necklace?"

"He was being mean to her," Rosa piped up again.

"So you were teasing Whitney?" Miss Greene turned back to Sean. "You know that isn't acceptable behavior. Go sit in the Time-Out Chair for ten minutes."

Whitney gave the other girl a withering glance. Rosa hadn't said three words all year. Why was she suddenly so talkative? "But, Miss Greene, I ruined his necklace," Whitney reminded her.

"Yes, you did. And I want you to apologize to Sean and give him yours. That was very naughty even if he was teasing you. But I'm sure it won't happen again. Now, go get the broom and dustpan and clean up the mess."

Whitney couldn't believe it. She had just done the meanest thing of her short life and she didn't even have to sit in the Time-Out Chair, much less have her father called in for a conference. She frowned as she swept the colorful crumbs into the dustpan. She hadn't planned on having to do *two* bad things. It had been difficult enough to do one.

She dumped the crushed cereal into the garbage, then mumbled an apology to Sean. Before she could think of some other bit of mischief, it was time for lunch.

In the cafeteria, she considered making a mess with her food or refusing to eat. But kids did that all the time and the only punishment they got was to miss recess. That wouldn't accomplish her purpose, so she waited until they were back in the classroom.

The afternoon lesson was to identify the different types of grain and dry vegetables. Miss Greene had canisters of popcorn, rice, wheat and several types of beans. Each student had a chance to feel the food and practice pouring it into measuring cups to the levels the teacher requested.

Whitney wished Miss Greene didn't have so many fun things planned for the day. It sure was making it hard not to go along with the group. For a few minutes, Whitney couldn't resist playing with the grains and kernels. They felt so good trickling through her fingers that she hated for her turn to end. Even more, she hated to mess it up for the rest of the class.

But a plan was a plan.

Taking the measuring cup, Whitney meticulously dipped a cupful of rice and poured it into the butter beans. She then took a cupful of wheat and poured it into the pinto beans. She was in the process of dipping into the popcorn when someone tattled to Miss Greene.

"Whitney! What on earth are you doing?" Miss Greene's words were edged with exasperation.

"I'm measuring the food. See, I mixed them all together," Whitney announced, waiting anxiously for the reprimand she knew must be forthcoming.

"Yes, you certainly did." Miss Greene studied the canisters for a minute, then sighed. "Well, that was certainly creative. I suppose I'll have vegetable soup this weekend."

"But, I . . ." Whitney's voice trailed off in disbelief.

"Now, class, we're going to cook the popcorn and have a snack. Thank goodness Whitney didn't mix it with anything."

Whitney slumped into her chair and rested her chin in the cupped palms of her hands. It was a lot more difficult being bad than she had ever imagined. How did Meagan and Sean make it look so easy?

"Whitney, don't you want to join us?"

Miss Greene's gentle voice revived Whitney's guilt feelings. She wanted to run to the teacher, throw her arms around Miss Greene's waist and tell her the whole truth. But she remembered how lonely her daddy was and how much she wanted a baby sister. In fact, she wanted a baby sibling so bad, she would even let them have a boy.

Whitney looked up at Miss Greene and wavered under the shine of concern in the teacher's eyes.

"I'm not very hungry," the little girl muttered.

Miss Greene pulled out a chair and sat down across from Whitney. Reaching out, she took the child's hands in hers. "Whitney, is something wrong? You've been acting... uh... unusual all day."

Mutely the girl shook her head. It was one thing to do something bad, but it was another thing to lie to Miss Greene.

"Is your father okay?"

Whitney nodded.

"Your grandparents?"

Again she nodded.

Miss Greene sat quietly for a couple of minutes, the creases of a perplexed frown peeking out between the feathery layer of her bangs.

"If you ever want to talk to me about some- thing... *anything* ... I'm always available. If you have a problem, I'll try to help you with it." Miss Greene hesi- tated, then added, "If someone is touching you where they shouldn't or having you touch them, you can tell me about it."

Whitney wasn't quite sure what Miss Greene meant. The teacher had talked briefly about people touching kids in their private places and how wrong that was. But no one was doing that to Whitney. Still, it might help her cause to not deny it.

When she didn't answer, Miss Greene smoothed the dark curls that had escaped from Whitney's ponytail. "I'm your friend, Whitney. You and I have a special secret, remember?"

The little girl nodded. How well she remembered that secret. And how much she wanted to add to it.

"If you have a secret with someone else, it's okay to tell me about it unless it's a surprise gift or something fun like that. Okay?"

"Okay."

"Are you sure you don't want any popcorn? It's almost gone, but I could make some more."

"No, thank you, Miss Greene."

"You may go to a play center if you'd like." The teacher stood and returned to the other students.

For several minutes Whitney sat, watching the kids eat popcorn and wishing she was with them. But she was depressed. Nothing was working out as she planned. She had overheard Meagan telling Jennifer that Meagan's parents were coming for a conference after school. Lucky Meagan.

Whitney got up and wandered across the room to the row of shelves that held a dozen or so games and about twice that many puzzles. Selecting a puzzle of two kittens sitting in a straw hat, Whitney sat at a table and dumped out the pieces. A couple slid off the slick surface and fell to the floor. When she leaned down to pick them up, the girl noticed a piece from another puzzle that had somehow hidden from the janitor.

She picked up all the pieces and tried to figure out in which box the stray piece belonged. What a mess it would be if the puzzles got mixed together. What an awful mess...

Whitney glanced back at Miss Greene, but the teacher was totally occupied popping another bowl of corn for the rest of the class. Taking the puzzles down one at a time, Whitney opened the lids and set them aside.

' When all of the boxes were open, she began dumping them on the floor, quietly at first, until the pile of displaced pieces grew. Her elbow caught on the edge of a box, flipping it to the floor and setting off a chain reaction that knocked the rest down.

The final crash caught everyone's attention, and they all hurried over to the play center where Whitney sat, surrounded by loose pieces of dozens of puzzles.

Miss Greene was obviously the most shocked of all as she stared at the mess. But before she could say anything, the bell rang.

"Okay, class. It's time to go home. Gather your things and line up at the door. And don't forget to wear shoes that tie on Friday. We're going to learn how to tie bows." She turned to Whitney and pulled her up, rolling her eyes at the waterfall of pieces that poured off the little girl's clothes. "You and I are going to have a talk about this on Friday. I hope you'll be having a better day then."

"I suppose you're going to tell my daddy about this," Whitney said, triumphantly, trying very hard not to smile.

Miss Greene glanced from Whitney to the puzzles then back at Whitney. "No, I don't suppose I will. You and I can handle this problem."

"But you called Meagan's parents," Whitney cried, sensing she was losing control of this one, too.

"Yes, I did. But that was because Meagan was bad once too often."

"How many times is *too often?*"

"It's not a fixed number. I just know."

"But if you call my daddy..."

Miss Greene managed a weak smile. "Don't worry, Whitney. I won't tell your daddy about this. Everyone's entitled to a really awful day. I've had a few myself."

"But..."

"Let's go. The parents will be waiting outside, wondering what's happened to us."

Whitney picked up her papers and stuffed them into her backpack, not caring that they were being hopelessly wrinkled. Yes, this was definitely the worst day of her life. So far.

But there was always Friday.

Chapter Six

Allison surveyed the disaster area of her room. There was still a sprinkling of crushed Froot Loops by the tables. A thin layer of beans, rice and wheat covered a countertop and spilled over onto the floor. And then there was the pile of puzzle pieces. She didn't even want to think about them. God only knows how many years it would take her to sort them back into the proper boxes.

And to make matters worse, Meagan's parents would be here any minute. What on earth would they think about the way Allison ran her classroom!

Allison picked up the beanbag chair the students used for silent reading and tossed it in front of the puzzles, hiding that mess. She then hurried to brush the mixtures of beans and grains into the garbage can, picking up pieces of popcorn as she went.

How had she lost control? The day had been so well planned. But the students had been wild.

To be absolutely fair, she admitted, it was mainly one student who had caused all the trouble—Whitney Sloane. Allison couldn't imagine what had gotten into the little girl. Usually she was the best of students, attentive, cooperative and friendly.

Allison hated to call parents in for a conference and used it only as a last resort to get the child's attention. She felt she was not doing her job properly if she couldn't find some way to reach her students and understand their problems.

Meagan's problems had been building. She was anti-social and mean spirited. No amount of talking to her had gentled her attitude. After meeting her parents at open house, Allison could understand that Meagan's behavior had been programmed into her by indulgent, adoring parents who devoted what little free time they had solely to their only child. Allison suspected the child had always gotten everything she wanted and had never learned to share or to be second at anything. The teacher needed to talk to the parents as much about their behavior as about Meagan's.

But Whitney's situation was entirely different. While she, too, wasn't accustomed to sharing or relating to other children, she had learned quickly. Even though some of the behavior required of her was clearly new, she always tried to get along. She worked hard and even helped others finish their tasks.

Until today. Allison could see there was something weighing heavily on the little girl's mind. She had been pre-occupied throughout the morning, not participating with her usual gusto. Allison had seen this withdrawal in children before, and it usually pointed to some sort of trouble at home. Little things upset children a lot more than adults realized. The children would misinterpret something that was said or done, or it could be an actual disturbing event that was occurring such as a divorce or the birth of a new baby.

In Whitney's case, however, Allison believed the child's problems were directly related to not having a mother. During her first five years, Whitney had been so involved with her father and grandparents that she hadn't known something was missing. But now that she was associating with other children, Whitney was seeing the role a mother usually played in a child's life. She was probably feeling the loss now more than ever.

But it had, after all, been one bad day in the month and a half since school began. Before she discussed Whitney's problem and possible solutions with Justin, Allison wanted to be more positive. She would watch Whitney closely on Friday. If the child exhibited any of the same angry behavior that she had today, Allison would decide what step to take next.

There was a knock on the classroom door, and she hastily dropped another handful of popcorn into the garbage before going to greet Meagan's parents. At the moment she must concentrate on this interview. As much as she dreaded calling Justin, she would face that possibility in two days.

"GOOD MORNING, CLASS." Allison began, as usual, on Friday morning.

"Good morning, Miss Greene," the children cheerfully called. It was the last day before a holiday weekend, so they were all in particularly good humor... and high spirits.

Allison drew an ice-cream stick from the cup, and although the name "Jennifer" was clearly printed on it, she announced, "Whitney is today's helper," then put the stick back into the cup before anyone could see the discrepancy.

Whitney held the flag proudly and led the class in the pledge and the song. Allison called the roll and had the children answer by naming a letter of the alphabet. She then gathered the children on the floor in front of the television set and played a movie about Christopher Columbus.

It was a short film, only thirty minutes long, but it allowed Allison time to observe Whitney. The child seemed cheerful enough today and was watching the movie intently. So far Allison had detected none of the pensiveness of Wednesday. *Thank goodness,* she breathed to herself. She really didn't like discussing the children's home life with a parent unless it was absolutely necessary. No matter how she approached it, it was always awkward.

For all her hesitation about spending any nonbusiness time with the man, she had to admit that it wasn't because she wasn't attracted to him. At the most unexpected moments the memory of his twinkling blue eyes or his slow, sexy grin would pop into her thoughts. And it would take a concentrated effort to push him out again.

If only there weren't so many other people involved, she might consider accepting his invitation to dinner. That is, if he should ever ask her again. After that one phone call, he'd made no further attempts. Allison had been perversely disappointed by that. Even though she'd turned him down, the fact that he accepted defeat so easily must mean he wasn't all that interested.

In spite of his short attention span where she was concerned, Allison still sensed that he was a kind and good man.

"Who can tell me the name of Christopher Columbus's ships?" she asked after turning off the video machine and the television.

Sean raised his hand.

"Yes, Sean."

"The *Ninja,*" he answered positively.

"Close. It was the *Niña.* Can anyone else name one of the other two?"

Meagan raised her hand.

"Yes, Meagan." The girl was noticeably subdued today, which Allison assumed was the result of Meagan's parents talking to her about how to respect other people's rights,

"The *Pinto.*"

"*Pinta,*" Allison corrected. "Thank you, Meagan. Anyone else?"

Rosa shyly lifted her hand.

"Yes, Rosa."

"The *Santa Maria,*" she answered, her voice barely above a whisper.

"That's absolutely correct, Rosa. Very good," Allison praised. The child seldom volunteered an answer and Allison was encouraged by the positive response. "Okay, students. Now repeat after me . . . the *Niña,* the *Pinta,* and the *Santa Maria* . . ."

They spent the rest of the morning acting out Columbus's voyage and singing the Columbus song. After lunch, as Allison watched the kids frolic like young foals let loose in the pasture, she breathed a sigh of relief. Whitney seemed to have bounced back to normal. So far there were no signs of the antisocial behavior she had exhibited earlier in the week. She was running and laughing along with the others as if she didn't have a care in the world.

Perhaps Allison was lulled into a false sense of complacency, but as she led the students back into the classroom, she thought the worst of it was over. Blithely she distributed bars of Ivory soap and showed the students how to scoop out the center so it looked like a little boat. Everyone got out their glue and scissors so they could cut a triangle out of construction paper and glue it to a toothpick for a sail.

Then, leaving their supplies on their tables, they all took their ships to the sink where they watched them float in a pristine armada that surely would have discovered something had there been anything to be found in the rectangular ocean.

Leaving their ships to dry on a dock of paper towels, Allison had all the children sit in the alphabet circle and take off one of their shoes. She then demonstrated how to tie a simple knot and a bow.

Mass confusion ensued as the children did everything to their shoestrings except tie them in bows. Allison went from child to child, guiding the short, clumsy fingers through the motions. She knew, from experience, that this wasn't a one-day project and she had it on her schedule every day for the next month.

"I can do it, Miss Greene," Meagan bragged, unable to hold back any longer. "See, my bows are perfect."

Allison was busy with Matthew so she barely tossed Meagan a cursory glance until she heard her scream. It was so bloodcurdling, so horrified that Allison was on her feet and across the circle before she even thought about responding. Standing in front of Meagan, Allison bit back a grin as she looked at Meagan's bowless shoes. Snipped next to the knot, there were four ragged strings where the bows used to be. But the actual bows, now limp and forlorn dangled from Meagan's fingers.

"Look what she did to my shoestrings," Meagan declared.

Allison wanted to say, *What a shame and they were so perfect.* Instead, she forced herself to hide her appreciation for the irony that Meagan had finally been on the receiving end, as she asked, "Who did that?"

"*She* did." Meagan pointed her finger at Whitney. "She's just jealous that I can tie my shoes and she can't."

"I can *too* tie my shoes," Whitney retorted defensively.

Allison looked at Whitney and saw the damning evidence still poised in her hand. Suddenly sober, Allison realized this was what she'd been hoping she wouldn't see. Not that she'd anticipated Meagan getting her shoestrings trimmed. It was an act of anger by a little girl who was trying to keep something bottled inside.

"You can not," Meagan taunted. With a toss of her head that sent her long French braid flying over her shoulder. "Your bows were all funny looking, not neat like mine."

"Are not."

"Are, too."

"Girls, that will be enough..." Allison tried to intervene.

"And the bows in your hair are ugly, too," Meagan sneered. "Did your mother tie them with her eyes shut? Or is she just stupid like you?"

Whitney gasped. She blinked her eyes, trying desperately to keep the tears from rolling out. Then, before anyone could stop her, she grabbed Meagan's braid and cut it off.

As if they were playing the Freeze game, no one moved or made a sound. Like statues, they all stared with silent shock at the long blond braid clutched in Whitney's hand. Allison knew she should do something, say something, but it had all happened so fast she couldn't believe her eyes.

Then slowly the antagonists began to react. Meagan's curious fingers lifted to touch the unraveling ends of her drastically shortened hair. Whitney stared at the unattached braid as if it were a snake about to strike, then her trembling fingers tossed it away.

Allison watched in what seemed to be slow motion as the once perfectly groomed piece of hair flew through the air. The students stumbled over each other in their haste to get out of the way so it wouldn't touch them as it arched toward the floor. When it finally landed on the carpet with a plop, it was as if that marked the end of the silence. Everyone began to speak at once, hushed whispers, nervous giggles, speculations on how mad Meagan's parents were going to be and what sort of punishment Miss Greene was going to give Whitney.

"Uh...class, go to your seats," Allison roused herself to say. "Whitney, give me the scissors. Now."

Without hesitation, the little girl handed over the weapon. Allison could see Whitney's whole body shaking as if her legs were barely able to keep her standing. But the girl's eyes never left Allison's. It was obvious that she recognized the gravity of the situation and was trying to steel herself for whatever Miss Greene did next.

Allison's heart tightened. She had never felt so sorry for anyone as she did for Whitney. The girl was terrified, but she was trying valiantly to be brave. Meagan's cruel teasing had almost justified a retaliation of some sort. But not something so drastic, so uncorrectable as cutting a person's hair. This was something Allison couldn't ignore. It was obviously a cry for attention, and it had to be answered.

Momentarily turning away from Whitney, Allison leaned over and tried to calm Meagan, who was sobbing hysterically. "It'll be all right. Now you can get your hair cut into one of those cute short styles. And if you don't like it, your hair will grow out fast. Honest, it will. Why, my hair grows so fast, I have to trim my bangs every month."

Meagan's tears dried to a sniffle. "Do you think I'll still look pretty with short hair? My mommy won't love me if I'm not pretty."

Now Allison felt doubly bad. Underneath that hard shell was a vulnerable little girl struggling to please her supersuccessful parents. She probably felt it was almost impossible to measure up to their expectations. It wasn't simply that she *wanted* to succeed; she felt she *had* to or her parents wouldn't love her anymore. And in desperation, she became ruthless to reach her goals of always being the first, the best...the prettiest.

Allison pulled the frail little body into her arms. "Your mommy loves you very much. It doesn't matter to her whether you have long hair or short hair, or if you can tie the best bow in the world or carry the flag better than anyone else. Your mommy loves you because you're her little girl. I talked to your parents and they're very proud of you, not because of what you've done, but because you're their daughter.''

Meagan leaned back and searched Miss Greene's eyes to see if she was telling the truth. The child must have been reassured by what she saw because she was calmer and more like her old self as she commented, ''My hair looks awful. Everybody's gonna laugh at me.''

Allison didn't comment, afraid Meagan would recognize the lie if the teacher tried to tell her her hair looked fine. In fact, it *did* look awful. All of the braiding on the top had unraveled and fallen around her face. The scissors hadn't cut evenly and, with the braid pulled to the left side when it was severed, the right side was longer than the rest.

''Let me see what I can do to fix it until you get home. I've got some barrettes and ribbons in my desk.'' Allison stood and instructed the rest of the class to go to an activity station. ''Meagan, you wait for me in the bathroom,'' she said, then turned back to Whitney.

''I know Meagan was being mean, but you shouldn't have cut her hair. You know that, don't you?''

''Yes, Miss Greene,'' Whitney whispered.

''What's been bothering you, Whitney? Is there anything you want to tell me?''

The girl shook her head.

''Has someone been hurting you?''

She shook her head again. It was the same type of response she had given to Allison's question two days ago. There were no visible signs of bruises or wounds on her and she clearly didn't want to talk about it. Allison was left with no choice.

"Whitney, I didn't want to do this, but I'm going to have to call your father."

A flicker of emotion touched Whitney's eyes. Was it fear? Panic? Before Allison could identify it, Whitney dropped her head, hiding her expression.

"Are you afraid of your father? Will he spank you for doing something bad?"

Whitney didn't speak but, once more, shook her head in response.

"I can't help you if you won't tell me what you're thinking."

Silence.

Allison's sigh was an admission of defeat. "I'll call him and arrange a conference. Just remember, you can talk to me anytime. I'll help you."

Still Whitney didn't speak. But the tenseness seemed to have left her as she walked back to her table. As Allison watched, she wasn't certain, but it looked as if the little girl was skipping.

"I CAN'T BELIEVE IT. Whitney's never done anything like that before." Justin was completely shocked by what Allison was telling him about the pigtail incident. Surely she was talking about some other child. "Are you sure it was Whitney? *My* Whitney?"

"I'm afraid so. I saw it happen," the teacher confirmed. "I'll admit I wouldn't have believed it myself if I hadn't been there."

Justin looked down at the round-tipped scissors that had supposedly done the deed. "I didn't realize these things were sharp enough to do that much damage."

"Neither did I," Allison admitted, a hint of a smile tugging at the corners of her mouth. "Most of them barely cut construction paper. I suppose the scissors caught the braid at just the right angle and a five-year-old's hair is still thin and very fine." She studied the pile of papers on her desk for a moment, and when she looked back up, all trace of humor was gone. "I hope it wasn't inconvenient for us to meet today. Monday is a holiday and I didn't want to let this go until next Wednesday."

"No problem." Actually he had had to reschedule a meeting in Breckenridge, but if Whitney was having trouble, there was no question which he would choose. "I thought she was doing so well in school."

"She has been...until now. Actually, her class work is still exceptional. It's her attitude that has gotten progressively worse." Allison took off the tortoiseshell framed glasses she had been wearing, meticulously cleaned them, then put them back on. "Usually, when a student undergoes such a dramatic transformation it's because of changes at home, such as a planned move."

He shook his head in a negative response.

"A new routine?"

"Nothing other than her school schedule."

"Are you spending more time with your job?"

"No, on the days she goes to school, I try to get it all done while she's away or after she's asleep so I can spend the evenings with her."

Allison hesitated for a split second before asking, "A new relationship? If you're seeing someone seriously or thinking of remarrying, Whitney might feel threatened."

"That couldn't be the problem. I've gone on only a few dates in the last couple of years, and none of them turned serious. I guess I've set my sights too high. When I marry again, the woman is going to have to be pretty special, and so far, I haven't met one who even came close."

"Oh...uh..." Allison shuffled through a pile of papers on her desk, straightened them, then put them back in the exact spot they had been before. "Okay, if it's none of those things, do you have any idea why her behavior has declined so dramatically?"

Justin considered the question. Until a few hours ago, he hadn't even realized there was a problem. And now, posed with the challenge of what went on in a five-year-old mind, he drew a complete blank.

"Like I said before, this is so unlike Whitney. Of course, she's had her share of tantrums and crankiness, you know, the usual childishness. I remember how scared I was of having to raise a little girl on my own because I hadn't been around kids all that much and those that I had known were obnoxious little brats. But I was lucky. Whitney hasn't ever given me any trouble. She's sweet, obedient and a really nice person. I've always been so proud of her."

Allison studied him silently for several moments. Although she kept her expression carefully closed, he sensed there was something else on her mind that she hadn't mentioned. He hadn't seen her wearing glasses before. And while he didn't doubt she must need them, probably for close-up work, he guessed she was wearing them during this meeting as a sort of shield. They served as a subtle reminder that she was the teacher, the person in authority.

She probably didn't even realize the psychology of why she was wearing them, but human nature and body language were things that had always interested Justin. His ability to read people and understand their motivations had helped him succeed with his business. People who weren't sure exactly what they wanted or couldn't put it into words could trust him to know what type of program they needed, a challenge he accomplished by first getting to know their personalities and the circumstances of their company.

But while he knew Allison was holding something back, he couldn't guess what that might be. Already today he had been rocked by the news of his daughter's escapades with the scissors. He couldn't imagine there was anything else Allison could tell him that would shock him more. He might as well hear it all.

"There's more to this conference than you've said, isn't there?"

For a moment longer she didn't speak, but her steady appraising gaze continued to focus on him.

"Yes, there is," she finally acknowledged. "Actually, today was not the first time Whitney displayed destructive behavior." She went on to inform him of the Froot Loops incident, the canister mix-up and the puzzle mess.

Justin listened in amazement. He was still having difficulty believing that Allison was talking about his daughter, the same girl who kept her own puzzles neatly stacked in her closet and had never lost even one piece. She always cleaned up her own cereal mess and was so careful when measuring ingredients that Justin let that be her job when they cooked something together.

"And when a child has such an abrupt personality change," Allison continued, "we have to consider the possibility that something has happened at home that has deeply disturbed that child. Bad behavior is often a cry for attention . . . or help."

"What are you suggesting?" Justin asked, wondering when she would get to the point.

"I know this is a painful subject for both of you, but I think Whitney has suddenly realized how much she misses her mother."

"But she didn't even know her mother."

"Yes, and I think that's part of the problem. She doesn't know exactly what it is she doesn't have. Perhaps she has learned enough about the other children's mothers that she's created a mental image of what a mother should be. While once it was enough to have you and her grandparents, she now sees there is an important piece missing from the family circle.''

He bristled at the insinuation. "I'm a good parent. Whitney has never lacked for love, discipline or attention. I admit that I've learned parenting through trial and error, but I can't believe a mother could have done anything for my daughter that I haven't.''

"Now, Mr. Sloane, I didn't mean to imply that you weren't a good parent.'' She frowned and shook her head. "I really hate dealing with relationship problems like this.''

"Miss Greene," he said stiffly. "Whitney and I do not have a relationship problem.''

"I didn't mean you and Whitney," she said, trying to explain. "I mean that Whitney is having a relationship problem with her mother. I can see that you've done an excellent job. Whitney is very bright and, in spite of the last few days, is well adjusted. But you know how five-year-olds are. They have single-track minds. She doesn't know how much she has. All she can see is the one thing she doesn't have.''

"Are you suggesting that I go wife shopping? Is there a factory outlet store at one of the Denver malls for unattached mothers? Or maybe I should run a personals ad in the local newspaper... *Wanted Mother: Young girl needs mother. Father is no longer adequate. Occasional sex might be required to keep up image of happily married parents.*''

Bright spots of color splashed across Allison's cheekbones. "No, of course not. I'm Whitney's teacher, not your romantic adviser. Your love life is of no interest to me. All I'm concerned with is your daughter's behavior.''

Her obvious discomfort made him regret his sarcasm. He reminded himself she wasn't discussing this because she was prying into his personal life, but because she honestly cared about his daughter's welfare. "I'm sorry. That was totally uncalled for." He shifted on the hard chair and leaned forward in an attempt to ease the tension. "I can't deny that Whitney's behavior at school is not at all in character with the girl I know. Maybe she does need a little extra attention. What do you suggest I do to help?"

"Perhaps you should simply talk to her. Ask her how she feels about mothers, in general, and hers, in particular. I don't know how much the two of you talk about her mother or how open you've been . . ."

"We don't make it a point to talk about Caroline. I've always tried to let Whitney lead the conversation, and we discuss her mother whenever she wants."

"That's good, but maybe she doesn't know the right questions to ask."

"I'll talk to Whitney about this tomorrow," he assured Allison.

"Good. I hope that helps," she commented. "If we can't get to the cause of her outbursts, she might need professional counseling. But even if it's all childish high spirits, something must be done quickly. I cannot have my class disrupted again."

She took her glasses off and set them down on the desk, unaware of the symbolism of her actions. Justin could see she was relieved that the sensitive discussion was almost over. She had presented the problem and her suggestions for its treatment to him and was now counting on him to resolve it.

"I expect Meagan's parents won't take her new haircut well," she continued with a wry arch of her delicate brows.

For the first time, Justin realized the incident could reflect badly on Allison. "They shouldn't blame you. With all those kids in your class, you can't be expected to keep up with every one of them all the time."

Once again a tiny smile played along the edges of her lips, but this time it was more in exasperation than amusement. "But that's exactly what *is* expected of me. Especially with kindergartners who are having their first school experience, I have to be not only their teacher, but their babysitter, their counselor, their guardian, and their pep squad to keep them from getting discouraged as they are bombarded with the basics of everything they'll need to know for the rest of their lives."

"Will you have to go to the principal's office?" he asked.

"Probably so," she replied with a notable lack of enthusiasm.

"It's no big deal. I spent quite a lot of time with my principal, too. Before I graduated, he and I were on a first-name basis." He grinned and was pleased to see she appreciated his humor even if it was only another of her small, nervous smiles. It suddenly became important to him that she not be forced to take the blame for this. She was a good teacher and his daughter adored her. Those were reasons enough to want to help her.

Less explicable was his sudden desire to see a real smile part her lips and a carefree twinkle dance in the depths of her eyes. He had heard her laugh with Whitney, and it was a warm, welcome sound in a house that had gone too long without a woman's voice, a woman's laughter, a woman's touch.

"You know, I agree that you need to know what Whitney's excuse is for her mischief," he commented. "In fact, I think you ought to hear it for yourself. And I think we'd get a more definite answer if both of us were there to ask questions and interpret the answers."

"Oh, do you think we should have another conference and include Whitney?"

"No, I think it should be a less formal atmosphere so she'd feel comfortable enough to talk. Maybe dinner tomorrow?" he asked casually.

Although she didn't move a muscle, he felt her withdraw. Before she could turn him down again, he added as a challenge he knew she would feel obligated to accept.

"It would give you an opportunity to see me in action as a father. And we can talk about families. You can gauge Whitney's reactions and give me your professional opinion. I want to get to the bottom of her problem as much as you do."

She hesitated and he could almost see her weighing the offer, measuring her personal feelings against what she believed was her duty.

"Where and when?"

It wasn't an acceptance, but he took it as such. "That Italian restaurant on Rose Street at six o'clock tomorrow evening." He stood and walked toward the door, almost reaching it before stopping to ask, "Should Whitney and I pick you up or would you rather meet us there?"

"That's only two blocks from my house, so I'll meet you there." Then, as if realizing she had been tricked into the agreement of dinner, she reached for her glasses and slid them back onto her nose.

Chapter Seven

"Table for one, Miss Greene?" the waiter greeted as she hesitated inside the doorway of the restaurant.

"No, Tony. Tonight I'm meeting someone."

"Good for you. It's about time you had someone to share your spaghetti with instead of always eating alone."

"It's not that kind of meeting." Allison hurried to correct his false impression. "I'm having a conference with one of the children in my kindergarten class and her parent."

"Is it a female-type parent or a male-type parent?" Tony prodded, a mischievous twinkle in his dark Italian eyes.

Allison knew it was hopeless to try to hide anything from Tony. "It's a male-type parent."

"Ah, then you *are* having dinner with a man."

"He's not a man...well, yes, he is a man...but that's not important. We're just trying..."

"He isn't married, is he?" Tony inquired. "Not that it matters. Some of my best dates have been with married women."

"No, he's not married. And no, this isn't a date," she insisted. "It's just a meeting and a meal that are happening at the same time. You shouldn't read so much into it. Have they arrived yet? Justin Sloane and his daughter?"

"Ah, yes, they're sitting in the back by the window. I'll take you to their table. Follow me."

Allison walked with him across the small dining room. The wonderful smells of tomato sauce, cheese and fresh garlic tantalized her senses and her stomach growled in response. To muffle the sounds, she pulled her coat tighter and crossed her arms over her abdomen. She'd been so busy trying to finish painting the house today that she hadn't taken time for lunch.

Tony pulled out her chair and, with a dramatic sweep of his hand, gestured for her to sit down. When she was settled, he handed out menus to all three guests and said, "I will be back in a moment to take your orders. Would you like cocktails?" At their negative response, he added, "Enjoy your meeting." As he turned to leave, he gave Allison a broad, suggestive wink.

She glanced at Justin to see if he had noticed Tony's teasing, but he was busy fumbling in the pocket of his sports jacket.

"Hello, Miss Greene," Whitney greeted with barely restrained excitement.

"Hello, Miss Greene," Justin echoed, a teasing glint in his eyes.

"Hi, Whitney and Justin. It's getting cold out there."

"There's a cold front pushing through tonight. No snow, just wind and low temperatures," Justin remarked.

Allison opened her purse and pulled out her glasses. She slipped them on and noticed that, almost simultaneously, Justin had put on a pair of his own. Their gazes met and he chuckled.

"You both wear glasses. How neat!" Whitney pointed out with glee. "Isn't that a confidence!"

"Coincidence," Justin corrected automatically. "I have to wear them for reading and close work. Staring at a computer screen all day doesn't help."

"I'm farsighted, too." Allison almost added that he looked much better in glasses than she did. They made him look intelligent and dignified. Her glasses made her look like the schoolmarm she was.

She picked up her menu, holding it a little higher than necessary to block Justin's amused scrutiny.

"I want pascetti," Whitney stated without hesitation, even though she was holding up her menu, imitating the adults.

"Spaghetti." Again Justin corrected her. "Have you eaten here before, Allison?"

"I eat here about once a week."

"Don't you know how to cook, Miss Greene?" Whitney asked. "I could teach you how to make soup, mashed tatoes, scrambled eggs and lots of other things."

"Thanks, Whitney, but I know how to cook. I just don't do it very often. It's not much fun cooking for only one person and a finicky cat."

"Well, you can eat with me and Daddy from now on."

Allison's gaze skittered over the top of her menu and met Justin's. He was still grinning, and Allison suspected he was having a much better time than she was.

"We'll talk about that later," Justin spoke up, apparently interpreting the hesitancy in her look. "So, Allison, how's the lasagna?"

"It's excellent. That's what I usually order here." She shut her menu and removed her glasses, carefully returning them to the case in her purse.

"Another confidence!"

"Coincidence," both Justin and Allison corrected at once. For a second longer, their gazes held, then they both burst into laughter. For all the innocence of the conversation, it was a very intimate moment. Almost as if they were a real family.

"I see your *meeting* is going well."

Startled, Justin and Allison turned their attention to Tony, who was standing next to their table, a pencil poised over his notepad.

"We've decided on the lasagna," Justin replied with admirable nonchalance. "And Whitney wants the—"

"Ah, let me guess. The very pretty *bambina* wants the pascetti, right?"

Justin nodded, but Allison could see he was biting his tongue not to laugh at Tony's playful pronunciation of spaghetti. It was sure to bring a comment from Whitney.

Tony took their ice tea and soda orders, then left.

"Daddy, why did he call me a deer?" Whitney asked, a puzzled frown creasing her forehead.

"He said *bambina,* not Bambi," Justin explained. "*Bambina* is an Italian word for child."

"Oh." She considered that for a few minutes. "*Bambina.* I like it. I think I'll change my name. *Bambina* Sloane."

"I don't think you should," Justin commented thoughtfully. "Remember, you're going to be a grown woman someday, and you'd feel pretty silly having everyone call you *child.* Besides, Whitney is a very nice name. You have no idea how many name-your-baby books your mother and I went through before we settled on Whitney."

"Okay, I won't *really* change it," Whitney agreed. "But you and Miss Greene can call me *Bambina* any time you want to. It'll be our *secret.*"

Allison recognized this as a smooth opening into the reason they were having dinner together. After a quick glance at Justin, she asked, "Do you have a lot of secrets, Whitney?"

"I have more secrets at Christmas. You know, secrets about presents to my grandmas and grandpas and my dad. And then there's my list for Santa. That's secret, too. And me and you still have our secret, don't we?"

Tony returned with their salads and drinks, and they waited to continue the discussion until he left.

"Yes, Whitney, we do. But do you have any secrets that make you sad? Secrets about someone else?" Allison prompted.

Whitney thought about it for a few minutes, then shook her head. "Sean hit me real hard with a kick ball once. But that's not really a secret."

Justin was sitting back, letting Allison conduct the interrogation. Allison guessed he didn't want her to think he was manipulating his daughter's answers by asking leading questions. She appreciated his cooperation and took advantage of the freedom to watch Whitney closely as she pressed the issue gently but firmly.

"Whitney, if something is bothering you, it's okay to tell me. I'm your teacher and your friend. I just want to find out why you've been acting so differently in class."

"Are you and Daddy having fun tonight?" the little girl asked.

Allison frowned. It wasn't like Whitney to drift off the subject even though she was only five years old. But maybe she was hiding something she'd rather not face and didn't want to talk about. "Whitney, that didn't answer my question," Allison persisted in her practiced no-nonsense teacher's tone.

"I can't answer your question until you tell me if you and Daddy are having fun tonight," Whitney insisted.

Allison looked at Justin, and his shrug told her to play along with Whitney if it meant they might get some answers to her behavior dilemma.

Was she having a good time? Allison considered how comfortable it was to be *with* someone instead of always eating alone. She thought of how warm it felt to be, at least temporarily, a part of this family. And she thought of the laughter she and Justin had shared over nothing really, just a silly reaction to a mispronounced word. Yes, she realized, she *was* having a good time.

"Yes, I'm having fun," she admitted to Whitney, who then looked at Justin expectantly.

"So am I," he acknowledged. "How about you, Whitney?"

The little girl giggled and clapped her hands together. "I'm having the *bestest* time."

"Now that we've answered your question," Allison said, trying to bring them back to the original subject, "will you answer mine? What caused you to do all those naughty things this week at school?"

The expression that crossed Whitney's face was not at all what Allison expected. She could have understood fear, pain, anxiety or even anger. What she didn't understand was that Whitney was trying to look contrite without quite concealing an expression of pure delight.

"I didn't mean to be bad. Not really," Whitney admitted. "I tried *everything* else, but you and Daddy wouldn't listen."

"What were you trying to tell us?" Allison asked.

"I love my daddy. And I love you, Miss Greene." Whitney's smile was wistful and innocent. "I want you to fall in love with my daddy so you can come live with us."

"But why—" Allison began, but Justin interrupted.

"You mean you were naughty in class so that Allison, uh, Miss Greene and I would get together this evening?"

Whitney nodded.

"So all of those pranks were just so I'd call your father and set up a meeting?" Allison was amazed at the intricacies of the little girl's plan. She had to admire her inventiveness.

"*You* wouldn't go to dinner with my daddy when he asked you," she accused. "When Meagan got into trouble you talked to her parents. I thought if I did something bad you would call my daddy. But you wouldn't. So I had to do another bad thing. I *wanted* to cut Meagan's shoestrings. But I didn't mean to cut her hair. It was just that she said something mean about my mother."

"Do you miss your mother very much?" Allison asked gently.

"I look at her picture. But I don't really remember her," Whitney mused. Then she added with renewed enthusiasm, "*Everyone* else has a mother. Some of the other kids even have two or three. I want a mother, too. And I think Miss Greene would be perfect, don't you, Daddy?"

Justin could have been embarrassed. He could have swallowed hard and shifted uncomfortably on his chair. But, to his credit and Allison's relief, he merely smiled and replied, "You know Miss Greene much better than I do. But I think she's a very nice woman and I wouldn't mind finding out for myself."

Tony arrived with their dinners and removed their salad plates, which gave Allison a few moments' reprieve as her mind whirled. In all honesty, she wouldn't mind getting to know Justin better, either. But she was a little old for a casual fling. Somehow she knew if she got any closer to this little family, it would break her heart to lose them.

After Tony left, both Justin and Whitney studied Allison, waiting for her answer. She decided to be as vague as possible and pull one of Whitney's tricks by evading the real issue.

"Whitney, I'll bet your father doesn't appreciate you playing matchmaker."

Whitney looked puzzled. "I don't never play with matches. I just want you to marry my daddy."

Allison started to explain what a matchmaker was, but the amusement in Justin's eyes stopped her. He was silently challenging her to make Whitney understand about love and marriage. And he was waiting for Allison to be the one to crush Whitney's childish dreams.

Well, Allison thought, *I refuse to be the bad guy in this scenario. I'll just go along with this game and let Justin be the first one to chicken out.*

"People shouldn't marry unless they're in love with each other," she began. "I don't know your father well enough to fall in love with him."

"But you could if you moved in with us," Whitney reasoned.

Justin's dark eyebrows lifted. It was apparent he was taking this conversation very lightly and leaving all the difficult answers to Allison.

"It's not a good idea for people to live together until they're in love. Even then, it's better if they get married first," Allison explained.

"Okay," Whitney replied, refusing to give up on her plan. "You and Daddy will just have to fall in love."

"How's your schedule, Miss Greene?" Justin teased. "Do you have enough spare time to fall in love this month?"

"I'm not sure," she answered in the same joking tone. "I'll have to check my calendar. But I think October is good month for falling in love. November has Thanksgiving and I'll be pretty busy with all the little Pilgrims and Indians in my class. Then in December there's Christmas, our annual holiday play and winter vacation. So I guess it will just have to be October.''

"Sounds good to me.''

Justin took off his glasses and placed them back in his pocket, thus removing any barrier between her and the power of his magnetic blue eyes. She felt her breath catch in her throat, and she could barely force herself to swallow a bite of the delicious lasagna.

"We'd better eat before our food gets cold,'' she murmured.

"I never have enjoyed falling in love on an empty stomach,'' Justin added, his expression a mask of innocence. Only the brilliance of his eyes and the playful curve of his sexy lips betrayed his subtle wit.

Oh, those lips. Allison could barely tear her gaze away from them so she could take her own advice and eat. It had been a long time since she'd dated anyone seriously, and she realized she was particularly vulnerable right now. She desperately hoped this little game wouldn't backfire, leaving her madly in love with a man who still hadn't let go of his wife. Georgetown was a small place and she couldn't afford to make mistakes if she wanted to continue living and working there.

On the other hand, it was nice to be with someone. It didn't bother her to eat alone. But it was a pleasant change to have company. She didn't realize how much she missed adult conversation until she and Justin exchanged their views on ecology, the Olympics and the upcoming elections. Surprisingly, they shared many of the same opinions, which led to even deeper discussions.

Justin told her about his computer company and the eccentricities of a few of his clients. Allison told him about some of the five- and six-year-old children she had dealt with in Boston and some of the amusing or bizarre things they had said or done.

Whitney listened with remarkable good manners, apparently so anxious that her father and her teacher get along that the little girl ate quietly, joining the conversation only when spoken to directly.

Although Allison no longer suspected child abuse, she still watched Whitney closely to see how she interacted with her father. It was clear they were devoted to each other. As much as Whitney thought she wanted a woman to join their family, Allison suspected the reality of having to share Justin would hit the child hard. Allison hoped that woman, whoever she might be, would anticipate the problem and try to soften the blow.

Tony brought the dessert tray and tempted them all with flaky pastries and rich cheesecake. Allison resisted but almost changed her mind while watching Whitney dig into a bowl of orange sherbet and Justin enjoy the cheesecake.

"Surely you're not watching your weight," Justin commented between bites.

"Who isn't?" Allison answered wryly. "But that usually doesn't stop me from eating dessert. I'm just a little tired tonight and the lasagna hit the spot."

"Did you have a lot of coloring tests to grade or alphabets to edit?" he teased.

"You're joking, but I do have about a zillion puzzle pieces to separate back into their boxes."

"That sounds like a job for our favorite little matchmaker," Justin offered. "Are the pieces at your house or school?"

"I brought them home so I could sort them in the evenings once it gets too cold to work on my house."

"What are you doing with your house?"

"Oh, the usual thing people do when they inherit a hundred-year-old house—I'm replacing every wire, every stick of wood and piece of plumbing." She laughed, then amended, "Actually, not *every* wire, stick of wood or piece of pipe. It just seems that way. Right now I'm merely trying to get the outside finished and I'm getting close. I was working on the porch railing today and there's still the picket fence to paint."

"My, what a resourceful woman you are. You tame wild children by day and rebuild old houses at night."

Her expression became sober. "Don't make fun of me."

Immediately apologetic, he said, "I wasn't. I'm genuinely impressed. I'm more electronically inclined but I surely can handle a paintbrush. And we can put Whitney to work on the puzzles. If you don't mind having a couple of helpers drop by tomorrow."

"I don't know if—"

"Oh, please, Miss Greene," Whitney cut in, apparently forgetting she was trying to be invisible. "I'm *really* sorry about the puzzles. I *like* to put them together. And I could play with your cat. I *really* like cats."

"In your spare time, maybe you can work on her use of *really*," Justin whispered to Allison as they stood up. "So what do you say? Is it on for tomorrow or not? Remember we have only a month to fall in love."

"Do you always give Whitney everything she wants?"

"No, not always." As he held Allison's jacket, her eyes were drawn to his. There was the familiar twinkle, but there was also a hint of seriousness as he went on, "Sometimes I do things just for me."

Allison ached to ask him into which category she fell, but she dared not. At this stage in their relationship—it was even too young and undefined to be called a relationship—she didn't want to hear his answer.

"Nine o'clock if you're serious," she answered, keeping her tone light and allowing every avenue of escape. "Two o'clock if you're afraid of blisters."

"Ha!" He finished buttoning Whitney's jacket and swung his daughter into his arms. "Whitney and I accept your challenge and we shall see you bright and early tomorrow morning. And we'll bring doughnuts."

"And doughnut holes," Whitney added.

There was a little disagreement over the bill as Allison tried to pay her share but Justin insisted on paying it all. "We got you here on false pretenses, or at least Whitney did," he reasoned. "It's only fair that I should have to pay the check and deduct it from her allowance. Let's see." He pretended to calculate. "At a quarter a week, she should have this paid off a few months before her eighth birthday."

"Oh, Daddy," Whitney sputtered.

When they reached the parking lot, Justin stated to Allison, "We'll drive you home."

"It's only a couple of blocks from here. I can walk," Allison began, but her protest was halfhearted. The wind had picked up and had a prewinter chill that easily penetrated her light jacket.

"We need to see where this place of torture that you call home is located. Besides, it wouldn't be good for morale if the kindergarten kids heard that their teacher froze in midstride as she was walking home from a parent-student conference."

"It's not that cold."

"It's not that far out of my way."

She gave up, sliding into the seat while he held the door open. She couldn't remember the last time a man had done that for her. It seemed that chivalry was no longer the "in" thing to do.

Whitney sat between them, her small body safely strapped into a seat belt, her head resting on Allison's arm. They had barely driven out of the parking lot when the girl suddenly grew heavier and her head began to slide.

"She's already asleep," Allison whispered, propping Whitney's head up in a more comfortable position.

"Matchmaking must be exhausting work." The white flash of Justin's grin was visible even in the dark interior of the car.

"Look, you two don't have to come over tomorrow. I'm not sure it's a good idea for Whitney to believe that, on a whim, she can manipulate adults into doing things they don't want to do. Oh, it's that house on the right."

He turned into the driveway and cut the engine. Before she could stop him, he was out of the car and walking around to her side. Carefully she rearranged Whitney so the girl was lying sideways on the seat, so deeply asleep that the movement didn't disturb her.

Justin didn't say anything until they were standing on the wide porch that stretched across the front of her house. "I'll admit that I've given Whitney her way more often than I probably should have. But if it mattered a great deal to her and didn't matter to me, I didn't see any reason not to if it wouldn't actually hurt her."

Sheltered from the wind and wrapped in the warmth of the low-wattage porch light, it was as if they were the only two people in the whole world. Allison unlocked the door, then leaned her back against the door frame as he continued.

"In this case, it didn't really matter one way or the other…"

Allison was shocked at the intensity of the pain that squeezed her chest. She had heard enough. Turning, she reached for the doorknob but was halted by the brush of his fingertips over her cheek. Gentle pressure forced her to look back at him.

"It didn't matter at first. I haven't done much socializing in the last few years, especially with people my own age. I thought it might be a nice change of pace to have a couple of dinners, maybe see a movie or two. Whitney would be happy that I was trying. If it worked out, it worked out. No pressure."

His hand slid over until his index finger touched her lips. Lightly it followed the curve of her mouth.

"But something happened while we were talking this evening. No, to be absolutely honest, I felt it the night you were at my house. I realized I wasn't interested in you as a generic date, but as a person. When it was suggested that we get to know each other better, I realized it wasn't just a game. I *really* did want to know more about you and spend some time with you," He chuckled. "Now Whitney's got me saying *really*."

He took a step closer until only inches of air that was suddenly quite warm separated them. "The meeting tonight was for Whitney," he said as he leaned toward Allison. "But this is for me."

She didn't move, she didn't resist. She waited… impatiently…for that first electric jolt when his lips touched hers. Slowly they moved across her mouth until their lips joined in a kiss that was both hungry and hesitant.

He was as breathless as she when he broke the contact. Looking deeply into her eyes, his smile was tentative, almost as if he were anxious that she was feeling the same surge of emotions he was.

"Now it's my turn to give you a chance to call a halt to this *game* because I'm willing to see how it turns out," he offered softly, apprehensively.

She found it endearing that he was as nervous and unsure as she was. A shaky grin separated her lips, which were still moist from his kiss. Her heart was pounding as if she had been doing aerobics, and her skin tingled where his fingers had lingered.

"October is a good month for falling in love, don't you think?" she asked as a wave of shyness swept over her.

"It's the *bestest* month," he replied with a sigh of relief, and pulled her into his arms.

Chapter Eight

"Miss Greene, you live in a dollhouse." Whitney's voice was filed with awe.

Allison studied the old house with a new perspective and could see how it did, indeed, resemble a dollhouse. The clapboard siding had received a fresh coat of pale blue paint. The eaves, complete with intricately curved gingerbread trim, and the boards around the doors and windows, were a bright white. Four carved columns and the spindles and rails of the porch had been stripped, and she hoped to finish painting them today to match the trim.

Built in a style that was popular in the late eighteen hundreds, the small two-story house was almost as tall as it was wide. There was a bay window on the right side in an area that Allison used as a breakfast nook and another bay window in the front of the house, which flooded the living room with light. Colorful stained glass panes gave the rooms a rosy glow, which added to the fairy-tale atmosphere of the charming Victorian building.

"You know, I remember thinking the same thing when I used to visit Aunt Millie during my summer vacations. I was a little older than you, Whitney, maybe eight. My parents let me fly out here every summer for about five or six years." Allison smiled at the memory. "The house was painted a lemon yellow when I inherited it, but it was this exact shade of blue when I stayed here as a child.''

"But why did you stop coming to visit your Aunt Millie?" Whitney asked. "Didn't you like it here?"

"I loved it here and I'm not sure why I stopped. I guess I must have gotten too busy with teenage things."

"Like boys," Justin suggested with a knowing grin.

"Like boys," Allison confirmed. "And talking on the phone for hours with my girlfriends. And..." She stopped. She had almost let slip that she had spent one summer in Europe with her mother, and other summers at their beach house at Cape Cod.

Allison felt a twinge of guilt that she wasn't being completely honest with Whitney. But she didn't think the little girl would understand the real reasons why Allison had suddenly started spending her summers away from home. It was the year her brother went to Vietnam that she had first come to Colorado for a visit. Before that, her family had always stayed at the beach house. But with Craig gone, it hadn't been the same. Splashing in the ocean or working on a suntan was so frivolous compared to the constant danger he was in, and no one could have a good time with the threat of losing him hanging over them.

Even after Craig came home, things had never been the same. It took years before the family felt comfortable at the beach house again. They tried to resume the carefree summer vacations when Allison was a teenager. That is, until Craig committed suicide. Even though she was in college, a mature young woman in her early twenties, Craig's death had marked the end of innocence, not only for her but the rest of her family. Her parents closed the beach house and eventually sold it, unable to live with the memories.

But Aunt Millie knew how much Allison had enjoyed her visits to the Rockies. It had been the perfect place to escape to when the girl hadn't been able to deal with the harsh realities of the Vietnam War era. Too young to understand the layers of politics, protests and pride, she simply knew it was tearing her family apart. With Aunt Millie in Georgetown, where the pace was slower and more old-fashioned, Allison felt comfortable and safe. Surrounded by the beauty and purity of nature, she could, for a while, almost forget her mother's worried tears, her father's long absences and her brother's letters filled with brave words that didn't quite hide his terror and repulsion of the death and destruction around him.

Aunt Millie had understood that those summers were some of the best of Allison's life. She had known Allison would love and care for the house and not let it be torn down to make room for condos or turned into a boutique or restaurant as so many of the old structures in town had been.

Allison poured coffee for herself and Justin and a glass of orange juice for Whitney while Justin arranged the doughnuts and cinnamon rolls on a platter.

"Did your aunt have any kids?" Whitney asked as she stacked doughnut holes into a pyramid shape on her plate.

"No, she didn't, but she loved children. She was a teacher, too, except that she taught fifth grade here at the Georgetown school." She didn't add that Aunt Millie had been married but that her husband died early in their marriage. Aunt Millie had never remarried, and Allison remembered sitting with the older woman on the front porch while Aunt Millie spoke about how sometimes true love only happened once and for her there could never be anyone to take Uncle Bob's place in her heart or life.

Allison took a sip of coffee and glanced over at Justin. Was that how it was for him and his Caroline? Could he ever truly love someone else? Was he attracted to Allison simply because his daughter needed a mother? Or was Allison his first tentative step back into the dating game?

It wasn't that Allison expected anything permanent to develop between them. He was a nice man, but even after the hours they had spent talking, she still barely knew him. And she certainly wasn't in love with him.

She drained her cup and set it back on its saucer. So what was wrong with accepting Justin as a friend and enjoying his companionship? That kiss last night hadn't meant anything. After all, it had been only one kiss. And the hug could mean anything from "I'm lonely" to "thank you for caring about my daughter."

But the sound of Whitney's laughter drifted into her thoughts. Allison enjoyed being around children. It was fun to share their joy of discovery and pride of achievement as they learned new things. Their minds and their bodies were in constant motion and the momentum swept everyone along with them.

And Allison could almost feel the rooms warm as the little girl's giggles chased away the shadows. It had been a long time since a child had lived here, and the house sighed its approval.

"What's your kitty's name?" Whitney was sitting on the floor with the calico cat happily curled in her lap.

"Her name's Curiosity."

"She's so pretty," Whitney murmured as she petted the cat's soft fur. "I wish I could have a cat."

"Uh-oh. We're about to tread on dangerous ground," Justin said, pushing back his chair and standing up. "Where's that paintbrush?"

"Coward." Allison sensed a pet was a touchy subject in the Sloane household.

"I just don't think it's fair for a pet to be locked up in a town house all the time. Our patio is barely big enough for a couple of chairs and a flower box."

Allison didn't comment. Her parents had always given her much the same argument, except their excuse was that they lived in the city. She'd already vowed she would let her children have a pet or two...if she ever had children. But it wasn't any of her business that Justin wouldn't let Whitney have an animal.

Allison picked up the cardboard box that was filled with mismatched puzzle pieces and put it on the table.

"Whitney, do you want to separate the puzzles, or would you rather play with Curiosity?" Allison asked.

"Whitney did that?" Justin asked, staring at the jumbled mess with disbelief.

Allison waited to see if Whitney would accept responsibility for her actions. And Allison was not disappointed.

"I'm *really* sorry about the puzzles, Miss Greene," Whitney apologized. "I didn't want to do it. I just couldn't think of anything else, but I know it was naughty. I'll fix them."

"I appreciate that you've offered, but I wouldn't mind if you didn't," Allison said, giving the little girl an honorable way out of the situation. "It won't be an easy job."

"I *want* to do it. I've worked most of the puzzles at school, so maybe it won't be so hard for me." Whitney looked down at the purring cat curled in her lap. "But would you mind if I put them on the kitchen floor? That way Curiosity could help me."

Allison doubted how much help the cat would be. In fact, once the pieces were spread out, Curiosity would probably only complicate matters when she discovered they were fascinating playthings. But Whitney seemed more than happy to deal with whatever the cat might want to do.

"Sure you can work with them in the kitchen. All the empty boxes are stacked in the utility room." Allison gestured toward the door on the opposite side of the kitchen. "Once you find all the pieces of each puzzle, put them in their correct box." Allison placed the box of pieces on the floor next to the girl, then grimaced as Whitney dumped it upside down.

"Okay," Whitney acknowledged. With one hand petting the cat and the other digging through the pile of puzzle pieces, she was already engrossed in the job at hand.

"And now, I guess it's our turn to get busy," Justin said as he carried his and Allison's coffee cups and Whitney's glass into the kitchen, carefully stepping over the scattered shapes.

"I'll give you a last chance to get out of the work," Allison offered.

Justin shook his head and chuckled. "You know, I'm beginning to get a complex. I know I told you that I spend a lot of time at my computer. I'm beginning to think you've classed me with the hopelessly nerdy section of the male population."

She peered at him with pretended skepticism. "Well, let's see how you pass the test."

"A test! And I forgot to study," he moaned. "I always hated pop quizzes."

Allison led the way to the garage. They opened and stirred the paint, then carried it and the brushes to the front yard.

Justin surveyed the work to be done. "Are you sure you wouldn't want a nifty candy-cane effect on your porch posts?" he asked.

"No, I think I'll settle for all-white trim, thank you. You'll be graded on the quality of your brush strokes and not on your creativity."

He started on one end of the porch and she started on the other. Since the porch floor had already been painted and the railing was not quite waist high, there wasn't a lot of surface to be covered. With two people working, the job went quickly and it wasn't quite one o'clock when they met in the middle.

As they both painted the last spindle, they suddenly seemed to lose control of their paintbrushes.

"Whoops," Allison said as her paintbrush slipped, leaving a white blob on Justin's hand.

Justin's rhythmic stroking never faltered, even though his hand extended slightly, painting a streak across Allison's cheek. "Oh, sorry. Did I miss the spindle?"

Allison walked around until they were both on the same side of the railing.

"Maybe your glasses are dirty and you can't see clearly," she commented, then leaned toward him and dabbed a large white dot in the middle of each of his lenses. "There, how does it look now?"

"Well, it looks like we're finished," he declared. "Everything's white. I guess I can go home now." He dropped his paintbrush into the can.

"Oh, no, you don't. You can't get out of it that easily," she accused, no longer able to keep from laughing.

"I hear you, but I can't see you." He held out his hands, groping for her as she squealed and tried to dodge him. It was evident that his vision wasn't totally impaired as he unerringly followed her around the side of the house.

He lunged forward, catching her by surprise. "Hmm, who could this be?" he mused as he held her against him with one arm and let the other hand wander over her face. "Whoever she is, she's soft, but she smells like paint."

Any desire to avoid being caught had melted the instant he pulled her against him. She was very aware of the pres sure of his body against hers and the sweet warmth of his breath as it followed the path of his fingers over her face.

"I wonder how she tastes," he murmured, and captured her lips with a sureness that proved either he could see through the white glaze or that he had incredible instincts.

As soon as their lips fused, it didn't matter that his glasses were paint-covered and hers had suddenly fogged over. All their other senses were overwhelmed by the surge of feelings the touch generated. Allison gasped, her open mouth becoming an invitation for the gentle exploration of his tongue.

Oblivious to the paintbrush still gripped in her hand, she wrapped her arms around his neck, pulling him closer... closer. For once she didn't stop to analyze whether or not he should be kissing her...or if she should be allowing it.

"I thought you were painting the porch," a voice accused, bursting unwelcome through the haze.

Allison and Justin automatically jumped apart, guilty looks on their faces as they turned toward the source of the interruption.

"Daddy, you've got paint on your glasses. And you've got paint on your face, Miss Greene. Boy, are you two messy."

Justin and Allison, who had both removed their glasses, looked back at each other and broke into laughter as soon as their eyes met.

"I can paint without getting it all over me," Whitney pointed out primly, which only made Justin and Allison laugh harder.

"I was just going to ask when are we going to eat lunch?" the little girl continued. "Me and Curiosity are getting pretty hungry."

"We were about to come inside," Allison finally managed to say. "We were just..." she noticed the paintbrush still in her hand "...going to clean our brushes," she finished, knowing it sounded lame, but her mind was still muddled from Justin's kiss.

"Yes, we finished painting the porch," Justin agreed. "But I couldn't see where I was going..." his eyes twinkled as his gaze never moved from Allison's face "...and Miss Greene was helping me find my way."

The implication brought a rush of color to Allison's cheeks. It suddenly dawned on her that, just seconds ago, she had been standing in her front yard in the undeniably intimate embrace of a man. Her neighbors would be shocked. She was shocked.

But she could still feel the pressure of his lips on hers and she wasn't sorry. In fact, if she regretted anything, it was that they *had* been in such a nonprivate place and that they had been interrupted. Her cheeks burned hotter at the thought. Justin was the first man in a long time who made her blood race and her temperature soar. Being with him reminded her that she was a woman—not just a teacher or a daughter or a sister, but a woman who had needs of her own.

It was in that instant that Allison knew she was going to spend as much time with Justin as possible. She still wasn't convinced he was as available as his widowed status might indicate. And she had no idea if there was any hope they would have any sort of future together.

But he made her feel good. He added a new sparkle to a normally ordinary day. And he made her laugh. It was worth the risk on the off chance it might work. The only thing she had to lose was her heart.

Whitney was studying them with an indulgent amusement. "Grown-ups," she said with a sigh, shaking her head as if she'd simply never understand them. Then she went back into the house.

Allison and Justin stood, silent for a moment longer.

"I guess we'd better get cleaned up," she spoke first.

"I guess so," he agreed, but neither moved.

"Your daughter thinks we're crazy."

"I'm beginning to wonder about us myself." He grinned. "I can't remember the last time I had a paint fight." He held up his glasses and surveyed the opaque surfaces.

"Me, either." Allison chuckled. "You looked pretty funny, sort of like Little Orphan Annie with those big white eyes."

"But I liked the result." His gaze suggestively returned to her lips. "Maybe sometime we'll be able to continue that particular discussion without being interrupted or without having Whitney asleep in the car."

"I seem to always be surrounded by children," she reminded him.

"It's an effective form of birth control."

"Justin!"

He shrugged, but his roguish grin was unapologetic. "I can't help it. When I get close to you I almost forget that I'm a thirty-three-year-old father. It's like I'm back in school."

"And you have a crush on your English teacher."

His expression grew serious. "Allison Greene, I never had a teacher like you. And the things I feel and think when I'm with you have absolutely nothing to do with elementary education." The twinkle returned and he added, "On the other hand, I've been out of circulation for a long time. Maybe you *could* teach me a thing or two."

"Justin!" she repeated. But she couldn't deny that his words excited her. In fact, everything about this man excited her.

They returned to the front yard where he picked up th paint can and his brush and took her brush. "I guess we' better get cleaned up and feed *our* children."

Although Allison knew he was jokingly referring to he cat as her child, she savored the sound of the term. *Ou children . . .* she could think of worse ways to spend the res of her life. She felt a sudden burst of pure joy. Here she wa with a wonderful man and his adorable daughter in a beau tiful town. Even the weather was perfect.

The chill of the previous evening had been chased away by the bright autumn sun, leaving the air comfortably warm Splashed up the sides of the mountains that surrounde Georgetown, large stands of aspens glowed like liquid gold The maples, cottonwoods and willows in town were also wearing their finest fall colors in all shades of red, yellow orange and green. Last night's wind had stolen some of the crisp, colorful leaves, spreading them like a rich Oriental carpet over the lawn.

"You know something else I haven't done in years?" she asked, sliding him an impish grin.

"Dare I guess?" he asked, one dark eyebrow arched pro vocatively.

She chuckled and nodded in mock dismay. "Yes, that, too. But I was talking about something a little more imma ture." She bent and scooped up a handful of leaves.

Justin eyed her suspiciously.

"When's the last time you rolled in the leaves?" she asked.

"As tempting as that sounds, I think I'll pass on it. I've got paint all over me and those leaves will stick every where." He started to turn away.

Allison deflated like a balloon whose string had slipped off. It was almost as if Justin were reprimanding her for acting so silly. For one brief moment, she had felt young and carefree again, as if anything were possible. She opened her fingers and the leaves trickled between her hands, falling down around her feet.

"Sure, let's go," she said, dusting her hands together. Her head was down and she didn't notice that Justin hadn't moved until she bumped into him.

"On second thought, I don't think that's an offer I can refuse," he said. Setting the paint can and brushes behind him, he scooped up an armful of leaves and lifted them over her head. "What happens every autumn?" He paused and let a couple of leaves leak between his fingers and float down on her upturned face. "The leaves all *fall.*"

"That sounds like a kindergartner's joke."

"Where do you think I heard it?" he asked.

She tried to dodge the avalanche, but he grabbed her and they tumbled to the ground. She squirmed out from under him and scooped a pile of leaves over him. But he caught her arms and pulled her to him. With his arms wrapped around her, they rolled over and over until they were both thoroughly covered in leaves.

"Uh-hmm." The sound of someone clearing his throat brought a halfhearted halt to their horseplay. Expecting to see Whitney, neither Justin nor Allison made any attempt to disentangle themselves or to stand up.

Lying on her back, Allison had to twist her head to look up. Instead of seeing a pair of small blue-jean-covered legs, her gaze traveled up to the bewildered face of a teenage boy.

"Uh . . . here's the pizza you ordered, ma'am," he said, shifting uncomfortably.

"But we didn't—" she began to say, but Justin's laughter interrupted.

"What kind of pizza is it?" he asked the delivery boy.

"Half plain cheese and half deluxe."

"Yes, that's ours." Justin disentangled his arms and legs from Allison and stood up. Without even asking how much it was, he reached into his billfold and pulled out a few bills. "Keep the change."

"Thank you, sir," the boy said, after giving them one last look that clearly mirrored his amazement that two adults would be participating in such a juvenile activity, he returned to his car and drove off.

"But how . . . ?" Allison sat up and began to brush the leaves off her face.

"Whitney. She must have given up on us. I've let her call out for pizza before, so I suppose she assumed we were too busy."

He held out his free hand and Allison let him help her up. Looping his arm casually around her shoulders, they shuffled across the yard, kicking up a spray of leaves in their path. Justin handed Allison the pizza and picked up the paint and brushes as they passed them, then he took them to the garage while Allison went into the house. With one hand, she tried to knock off as many leaves as possible, but she could feel pieces of them still stuck in her hair and inside her clothes.

Whitney didn't ask, but from the way she surveyed Allison's appearance, it was evident she noticed.

Not that anyone wouldn't notice, Allison thought as she peered into the mirror. She had pulled her hair back into a ponytail so it wouldn't get into the paint, but so many tendrils had escaped the band and there was so much debris lodged in it, she had to take her hair down, comb it out and refasten it.

Unfortunately, the mess was now on the bathroom floor. But the smell of pizza lured her back to the kitchen. Justin was already there, looking remarkably fresh with only a few particles of leaves glued to the spots where paint had spattered onto his old sweatshirt. His hair was neatly combed and his glasses, which were lying on the table, were sparkling clean.

Whitney had set the table, complete with napkins and flatware and even glasses of cola at each place. "We need to sit down *right* now or the pizza's gonna be cold. Daddy, you know how you hate cold pizza."

In some ways Allison thought Whitney's mothering was cute, but in other ways, it alarmed her. The little girl was showing a remarkable amount of responsibility for one her age. Just as Justin needed to be cajoled into relaxing and letting go a little, Whitney needed to be reminded she was a child. She should have been outside rolling in the leaves with Justin and Allison instead of staying inside and playing housekeeper.

"Whitney, I think you should help us paint the fence this afternoon," Allison announced. "Would you like that?"

Whitney's eyes brightened, then she shook her head, "No, someone has to clean off the table and finish the puzzles."

"I'll do the dishes while you and your dad get started on the fence. And we can finish the puzzles any time."

Whitney looked to her father for confirmation. At his nod, she smiled. "I like to paint. I promise I'll do a good job and I'll try not to spill."

"I'm sure you'll do a terrific job," Allison assured the girl. "I've seen how well you paint your pictures in school."

The child beamed under the praise and waited impatiently for her father to finish eating so they could get to work. As Justin was following her out the back door, he leaned toward Allison and said, "Was it my imagination or did I hear Tom Sawyer whistling?"

Allison laughed. "Hey, it worked back then and it still works today. I know a good thing when I see it."

"Do you really?" Justin flashed her a teasing wink and shut the door behind him.

She did indeed, and she knew Justin and Whitney were the two best things that had happened to her in a very long time. They seemed to be enjoying spending their time with her now. But there was no doubt that the father and child were very close. How much longer would they allow an outsider to share their lives? They had had each other for so long. Was it possible for anyone to ever truly become a part of their compact, close-knit family?

Allison rinsed the dishes and loaded them into the dishwasher while Curiosity sat on the kitchen stool and meticulously cleaned her paws and face. As Allison passed the stool, she stopped to scratch the cat's back.

"So, Curiosity, you like that little girl, don't you? It's nice to have a child around, isn't it? Yeah, I sure do like that little girl, too. And her daddy... well, I could get used to having him around, too."

Curiosity stretched and curled into a contented position on the stool's cushion.

Allison stepped around the puzzle pieces that were still in the middle of the floor and was surprised at how many Whitney had been able to put together in so short a time. The child was truly gifted. But she was also much too intense. Allison decided it would be her goal as the girl's teacher and friend to help Whitney learn how to be a kid. And if she made Whitney's father remember how to play in the process, so much the better.

Justin and Whitney worked together well and were moving along the picket fence in rapid procession. Allison found another paintbrush but hesitated to join them. She enjoyed listening to Whitney's chatter and Justin's baritone responses and occasional laughter. It was a comfortable moment... a wistful moment. Allison wanted, more than almost anything, to belong to them and for them to belong to her.

"Come on, Miss Greene. You can paint with me. See, I'm doing a real good job, aren't I, Daddy?"

"You sure are, sweetheart." Justin looked up at Allison. "Yes, come join us, Miss Greene. We're having so much fun you won't want to miss a minute of it."

"Sarcasm will get you pizza for dinner, too," she threatened, intercepting his mischievous grin.

"Oh, no!" he declared.

"Oh, boy!" Whitney exclaimed at the same instant.

Allison enjoyed herself so much she almost felt guilty. Getting her fence painted became the least of her objectives as she and Whitney and Justin talked and laughed, making the task go quickly—almost too quickly.

As the shadows filled the canyon, the chill of the evening began to return. Justin sent Whitney inside and even tried to talk Allison into going indoors while he finished alone. But Allison reasoned it was her fence, and she should certainly help. It was almost too dark to see the final strokes their brushes made as they painted the last two pickets.

Justin stood and stretched. "Now I remember why I decided on a career with computers. It was a desperate attempt to escape manual labor."

"Ha, but it caught up with you when you least expected it."

"A lot of things are like that." He tamped down the top of the paint can and dropped the brushes into a bucket of clean water.

"Oh, really. Such as?" Allison prompted.

"Such as having your kid get old enough to start to school," he said.

"Such as your thirtieth birthday," Allison added.

He nodded. "Such as your fortieth birthday."

They both groaned their response to that thought.

"Such as having your daughter set you up with her teacher." Allison was sorry she said it as soon as it slipped out, because she knew it sounded as if she were fishing for some sort of confirmation.

Justin looked up from the brush he had been washing and flashed her a tender smile. "Remind me to thank her for that."

Allison's heart soared. It was such a simple comment to give so much pleasure. "Not all of my parent-teacher conferences go so well."

His expression took on a fierceness. "They'd better not."

"This is a very special situation," Allison assured him, delighted at the hint of possessiveness in his reaction.

"How about another roll in the leaves?" he murmured, wiggling his eyebrows roguishly. "It's dark outside and no one could see us if we—"

"Daddy, when are we going to eat dinner?"

Allison and Justin looked through the garage door opening and saw Whitney standing on the back porch holding Curiosity.

"Like I said, maybe someday we'll have a chance to finish a whole conversation without having her interrupt us." Justin sighed. "Or better yet, maybe we'll be able to find out what happens after a conversation. It's been so long I can't even remember."

"Such as what?" she repeated, hoping he didn't see the anxious tenseness of her smile.

"Such as . . . falling in love."

"Daddy, I've changed my mind," Whitney announced, breaking the mood as she walked into the garage. "I don't want Miss Greene to move in with us."

Allison paused, her hand poised over the paintbrush Justin was handing her to dry. If Whitney no longer was interested in getting Allison and Justin together, Allison wouldn't have a chance to fit into their family, no matter how Justin felt. And almost as much as the thought of not seeing Justin hurt, the fact that the little girl was so fickle that she didn't want Allison around anymore hurt more. She believed they were close...very close to being a real family. A lump rose in her throat so quickly that she couldn't form the words to ask for a clarification. Fortunately, Justin asked the question for her.

''Why not, Whitney?'' His expression was equally surprised.

Whitney looked from one adult to the other and gave them a satisfied smile, as if she had it all figured out. ''Because I've decided me and you should move into this magical house with her.''

Chapter Nine

"Good Morning, Miss Greene."

The voice over the telephone brought Allison immediately awake. She glanced at the clock and saw it was after eight. "Oh, no, I overslept!" She threw back the covers and was sitting on the side of the bed before she finished speaking.

"Calm down, sleeping beauty," the voice cut in. "It's a holiday. There's no school today."

That's right; it was Columbus Day and she had every right to sleep in. As she relaxed back onto the bed, her thoughts of school were replaced by the identity of the voice on the other end of the telephone line.

"Good morning, Mr. Sloane," she said, her tone softening. "I'm surprised you're up so early. After all that moaning last night when you left here, I thought you'd be in bed all day."

"I *am* in bed." His voice was low and suggestive. After a breathless pause, he added, "Alone . . . and lonely."

A tingle shot through Allison's body at the mental image of him reclining against his pillows, a sheet draped low across his hips. *Pull yourself together,* Allison admonished herself. *You're acting like a love-starved old maid.* So what if she fit that stereotype more than she cared to admit? Her

Get 4 Books FREE

SEE BACK OF CARD FOR DETAILS

DETACH ALONG DOTTED LINE AND MAIL TODAY! – DETACH ALONG DOTTED LINE AND MAIL TODAY! – DETACH ALONG DOTTED LINE AND MAIL TODAY!

very feminine reaction was merely a reminder that she wasn't all *that* old. Her desire to love and be loved was still alive and well.

"What are you wearing?" he asked, sharing her wayward thoughts.

Allison looked down at the warm but not very romantic cotton flannel gown. Should she tell him the truth or should she describe a slinky silk nightie that would make him salivate? It wasn't that she didn't own sexy sleepwear. Her mother always sent her something terribly expensive from her favorite boutique for birthdays and Christmas, as if the older woman couldn't imagine what sort of things Allison might need now that she lived in the "wilderness." Or maybe her mother thought Allison wouldn't be able to find nice lingerie now that she couldn't run into Boston to shop.

But Allison felt silly wearing sexy negligees around the house. Curiosity's claws snagged the soft material and the thinness did nothing to block out the cold. So the gowns stayed hidden, neatly folded in her lingerie drawer next to a daring black-lace teddy and bikini underwear that she had bought for herself on a whim. But she didn't wear them, either. Somehow sexy underwear seemed out of place in a classroom, even well covered by "teacher clothes." Except for occasional lapses such as paint fights and leaf attacks, Allison could be counted on to be the logical, sensible woman everyone expected her to be.

"Don't tell me, let me guess," he went on, easing her dilemma. "Something soft and sensible."

Sensible!

"Probably pink with long sleeves and a high collar."

Long sleeves and a high collar!

"But with lots of lace and bows."

Allison didn't know whether to laugh or cry. He had described her gown so accurately he might as well have been sitting in her room staring at her.

"It's blue," she muttered, perversely pointing out his one error. Did he think she was so lacking in sex appeal that he automatically assumed she would be wearing a granny gown?

He was silent for a moment, then he whispered, "I'd like to see you in it. I'll bet you look beautiful."

Beautiful? He thinks I would look beautiful? Allison sighed, immediately forgiving his "sensible" comment. "Now you have to tell me what you're wearing." She closed her eyes and summoned a mental picture. He had a daughter, so he too had to dress sensibly. Judging from the slightly preppy style of clothes he wore, the way he had his hair cut, his businesslike wire-rimmed glasses and his precise, analytical train of thought, he not only wore pajama bottoms but the tops, as well.

Before he could answer, there was the muffled sound of the phone being jostled against his ear, followed by a cheerful, "Who're you talking to, Daddy? Grandmother? Are we going to see her today?"

It was evident he turned away from the phone as he answered, "I'm talking to Miss Greene. And if you'd be still, I'll finish asking her if she'd like to go with us."

"Yes, yes, *yes*," the little girl squealed. "That'd be *so* much fun. We could go shopping and she could buy me some *neat* clothes."

"Shopping?" Justin echoed weakly and with an obvious lack of enthusiasm.

"Yes, shopping. For *girl* things."

Justin resettled the phone against his ear. "Did you hear all that?" he asked Allison.

"Most of it."

"So how about it? Would you like to go with Whitney and me to Denver? I have some work to deliver, then we'd have the rest of the day free. I sort of thought we'd spend it going to a movie and out to eat, but it sounds like Whitney would rather go shopping. Does any of that strike your fancy?"

Allison considered the list of boring, ordinary things she had planned on doing that day. It was an easy decision to put off cleaning out the refrigerator and crushing her aluminum cans so they could be recycled. "Sure, I'd like to go with you and Whitney."

"Great. Could you be ready about ten? Have you had breakfast?" he asked, then answered his own question before she had a chance to speak. "No, I guess not if I just woke you up. If you can wait, we'll catch breakfast on the way, then we can eat an early dinner in late afternoon. Okay?"

"Okay," Allison agreed, amused by his obsession with planning everything to the smallest detail.

"Is she going with us, Daddy?"

"Yes, she is. Now hurry and get dressed," he spoke to Whitney, then returned to Allison. "We'll be by to pick you up in . . ." He paused, and Allison guessed he was looking at a clock before he continued, "One hour and twenty minutes. And Allison . . ."

"Yes?"

"I'm glad you're going with us."

Allison was smiling as she returned the receiver to its cradle. He thought she looked beautiful and he was glad she was going with them. She hadn't had a chance to look outside yet, but she knew, without a doubt, it was going to be a perfectly gorgeous day.

JUSTIN KNEW he should get up and get dressed, but for several minutes after he hung the phone up, he remained in bed.

He'd surprised himself when he told Allison she was beautiful. He remembered the first day of school when he had thought she looked rather plain. Not unattractive really, just ordinary.

What had she done? When had she grown so beautiful? What miracle had made a passably pretty woman become a fascinating creature who made his body ache to possess her?

He must not have gotten a good look at her before. Or maybe he'd judged her too quickly. He thought about how she'd looked yesterday, half-buried in leaves, her hair spread out. Funny, before that moment he had thought her hair was brown—plain brown. But yesterday he'd seen the rich red and gold highlights of autumn mixed in with the brown.

Her eyes—silly how he had thought they were an indecisive hazel. Since then, he'd seen them sparkle like newly polished emeralds, and he'd watched them warm to a sizzling golden brown that could melt his bones with a glance.

When she suggested they roll in the leaves, he thought she was joking. He was too old for playing around like a kid. Even when he was younger, he hadn't done things like that. On the days he wasn't staying after school for computer club or student council meetings, he'd been helping his father at the family's electronics store.

From the time Justin was old enough to know one end of a screwdriver from the other, he had watched his father put together and repair televisions, radios, small appliances and anything that contained tubes, switches or wires. While other boys were outside playing, Justin was content to observe, learn and, eventually, help with the repair and reassembly of all types of electrical equipment.

Justin had been small for his age and not very athletic. It wasn't until he was a junior in high school that a spurt of growth had taken him to his current height of six feet and added the bulk that made the girls start to notice him. But years of being a nerd had left him shy and totally lacking in self-confidence. It was only when he was involved in an electronics project or in front of his computer screen that he had absolute faith in his abilities.

That was until he met Caroline. She was beautiful, elegant and bored with the social life on the University of Colorado campus. For a reason Justin never quite understood, she was attracted to him. She made it clear, almost from the first moment they met, that she planned to marry him.

Justin thought she was joking. Caroline was every man's best dream, and Justin didn't know how to handle his unexpected blessing. But she persisted, showering him with affection and compliments, building his ego and making him feel as though he could conquer the world. How could he help but fall madly in love with her?

During their entire courtship, he never stopped expecting her to tire of him and move on to someone new. He was amazed and thrilled when she accepted his proposal, or to be more accurate, he accepted hers.

The fantasy continued through their first years of marriage. Justin grew to accept Caroline's love and not constantly question it. She encouraged him to start his own business even though he didn't actually do it until after her death. She gave him the confidence to approach new clients and, unwittingly, the strength to carry on without her.

Justin had been devastated by her death. If it hadn't been for Whitney, he wasn't sure how he would have made it through the nightmare. The one thing about which he had been certain was that he would never fall in love again. How could any woman ever equal Caroline in his eyes or in his heart?

Then Miss Greene entered his—and Whitney's—lives. At first Allison seemed to be Caroline's exact opposite. They certainly didn't look anything alike. Caroline had been refined, poised and totally self-confident while Allison was almost like Justin's female counterpart, quiet, studious and self-conscious enough to hide behind the dubious shield of her glasses.

But there was an impulsive side to her that fascinated him even while he wasn't sure how to relate to it. As a child he hadn't played in a pile of leaves although he had certainly raked his share of them. His first response yesterday to Allison's suggestion had automatically been negative. Then he'd seen the disappointment darken her fascinating eyes. And he suspected it wasn't because she wanted so desperately to tumble around the front yard. But rather it had been that she was disappointed in him because he wouldn't relax his inhibitions enough to do something completely frivolous.

He'd never thought it possible that he would care deeply about another woman—until Allison Greene was thrust, by fate and by his daughter, into his life. He knew it was too soon to include the word *love* in the description of their relationship. But he was, for the first time in years, willing to let things develop naturally and even encourage them a little. Allison was an intelligent, interesting woman. And she, without obvious effort, made him feel he was an intelligent, interesting man.

He thought of how appealing she had looked yesterday, with her cheeks flushed and her hair tousled. His body stirred and hardened at the memory of her firm, full breasts pressed against his chest and the innocently provocative taste of her lips. Every time she moved beneath him during their playful wrestling, the sweet friction of her stomach against his groin had brought a response so immediate it had almost been embarrassing. He was glad she hadn't seemed to notice. Justin was equally relieved they had been interrupted by the pizza delivery boy because it had allowed him a few moments to slow down his raging libido. And raging libido was something Justin wasn't accustomed to dealing with.

He could hear the sound of Whitney brushing her teeth in her bathroom, and he thrust his pajama-covered legs out of the covers. Even before she was born he had always worn pajamas. He couldn't imagine sleeping an entire night in the nude, partly because Caroline hadn't thought it was dignified and partly because he had grown up self-conscious about his body.

As he took a quick shower and shaved, he realized he was smiling. He was looking forward to spending another day with Allison...another day of surprises. Although he thought he had everything well planned, with Allison and Whitney along, there was every chance something unexpected would happen. A week ago that would have upset him. But today, he was looking forward to it.

Allison was ready and sitting on the porch swing when he and Whitney drove up. He stopped in front of the white picket gate, got out of the car and waited for her on the passenger's side.

"You look terrific," he told her as soon as she reached the car. "And not at all like a kindergarten teacher."

"Oh, and exactly how are kindergarten teachers supposed to look?" she asked, sliding into the seat next to Whitney.

He had to tear his gaze away from the enticing stretch of nylon-covered leg revealed when her skirt clung to her thigh.

"They certainly don't wear clothes that fit like that." He punctuated the statement with a low wolf whistle. Even with a paint smear on her cheek and leaves in her hair, he had thought she was beautiful. But dressed in a teal-colored sweater and skirt that showed off her petite body to its best advantage, he thought she was a knockout.

"This old thing?" Her tone was light, but he could tell by the gentle pink of her cheeks that she had taken extra care when dressing for the day.

"Miss Greene, you look *real* pretty," Whitney said, adding her opinion. She reached out and stroked the soft cashmere of Allison's skirt. "I want a sweater this color. Do you think we could find me one just like yours?"

Allison nodded. "We'll try. I guess I'd better fasten my seat belt before we leave."

Whitney pointed down to the belt fastened firmly across her stomach. "See, I've already got mine on. I remembered," she stated with obvious pride.

Justin hurried to fasten his seat belt before they turned their attention to him. "Okay, ladies. How about brunch in Idaho Springs?"

"At the Sugar Plum, Daddy? Could we eat at the Sugar Plum?" Whitney squealed.

"If Miss Greene doesn't mind."

Allison shrugged. "Any place is fine with me. I'm not familiar with any restaurants outside of Georgetown."

"The Sugar Plum is really cool," Whitney added. "They make neat little cookies in all sorts of shapes and put them on their Christmas tree."

"I don't think the Christmas tree will be there yet," Justin reminded her. "But they have good food."

They turned onto the entrance ramp and eased onto the highway. "I couldn't help noticing how nice your house looks," Justin went on, flashing Allison a teasing look. "Whoever painted that fence and your porch sure did a terrific job."

"You think so?" Allison pretended to consider his comment. "I suppose they were worth what I paid them."

Whitney's frown reflected her bewilderment. "Did we get paid anything, Daddy?"

"No, Whitney, we didn't. Not a penny." He held out his hand, palm up, toward Allison. "And just look at those blisters."

"Oh, poor baby," Allison said. She lifted her hand and touched one small swollen bump.

"Ouch!" He jerked his hand back. "You touched my blisters."

Allison held out her hand. "See, I have one, too. Do you want to touch it?"

His glance wandered past her hand and on to the fluffy material that hugged the swells of her breasts. "No, thanks. But I wouldn't mind feeling how soft that sweater is."

Over Whitney's head, he and Allison exchanged a look that was tentative and bold at the same time. Neither was familiar with the dating game and they were moving forward one cautious inch at a time.

"It feels real good," Whitney innocently concurred.

"I'll bet." Justin had no doubt that it would.

Again that pretty flush he was becoming so accustomed to seeing washed across Allison's cheeks.

They moved to a safer subject for the few miles remaining before they turned off the highway and into Idaho Springs. An old silver-mining town, it boasted a population more than twice that of Georgetown. Like Georgetown, many of its residents and businesses were housed in structures that had been built more than a hundred years earlier, when the economy of the area was booming.

Justin parked in front of the restaurant and they enjoyed a comfortable, casual meal. As they were leaving, the proprietor gave Whitney a decorated cookie "for the road."

The child carefully wrapped the cookie in a napkin and cradled it in her lap as if she had received a valuable treasure.

It was another picture-perfect autumn day. The rugged layers of the Rockies surrounded them, their jagged peaks still free of snow except for the glaciers that hid in the shadows year-round. Vivid yellow aspens were startling against the dark green pines, firs and spruces. Even the wildlife was enjoying the last of the season's sunshine as a half-dozen bighorn sheep grazed on the side of a mountain and a mule deer doe and her half-grown fawn nibbled on a bush at the edge of a meadow.

It became a contest to see who could find the most animals. When they passed a herd of buffalo, Whitney surged into the lead.

"I have a sneaky feeling she knew they'd be there," Allison said.

"She did," Justin admitted, earning a giggle from Whitney. "The state raises them in a pasture that has a tunnel so they can cross safely under the highway, so Whitney knew they would be on one side of the road or the other. Usually, there's a big herd of elk off to the right, but they must be bedded down in the trees."

"Are we going to see Grandmother and Grandfather today?"

"If we have time. I thought you wanted to go shopping," Justin replied.

"Yes, I do." Whitney sighed. "But I want to see Grandmother, too."

"We'll see," Justin answered, intentionally vague. Caroline's parents were not two of his favorite people, but Whitney loved them.

As he promised, it didn't take long to deliver the computer programs and explain them to the operator in charge. Then, also as promised, they headed for the nearest mall.

Justin was very familiar with Whitney's wardrobe. He knew her closet was full of pretty dresses and her dresser drawers overflowing with nightgowns, socks and panties. He couldn't imagine what sort of "girl" things she wanted to buy.

But he played along, following her and Allison through the stores, trying to be patient.

"I want some of these," Whitney stated positively as she pointed to a rack of stone-washed jeans.

"You have a pair of blue jeans, Whitney," Justin reminded her.

"*One* pair and they're so... blue," the girl replied. "I want some of these."

"But they look like they're older than you are."

"Daddy, that's what *everyone* is wearing. Everyone except me. I have to wear dorky dresses to school every day."

"*Dorky* dresses?" Justin repeated in exasperation. "Those dresses are very cute. You always look nice and neat."

Whitney sighed. "But, Daddy, I look like a nerd. *None* of the other girls wear dresses."

A nerd? His daughter looked like a nerd? It was a word that hit too close to home for comfort. He turned to Allison for advice. "No one wears dresses anymore?"

"Well, not often," Allison admitted. It was apparent she knew she was being involved in a family discussion and wanted to avoid taking sides. "Most of the girls wear slacks and jeans. We have two recesses a day and in class we're on the floor a lot, so pants are more convenient."

Justin shook his head. He'd put a lot of thought into what his daughter should wear to school. She'd tried to talk him into adding a few pairs of pants to her wardrobe, but he had insisted on dresses. Now Allison was telling him they made her different from everyone else. Of all the things he wanted most for his child, he wanted her to fit in and get along with the other kids.

"Okay, let's see if they have your size," he finally agreed. He didn't miss the triumphant look that Whitney gave Allison. Females. How could he ever hope to understand them?

Whitney and Allison selected several pairs of jeans in different degrees of fadedness, then continued their prowl of the girls' department.

"So what does a person wear with jeans in that condition?" he asked in all sincerity, but received a reprimanding frown from both Allison and Whitney. "All right, I'll be quiet and stand near the cash register," he muttered.

Allison and Whitney chose an armful of tops and blouses and took their selections into the dressing room. Justin waited outside the draped doorway, feeling very conspicuous standing alone, surrounded by mothers and daughters and racks of little girls' clothes. For not the first time, he wondered how different his life would be if Whitney had been a boy. However, it was more curiosity than a genuine wish. He simply couldn't imagine life without her.

She paraded out, modeling each outfit for his approval. He had to admit that she still looked adorable and very feminine whether she was in pants or a dress. As the saleswoman totaled the bill, he was startled that clothes so little could cost so much. But he knew it was a small price to pay for avoiding permanent nerddom.

They made another stop in the shoe department for a pair of ridiculously overpriced tennis shoes with not one but two sets of shoestrings, then they headed toward the exit.

But as they walked through the men's department, Whitney stopped at a rack of stone-washed jeans.

"Here, Daddy. You need to get you a pair of these, too."

"I *need* them?" Justin repeated skeptically. "What for?"

"So you can be cool." Whitney made it all sound so simple.

Justin looked down at his neatly pressed slacks and thought of the one pair of jeans he owned. They were brand new, dark blue and still folded on the top shelf of his closet. His preference was for chinos. But he had no objections to being "cool." Maybe it was time for a change.

He looked through the tabs until he found his size. "And I suppose you think I should buy a new shirt, too."

"Of course," Whitney replied without hesitation. "You need something purple or pink."

"Pink! When I was growing up, guys never wore pink," Justin mumbled, but noticed no one was listening. Allison seemed to be getting as much pleasure out of updating his look as Whitney was.

"Here, try these on." His daughter thrust a handful of shirts at him and he groaned. The only thing he hated worse than shopping was trying on clothes. But he humored her and took them into the men's dressing room.

As he looked in the mirror, he had to admit they didn't look all that bad. Instead of buying one, he ended up with three.

"I'm going to have to dig up a couple extra clients to pay for this shopping trip," he complained, but it was more because he felt they expected him to than because he meant it. "So, where's the women's department? We might as well get Allison a pair of faded jeans. We wouldn't want her to look overdressed when we're out doing *cool* things."

"No, that's not necessary," Allison protested.

But just as they hadn't listened to him, he didn't listen to her and propelled her to a saleswoman. "We'd like a pair of jeans just like these for her." He indicated a still-sputtering Allison.

"Hmm, about a size five or six," the saleswoman guessed, and Allison nodded.

"That's the same size I wear," Whitney declared, delighted to share something so personal with Miss Greene.

The saleswoman led them to yet another pile of jeans and took out a pair for Allison. "Here, these should fit. The dressing rooms are right over there."

"But—" Allison began.

"No buts," Justin cut in. "Whitney had to do it. I had to do it. It's your turn, although it is a shame to cover up those gorgeous legs."

Allison gave up and took the jeans into the dressing room. She didn't wear them out so they could see them, but she nodded when she returned. "They fit fine, but I can't let you buy these for me. I'll pay for them."

He waved away her offer. "Consider them a gift for helping us shop. Without you, Whitney would be doomed to wearing dorky dresses and being a nerd and I'd be uncool for the rest of my life."

"Yes, Miss Greene," Whitney chimed in. "You *have* to take them. If you don't wear yours, then my daddy won't wear his and he'll always look like he does now."

Allison smiled and threw up her hands. "I give up. It's a conspiracy."

But Justin wanted further clarification of Whitney's statement. "So what's wrong with the way I look now?"

"Let's go, Daddy, so we can go to Grandmother's."

"Wait a minute. What's wrong with the way I look?" Justin repeated, but Allison and Whitney were already walking away, laughing and talking together like best friends.

Chapter Ten

"So this is where Caroline's parents live." Allison looked around the neighborhood, recognizing the grandiosity of the superwealthy. Huge homes built by the rich for the even richer sprawled across lots that were at least a half acre in size. Although Allison wasn't familiar with the property values in Denver, she guessed these mansions were in the half-a-million- to three-million-dollar range.

Cherry Hills. Even the name was pretentious. There were no hills, and as far as Allison could see there were no cherry trees of any size to be worthy of the name.

Every driveway they passed had a Mercedes, a BMW, a Volvo or a fancy European sports car parked on it. Gardeners worked on the perfectly manicured lawns, flower beds and sprinkler systems, preparing them for winter. Signs warning of security protection were posted in every yard, and cedar or stone fences shielded most of the backyards from view.

It wasn't that Allison begrudged any of these people their money and possessions. They probably had the ulcers and therapy bills that usually went along with such wealth. It was just that she recognized the life-style and was very glad she didn't share it. She hated to think about the sadness and loneliness that hid behind some of those ornately carved doors.

She'd been there. Not in this exact neighborhood, but in one very much like it. She knew from experience that money did not guarantee happiness. Her mother's friends were shallow, unhappy creatures, more involved in their charities than they were in their own families. Her father's friends were ambitious to a fault, sometimes ruthlessly so.

Allison had grown up in an atmosphere that left her emotionally insecure. But even while she recognized that fact, she hadn't been able to overcome it. She felt that nothing she did was good enough. She knew her mother had been disappointed that Allison wasn't prettier. For her eighteenth birthday, her mother had given Allison carte blanche at the best plastic surgeon in Boston. Allison's mother had always thought her daughter's features were too strong and had recommended Allison add an upward tilt to her nose. More prominent cheekbones would bring a refined elegance to her face, and a reformation of her jawline would take out some of its squareness.

But Allison had resisted the changeover, keeping her straight nose, perfectly adequate cheekbones and stubborn jawline. She'd donated the gift to the children's hospital to be used on a child with birth defects whose parents couldn't afford the treatment. It hadn't been simply a matter of moving to Colorado because Aunt Millie had left her the house. Allison hadn't left Boston; she had escaped—escaped from a life-style similar to the one surrounding them—escaped to a gentler, kinder way of life where maybe, just maybe, she might make a difference in a young child's life.

"This is it," Justin confirmed as he turned into the driveway of a huge French colonial.

Whitney had unbuckled her seat belt and was impatiently waiting for either her father or Allison to get out of the car so she could exit, too.

"Would you like to come in with us? I have no idea how long we'll be in there."

Allison started to say that she would wait in the car, but there was something in his expression that made her change her mind. He looked as if he were about to go into a lion's den, and he didn't want to go alone.

"Sure, I'd like to meet Whitney's grandparents," Allison said, and noted the immediate relief on his face.

Whitney slipped one hand into Allison's and the other into Justin's as they walked to the door. The cozy family scene didn't escape the scrutiny of the tall blond woman who opened the door.

"Hello, Justin," the woman stated with no semblance of welcome.

"Hello, Charlotte." Justin nodded toward Allison. "This is Whitney's teacher, Allison Greene."

"Hello," Charlotte responded briefly. Her gaze swept over Allison, then fell on Whitney. The woman's severe facade slid away as she knelt in front of the little girl and said in a much warmer voice, "Hello, my beautiful little Whitney. Come give Grandmother a hug."

Whitney released Allison and Justin's hands and ran into the older woman's open arms. The affection between the two was obvious and completely genuine. Whatever hostility Allison sensed from the other woman, none of it was focused on Whitney. The teacher in Allison admired the grandmother's devotion to her grandchild. But the woman in Allison resented the barely restrained distaste for Justin.

"Come on in, Whitney. Grandfather's in the garden. Wait until you see the new bird feeder he put up. The birds love it." Charlotte took hold of Whitney's hand as she turned to usher the child into the house. Almost as an afterthought, she glanced over her shoulder and said, "You two can come in if you'd like."

Justin sighed and gave Allison an apologetic arch of his eyebrows. "How can we refuse an invitation like that?" he muttered, and casually draped his arm around Allison's shoulders.

Allison wasn't sure how to interpret the gesture, whether it was because he wanted Allison to feel more comfortable or to bolster his own morale. Whatever the reason, she couldn't help but notice how natural it felt...and how good.

Allison and Justin walked through the large entry hall with its gently spiraling staircase that led to the second floor and into a gigantic den. Whitney and her grandmother continued through the patio door to the redwood deck, completely ignoring her other guests.

"Do I sense a little chill in the air?" Allison whispered to Justin.

"She wasn't too thrilled about her daughter's choice for a husband," Justin replied, keeping his voice low.

Allison's dislike for the woman grew, but it didn't surprise her that Caroline's mother should so quickly and unfairly judge Justin. Allison would say it was typical of the woman's class, but that would mean Allison was being judgmental, too.

"And she never has forgiven me for Caroline's death," he added harshly.

Allison suspected some of that harshness was directed toward himself because she truly didn't believe he had gotten over the tragedy yet, either. She felt it was time both Justin and Charlotte let it go.

"That's ridiculous," Allison chided. "I didn't know her, but I'll bet Caroline would want the two of you to put all this behind you, if only for Whitney's sake."

"If it wasn't for Whitney, I'd never darken this door again," Justin retorted. "I've put up with this for five years just because I believe Whitney should know her relatives, especially both sets of grandparents. And the one thing I don't doubt is that they love her."

"Yes, I can see that they do. And she loves them." Allison reached up and gripped his hand where it rested on her shoulder. "It was wonderful that you gave her this. There are few enough people in her life as it is."

He looked down at Allison, and some of the pain and anger ebbed away from the stormy blue depths of his eyes. "I'm glad there's one more now."

His hand tightened on her shoulder and for a moment Allison thought he was going to kiss her. But he pulled back, apparently remembering they were in his in-laws' house under less than friendly circumstances.

Whitney and Charlotte returned to the den with the little girl chattering about the birds she had seen. Justin glanced at his watch.

"Whitney, tell your grandparents goodbye. We've got to leave now if we want to make the three-thirty show of *101 Dalmatians.*"

"Why don't you let Whitney spend the night with us, Justin?" Charlotte suggested. "She doesn't have school tomorrow and we can bring her home."

Allison felt Justin stiffen and could almost hear his mind working to think of a legitimate reason to refuse. She felt it showed a remarkable desire to keep up the relationship for Whitney's sake, especially when Caroline's father, who had remained on the porch, was either totally impolite and was making no attempt to be civil to Justin or else he couldn't force himself to be in the same room with his former son-in-law.

"Whitney, would you like that?" Justin asked his daughter.

"Yes, Daddy. Oh, please let me stay. Grandmother said she'd take me to Baskin-Robbins."

"Then I guess I'll see you tomorrow," Justin conceded. He handed her the car keys. "Why don't you run out and get a change of clothes?"

She hurried to obey, returning a couple of minutes later with one pair of jeans and a shirt.

"Good Lord, child. Don't you have any better pants than these?" Charlotte exclaimed. "They're all faded."

"Grandmother," Whitney responded with the same sigh of exasperation she had given her father earlier in the day, "that's the way they're *supposed* to look. They're brand-new."

"They look tacky. Why, in my day, I'd never let my child go out dressed in rags like—"

"Come give me a kiss, Whitney," Justin interrupted. "It's time for Miss Greene and me to leave." The child ran into his arms and gave him a fierce hug.

"I love you, Daddy. Don't worry about me."

"I'll try not to." He smiled and returned her hug.

"You and Miss Greene will just have to have fun without me," the little girl said.

"I'm sure they will," Charlotte muttered tartly. "Now run put your clothes in your bedroom. Then we'll see if Grandfather will get the barbecue grill going so we can have hamburgers for dinner."

Whitney stepped away from her father and, with a last wave and goodbye to both him and Allison, she took her clothes and ran down the hall.

"Walk, please," Charlotte called after her, and Whitney slowed to a clumsy skip.

Justin leveled his gaze on Charlotte, and although he didn't speak it aloud, Allison felt he was warning the older lady that she'd better take very good care of his daughter. Charlotte returned his gaze with a haughty tilt of her head as if to say she had raised a daughter and she could certainly take care of Whitney.

"Goodbye, Charlotte. I'd appreciate it if Whitney was home by dark."

Charlotte nodded and walked them to the door, although it felt more like a police escort than a friendly farewell.

"It was nice to meet you," Allison lied politely.

"Yes, you, too," Charlotte returned with equal insincerity, forced through a courtesy that was too deeply inbred to be denied.

Neither Justin nor Allison spoke until they were out of the neighborhood, as if anything they said would be overheard. Finally, breaking the silence, she said, "Now I know why you moved away from Denver. Living within twenty miles of those people would keep me awake nights."

"Yes, that was one of the reasons. You wouldn't believe how much they interfered when Whitney was a baby. They even threatened to take me to court to gain custody of her."

"How awful. What stopped them?"

"I threatened to take Whitney and move to a place where they'd never see us or hear from us again. I guess the possibility of losing her forever was enough for them to make an effort to get along."

"Not much of an effort."

"I know. They make it as uncomfortable for me as possible. But they're very good to Whitney, and in their own way, they're good for her. And, of course, she's crazy about them."

"It's admirable that you've been able to keep from expressing your true feelings about them to Whitney so she can make up her own mind."

He shrugged. "She's all they've got left of Caroline."

And all you've got left of her, too, Allison thought.

"So, enough about my in-laws, we need to decide what we're going to do this evening."

"I'm still game for a movie and a meal," she answered.

"101 Dalmatians?"

"Not really. I saw that when I was about seven or eight. I loved it then, but since Whitney isn't with us, I'd rather see something else."

"I tossed *The Denver Post* in the car this morning because I didn't have time to read it before I picked you up," he said. "Why don't you look up the movie page and see what else is showing."

She found the newspaper and turned to the entertainment section.

"I think there's a sequel to that mouse movie. Is it out yet?" he asked.

Allison gave him an amused look.

He realized he was still programmed to think like a dad and chuckled. "It's been a long time since I've gone to see a movie that wasn't rated 'G.' If I want to see anything racier, I have to wait until it makes it to the video stores. Even then, it's too much trouble to find the time to watch it when Whitney's asleep."

"I had something a little more adult in mind. At least a 'PG.'" She glanced through the selections. "How about that new Robin Williams movie, you know, the one about Peter Pan?"

"The last Peter Pan movie I saw was animated by Disney," he teased.

"You *do* need to get out more."

They found a theater that was close and, their arms loaded with popcorn, nachos and colas, they munched their way through the movie.

"Still hungry?" he asked when they were back in the car a couple of hours later.

"Sort of."

"Italian, Mexican, Chinese, seafood or good old American steak?"

After some discussion, they decided on a well-known steak house and enjoyed a pleasant, peaceful meal. After resisting the dessert tray, Justin leaned back in his chair.

"You know, I almost feel guilty. As much as I love Whitney and like spending time with her, I've really enjoyed this."

"Maybe you've let the line between being a parent and being a friend get a little hazy. You need some time away from Whitney just like she needs time away from you every once in a while."

There was a spark of desire in his eyes as his gaze met hers. "I haven't needed the time alone...until now." He reached out and captured her hand in his. The pitch of his voice was lower, huskier as he continued. "Let's go home."

They kept up a normal conversation about school, the weather, the world situation...everything they could think of except what was really on their minds. The anticipation of what might happen settled low in the pit of Allison's stomach like heavy, liquid heat. She had no idea how far things would go, or even how far she'd like them to go. The one thing she knew was that, for once, they would be alone.

He parked the car in her driveway, but before he turned off the engine, he paused, his fingers on the keys, and looked at her. "It's late."

"Yes, it is." She knew she had to get up early the next day and teach the Rams class. Instead of feeling grateful that he was ready to call it a night, she was disappointed. "Would you like to come in for a cup of coffee... or something?"

His fingers moved and the car fell silent. "I'd love to come in for a cup of coffee... or something."

He took her hand as they walked to the back door, letting it go only long enough for her to unlock the door and open it. She flipped on the lights and shut the door behind them, then he whirled her around and pulled her into his arms.

"I've been waiting all day for this," he breathed against her lips. "Heck, I've been waiting all weekend for this."

He cupped her face in his hands, then let his fingers slide until they were buried deeply in the thickness of her hair. "I know now why I passed up dessert. There was nothing on that tray that looked as good as your lips...." He lowered his mouth to hers and moaned as she returned his kiss with an unrestrained passion she wasn't aware she possessed. All she could think of was getting closer to him, feeling the warmth of his body, having him satisfy the hunger, the ache throbbing deep inside her.

She wrapped her arms around him, holding on when her knees threatened to buckle beneath her. But by leaning on him, she could feel the full extent of his stimulation, pressing hard and hot against her. It excited her... and it frightened her.

To give in to the physical urges of their bodies without any sort of emotional commitment would not be the act of a responsible adult. And she and Justin were, above all else, responsible adults, however much their senses were aroused.

Her hands moved from his back to press gently against his chest. The pleasure his kiss promised almost made her change her mind. It wasn't until his mouth lifted, momentarily breaking the bond of temptation that she was able to say, "Coffee. I think we'd better get that coffee." It was more of a gasp than normally spoken words.

If he'd offered any resistance, she doubted her resolve would have held firm. But as he stared down at her, his eyes struggling to focus, his ragged breath whispering between his half-closed lips, she could almost hear his thoughts echoing hers.

After a few tense seconds while his logic fought with his passion, he took a step backward, completely severing the physical connection.

"Coffee, yes, you promised me some coffee." His voice wasn't any more steady than hers, and it was obvious his body wasn't going to let him forget the abrupt and unsatisfactory ending to their lovemaking. "Or maybe you have something cold, icy cold," he suggested wryly. "Like a shower?"

"Good idea. Or you could stand in front of the freezer and fill our glasses with ice."

He chuckled, but he followed her suggestion, standing with the door open for several minutes longer than necessary while Allison took a bottle of cola from the pantry and opened it. He held out the glasses and she filled them, then they sat down at the breakfast room table.

Sitting across from each other, they sipped their drinks and let their bodies calm down.

"I'm sorry about...well, you know..." he began. "I didn't mean to jump on you the minute we stepped in the door. I don't usually do things like that."

"That's okay," she replied with a smile. "I don't either. I guess I'm just a sucker for tall, dark and handsome." She kept her tone light and hoped he wouldn't see how deeply he had touched her.

He looked around the room. "Tall, dark and handsome? Where is he? I'll challenge him to a duel."

Allison laughed at his self-deprecating wit. "How exciting. I've never had a duel fought over me before."

His expression became serious. "Either you've been hiding away in a nunnery or all the men in your life have been fools."

She shook her head. "There haven't been all that many men in my life. I suppose I've been so busy trying to find out who I am that I haven't had time to look for anyone."

"Can I help? I'm good at finding things. Almost every day I have to look for a lost shoe, a lost button..."

"I'm not sure I'd know what to do with a man if I found him," she admitted, still attempting to keep up the banter. "What happens after the duel?"

"According to all the fairy tales, you and your champion will live happily ever after."

"Is that a promise?"

"Happily ever after is something no one can promise." There was a hint of melancholy to his words as he continued, "It can be here today and gone tomorrow."

"It's tomorrow I'm worried about." She lowered her gaze to the dark liquid in her glass, studying the bubbles that were clinging to the side as if they were the most interesting things on earth. Absently she rubbed the bridge of her nose and wished she had her glasses. Somehow they helped her keep enough of a distance so she could think more clearly. "I'm not interested in a one-night stand," she added after a few silent minutes had passed.

"Neither am I."

Once again she let her gaze meet his. "I read fairy tales to my students every day. I still believe happily ever after is possible."

"I wish it *was* possible." The pain, deep, unforgiving pain, clawed through his voice. "God, how I wish it was."

Chapter Eleven

"This week we're going to be talking about autumn. How many of you have noticed that the leaves are changing colors and falling down?" Allison asked her class.

All of the children nodded their heads.

"Today we're going to make pictures of trees," she continued. When everyone was settled on their chairs, she showed them a picture, then demonstrated how to draw a trunk, tear tissue paper into very small pieces and glue them onto the construction paper in clusters on the tree and the ground so they looked like leaves.

The children were hesitant at first, tearing off one tiny piece at a time. But as Allison encouraged them and they began enjoying themselves, their leaf-making grew much more uninhibited. The tabletops and the floor around each child began to look like Allison's front yard after a stiff wind.

Thinking about her own yard with its thick layer of leaves made her also think about Justin. He, too, had hesitated at first, but his inhibitions had slipped away as they tossed handfuls of leaves into the air and scrambled through the wind-made piles.

For a moment his eyes had lost their haunted look. For a moment he wasn't thinking of Caroline or even of Whitney. For a moment all of his attention was focused on Allison.

Again last night she had had his full attention. She didn't doubt that they would have ended up in her bed if she hadn't pulled away. Her fear hadn't been about the lovemaking. She had no doubt that would have been wonderful. What she was afraid of was afterward while she lay in his arms. He would be looking at her but seeing Caroline.

Aunt Millie had told Allison that that was always what happened to her. Not that she had slept with other men, but her aunt had tried dating after Uncle Bob's death. But, she said, every time another man kissed her, she automatically closed her eyes. But when she opened them and looked into the face of her date, she had been disappointed. Always it was Uncle Bob she was thinking of when she was with other men. And always, until the day she died, it was Uncle Bob she loved.

"Miss Greene, Jason used all the red. We don't have any red leaves on our trees," a girl named Rachel tattled.

"I wanted a cherry tree," Jason retorted. "I don't like those other colors."

"Jason, these are supposed to be leaves, not fruit. Cherry trees don't have cherries on them in the fall. Now tear up some yellows and oranges and put them in your tree so it will look more like leaves." She took a piece of red tissue paper off her desk and tore it into three pieces before handing it to the other occupants of Jason's table. "Here you go. Now you all have red leaves."

She returned to her desk and sat down. Slipping her glasses on, she reread the note from Mr. Gibson. The students' bickering had reminded her of the summons to his office after school. It was not something she was looking forward to. He hadn't mentioned the subject of the conference, but Allison had no doubt it was about Meagan's hair.

Actually, she hadn't been surprised by Mr. Gibson's note. She'd been expecting it all day. Meagan's parents wouldn't let something so drastic pass without some sort of comment. And Allison understood their concern. To anyone who had not been in the room on that day, it would certainly seem as if she hadn't been in control of her class.

Remembering how quickly Whitney had moved and how smoothly the blunt-tipped scissors had sliced through Meagan's braid, Allison knew no one would have been able to react fast enough to have stopped the incident. And it sure wasn't the type of thing that could have been anticipated.

Still, she was the teacher, the only adult in the room. She was responsible for everything that happened, and now it was time to try to explain the events of that day to the principal.

She had taught in some of the toughest schools in Boston. Behavior there had always been a problem for the older grades, but Allison had rarely had trouble with her students. Not that they were close academically to the students in Allison's current classes. Most of her Boston students hadn't accomplished even the basic skills such as counting to ten and reciting more than four or five letters of the alphabet before their first day of school.

Although the majority of students in the Georgetown-Silver Plume-Empire area came from families that fell in the poor to middle-class range, at least their parents cared enough to work with them and prepare them for class. Allison loved working at the school. She knew how lucky she was to have this job and she definitely didn't want to lose it.

But this was her second conference of the year and it was only October. She doubted that would look good on her record. Hopefully Whitney's mischief had ended now that she had succeeded in getting her father and teacher together. Well, not *together*, exactly. But at least they were exploring the possibilities.

Hearing Whitney's side of the story would probably help Allison's case. However, it wasn't Whitney's class day and even if it had been, Allison would never have put the child in the awkward position of defending her actions. Besides, Mr. Gibson wouldn't approve of a child planning bad behavior in order to force Justin and Allison to meet with each other. And he probably wouldn't be too thrilled that the ploy had worked. Allison knew there wasn't an official policy against parent-teacher fraternization. She just wasn't sure she wanted to openly test the unwritten rule.

That didn't mean she didn't want to see Justin again. But then, that might not be her choice to make. Last night he hadn't asked for another date or even mentioned it in passing. He hadn't stayed long after she ended their rather heated embrace. As soon as he had finished his drink, he made an excuse about getting some work done since Whitney wasn't home and then he left. Justin hadn't even kissed her goodbye.

Allison was distracted for the rest of the day. And the worst part of it was that she didn't know whether to hope the day went slowly or quickly. Anxious thoughts of the meeting with the principal and the uncertainty of what was happening with Justin made it difficult for her to concentrate on the class. Luckily she had planned activities that kept the children busy with a minimum of supervision, because her body was in the classroom but her mind was miles away.

"Miss Greene...Allison...overall we're pleased with your work here. However..."

Allison hated "howevers," especially when they were being spoken by her boss. She kept her back straight and her eyes focused on the man who was sitting behind a large desk. It took all her willpower to keep her hands loosely folded in her lap and to keep from squirming on the hard wooden chair. She hated confrontations such as these. It made her realize how her students must feel when they were in her position.

"I'm a little concerned about the extreme activities going on in your classroom. First, there was the...er...photo incident, and now this." The principal picked up a pen and idly tapped it on the wooden desktop. "Mrs. Williams, your predecessor never seemed to have these problems. Now I'm not saying it's all your fault. I realize every class is composed of different children and one never knows how these children will interact. But it is the job of a schoolteacher to anticipate and avoid crises in the classroom."

Allison had no defense. Not that Mr. Gibson was giving her an opening to reply.

"Meagan's parents don't want to press this issue. However..."

Allison grimaced. There was that word again.

"They *did* point out to me several times that you had just called them in for a conference about their daughter's alleged unacceptable behavior. They suggested that, perhaps, you were mistaken about Meagan and that all of the incidents you attributed to her were, indeed, caused by this..." he glanced down at his notes "...Whitney Sloane."

With an emphatic shake of her head, Allison simply could not let that accusation pass. "There's no doubt it was Whitney who cut Meagan's hair, but there's also no doubt that all of the incidents I attributed to Meagan were definitely done by her."

He shrugged. "That's a moot point. The problem I am forced to deal with today is your lack of control in your classroom. Your references were glowing and a special notation was made about how well you handled the children, so I can assume this is not a flaw in your training or experience.'' He made a notation on the inside cover of the file folder that was open on his desk.

Losing a fraction of her composure, her hands clenched into a frustrated fist.

''Because I believe in you and I believe in giving people the benefit of the doubt, I'm willing to give you one last chance to prove you're capable of handling this position.'' He jotted another note on the file and closed it with a decisive thud. ''Any questions?''

Her teeth were too tightly clenched for her to have forced a question out even if she had had one she thought he could answer. Instead, she shook her head.

''Good. I trust this will be our last official meeting until the end of the year.'' He held out his hand. ''Good evening, Miss Greene.''

She uncurled her stiff fingers and shook his hand. Although she had intended to return to her classroom and clean up the tissue paper shreds that the children had missed picking up, Allison bolted for the exit. All the way home she replayed the conversation in her mind, getting angrier with every mile. By the time she unlocked the door and walked into her house, she was ready to call Mr. Gibson and tell him he could take his job and—

The ring of the telephone interrupted her hostile thoughts.

''Hello,'' she shouted into the mouthpiece.

For a moment there was a stunned silence on the other end of the line.

''Allison?''

A trace of tension eased out of her. ''Hello, Justin.''

''Bad day?''

''It was too awful to be bad.'' Allison kicked off her shoes and dropped onto a chair.

"Was it the kids?"

"The children were terrific. In fact, if it wasn't for this house and those children, I'd be on the next plane to Boston."

There was another moment of silence. "There's nothing else keeping you here?" he asked, his tone flat and totally devoid of emotion.

Allison closed her eyes and counted to ten. How dare he get his feelings hurt when she was the one who had had a miserable day worrying about where, or even if, she fit into his life. "I don't know," she answered honestly. "Is there?"

"Allison, I missed you today."

His unexpected confession stripped away the prickly shell her fears had created. "Did you really?" she couldn't resist asking, suddenly desperate to hear him repeat it so she could listen for any hint of insincerity.

"Allison, I *really* missed you today," he repeated with emphasis. "I didn't get anything done. I guess I couldn't get last night off my mind."

"Neither could I," she admitted.

"I'm sorry if you felt rushed. I'm not sure what came over me." She heard the sound of his chuckle. "Actually, know exactly what it was, but I thought I had it under control better than that."

"I don't feel rushed. I just feel confused."

"I hate to tell you what I felt, but it starts with an *h* and rhymes with corny. I think I spent an hour in the shower hoping the cold water would make me forget how much wanted you."

"It didn't work, did it?" she asked.

"No, it didn't. How did you know?"

"Because I wasted a few gallons of water myself."

She thought she heard a muffled groan, but his voice sounded controlled when he asked, "Remember that duel I was talking about?"

"Yes."

"Well, I fought it with myself."

Her eyebrows lifted wryly. "Who won?"

"I wasn't as concerned about winning as I was about losing. I realize that finding lost shoes and socks wasn't anything compared to finding someone I care about. I can't guarantee happily ever after. But I'll help you search for it. And no one will be happier than I if we find it."

"Justin, I—" she began, but he cut her off as if afraid to hear her tell him she wasn't interested in the risk.

"Allison, I don't want to lose you," he whispered, his voice strangely ragged.

Her heart seemed to be beating in her throat, making it difficult for her to speak. He had said what she wanted to hear. At this particular moment he might even believe it. But Allison wondered how long it would be before he wished she was Caroline. Allison wasn't sure she could handle his disappointment and eventual disinterest. On the other hand, she wasn't sure she wasn't denying herself a chance at happiness because she was being overly cautious.

"I'm not going anywhere," she responded softly. "Or at least I'm not planning to. My principal might have other ideas."

"Oh, no. Is that why you were late?"

His genuine concern was like a telepathic message. It was almost as if she could feel his long, strong fingers squeezing her tense muscles, working the tightness out of them and soothing her frayed nerves.

She leaned back in her chair and propped her feet up on the cushion of one of the other chairs. "Yes, I'm afraid Mr.

Gibson is very concerned about how often I lose control of my students. But he's decided to give me one more chance."

"How generous of him," Justin sputtered sarcastically. "I doubt that a teacher with your intelligence and compassion has darkened the door of that school since he's been there. I'll bet he wouldn't know a good teacher if one slapped him in the face."

"I was tempted." For the first time that day Allison was able to laugh. "What a stuffed shirt. He acted as if I was totally incompetent." She went on to repeat the dialogue, omitting only the part about Meagan's parents trying to implicate Whitney in Meagan's misbehavior. It would serve no purpose for Justin to get mad at Meagan's parents even though they were almost as pompous and unbearable as the principal.

"I'm sorry you had to go through that," he said when she had finished. "Whitney shouldn't have cut off that girl's hair, but I can't be angry with her. She *did* force you and me to notice each other. Not only couldn't I punish her, but it was all I could do not to give her a special treat."

"You wouldn't dare do that. Even though her intentions were good, she can't be left to believe that sort of behavior is acceptable."

"I know. She and I had a long, father-to-daughter talk and I'm sure she understands. In fact, she knew all along that what she was doing was wrong."

"Speaking of Whitney, I assume she isn't home yet."

"No, and it's almost eight o'clock. I was hoping we could come over to see you tonight, but now we won't be able to. As soon as Whitney gets here, it's going to be time for her bath and bed." His sigh was clearly audible. "I know it would lead to another lengthy stay in the shower, but I wish I were with you now...hugging you...kissing you."

The longing in his voice so echoed hers that her body responded to his words as if he were actually touching her.

In the background she could hear the sound of a doorbell, followed by Justin's apologetic, "I guess I'd better go. That's probably Whitney. How about dinner tomorrow night?"

They quickly agreed on a time before hanging up. For several minutes Allison didn't move as she thought about how lonely her life had been before that fateful parent-teacher conference last Friday. Had it been only five days ago? And already she was dreading going a whole day without seeing him. It was all very high schoolish, and if she wasn't enjoying the excitement of the moment so much, she might have felt silly.

It reminded her of one of the projects she planned for her students, which was to take fluffy balls of yarns, glue eyes and feet on them and then she would tell the children the story of the warm fuzzies and the cold pricklies, two very strong and totally opposite feelings. Allison had experienced cold pricklies on several occasions in her life, including when her brother went off to war, the news of his wound and, worst of all, his eventual death. Allison's unemotional relationship with her parents hadn't exactly been cold, but it certainly had never been warm, either.

Her relationship with Aunt Millie had been a warm fuzzy. Aunt Millie had always encouraged Allison to live her own life and not feel forced into her parents' mold. And Aunt Millie had been fun to be with, whether they were making popcorn balls or staying up late at night to put together a jigsaw puzzle.

Justin was also a warm fuzzy. He made Allison feel pretty and desirable, which was something no one else had ever done, not even the men she had dated back in Boston. He reminded her she was a woman and gave her hope for a future together as a real family. But even if it didn't work out, at least for a while he was making her feel good. Surely the risk was worth the happiness, however temporary.

"DADDY, I WANT TO BE a *dinosaur*. They're *so* cool." Whitney's lower lip protruded petulantly.

"Little girls don't dress up like dinosaurs. Little girls are princesses or ballerinas."

"But I don't *want* to be a princess or a ballerina. I want to be a dinosaur."

Justin glanced at Allison, his eyes begging for help. But she didn't think he'd approve of her opinion, so she kept quiet.

They were sitting on a blanket spread next to the gazebo in the park across from Allison's house. The remains of a picnic lunch were scattered across the blanket, but they were all enjoying the sunshine too much to clean up the mess. Somehow, as it always seemed to in the past two weeks, the conversation had turned to what Whitney was going to be for Halloween.

"You'd make such a pretty ballerina," Justin persisted. "I don't see why you can't wear that pink outfit you wore in the last dance recital."

"Because it makes me look like a girl," Whitney retorted in total exasperation.

"I hate to be the one to break it to you, Whitney, but you *are* a girl." Justin was clearly bewildered.

"I *know* that, Daddy. But I don't have to be a sissy. And ballerinas are sissies."

"I thought you liked taking ballet lessons," Allison commented. She had sat with Justin in the observation room and watched Whitney prance and pirouette more or less as instructed by the lithe, young dance teacher at the Thursday afternoon lessons.

"I do, but I can be a ballerina every week. This is *Halloween.* I'm supposed to be something scary."

"I'd rather you be pretty," Justin repeated.

"*Daddy!* Pretty is not scary. Tell him, Miss Greene. I *can't* be a ballerina."

"Yes, Allison," Justin agreed. "Tell us that it's perfectly acceptable to be pretty on Halloween."

Allison cleared her throat, reluctant to jump into the middle of a domestic disagreement. But they both stared at her, impatiently waiting for her answer and forcing her to take sides. Trying to be as diplomatic as possible, she looked at Whitney as she said, "I've seen a lot of girls who look pretty for Halloween and they get just as much candy as everyone else. But," she turned to Justin, "I don't see anything wrong with Whitney being a dinosaur if that's what she wants to be. I think she'd make an excellent terraverdesaurus."

Justin started to argue, then frowned. "There's no such dinosaur as a terraverdesaurus."

"Of course there is...in Whitney's imagination. We've been reading a story about a dinosaur who was bored being a brontosaurus, so he made up a species that sounded more exotic. The moral of the story is to be happy with who or what you are."

A smile replaced the frown, and Justin reached out to tuck a wayward strand of hair behind Allison's ear. "Are you happy with who and what you are?"

"Sometimes," she admitted. "More so lately."

He leaned over and gave her a slow, sweet kiss. "I was hoping you'd say that."

"So can I be a terraverdesaurus?" Whitney interrupted.

Allison had grown accustomed to the child's bad timing. But Allison wasn't sorry that she and Justin hadn't had a chance to be totally alone since that Monday night in Alli-

son's kitchen. With Whitney always around, they could talk
and laugh and even sneak a kiss or two, but since there was
no possibility of things getting any hotter, they felt safe
enough to relax. It gave them time to develop a friendship
rather than have their hormones explode into a sexual
frenzy.

Not that Allison didn't want that friendship to eventually move into a more physical relationship. Allison realized that. But by spending the past two weeks on low-key,
fun, family dates, they'd given themselves a little breathing
room so they could decide how far and how fast they wanted
to move.

"Halloween is this Thursday," Justin said after giving
Allison a special, intimate smile and settling back against the
side of the gazebo. "I don't see how we can find a dinosaur
costume of any breed in such a short time."

Whitney's eyes filled with tears. "But, Daddy, you *knew*
I wanted to be a dinosaur. I've told all my friends and now
they're going to laugh at me."

"How will your friends know what you are?" he asked.

"They wear their costumes to class on Halloween and, for
Whitney's class, the day before. All week they've been
talking about their costumes, and we've made drawings of
what we'll look like on Halloween," Allison explained.

"And Whitney thinks she looks like a dinosaur," Justin
muttered without enthusiasm. "Well, I don't see what we
can do about it now. It's just too late. I'm sure there aren't
any dinosaur costumes within a hundred miles of here."

"I'm not bad with a needle and thread and I have a costume book at home. I suppose Whitney and I could put together a pretty decent terraverdesaurus." Allison watched
Justin's reactions carefully, not wanting to suggest something to which he was adamantly opposed.

But before Justin could respond, Whitney was on her feet, jumping up and down and sending her ponytail bouncing wildly around her head. "That would be *so* neat."

Justin gave in with a resigned sigh. "I guess that means we'll be spending the rest of the day *sewing.*"

"And shopping for terraverdesaurus material," Allison added. "Did you have something else in mind?"

He shrugged and shook his head with good-natured acceptance. "I had hoped . . . but I don't think it's meant to be."

Allison knew exactly what he was talking about. The subject was never far from either of their minds, especially when they were together, seeing each other . . . touching . . . kissing when Whitney was distracted. They had discussed it and both agreed that even though Whitney was one hundred percent behind the relationship, it wouldn't be responsible for them to flaunt their sexual attraction in front of the child. While Whitney encouraged frequent dates, she simply had no concept of how grown-up men and women interacted, especially in the bedroom. As mature as she was in other ways, she was still an innocent when it came to men and women dating and marrying.

"You're a wonderful father. Someday your daughter will thank you for all your sacrifices."

"And she has no idea how great those sacrifices are," he moaned as Whitney grabbed his hand and tried to pull him up.

"Let's go, Daddy. We've got to make my costume."

"Let's go, Allison," Justin echoed as he let Whitney think she was pulling him up. He stood and held out his hand to Allison.

They gathered up the picnic supplies and walked over to her house. Curiosity, who had been chasing birds and keeping a close watch on the squirrels, followed on Whitney's heels.

In the living room bookshelf, Allison found a book on how to make children's costumes, and she and Whitney sat down at the breakfast table and began to flip through it. Justin stood behind Allison, his hands resting casually on her shoulders as he offered his comments and suggestions.

His patience was thoroughly tested by Tuesday evening, when Allison was still working on the costume. It was more complicated than she expected and took all her spare time. They had even had to drive into Denver to find enough green felt. Whitney helped whenever possible, but having the little girl and the teacher focused on the project left Justin as the odd man out.

Whitney stood, wiggling anxiously, her small body completely covered as Allison knelt in front of her and made the final adjustments. Only her face was visible through the open mouth of the dinosaur's face that was really a hood attached to the body by a row of jagged ridges that ran from the top of her head to the end of the stiff three-foot-long tail.

"There, all finished," Allison said after taking a pin out from between her lips. She leaned back, sitting on her heels, and studied her handiwork. "Not bad, even if I say so myself."

Whitney lifted her arms and growled with all the menace a five-year-old girl could muster. Moving her feet with the slow, heavy pace of Godzilla advancing on a Japanese city, she walked toward her father.

He looked up from the book he was reading and feigned terror. Leaping to his feet, he ran across the room and knelt down behind Allison, holding her in front of him like a shield.

"Help, save me from the dreaded terranovasaurus."

"Terranova is the name of the hunk on *Wiseguy*," Allison corrected. "Whitney is a *terraverdesaurus*."

He stood, pulling Allison up with him. "I knew that," he joked. "I was just testing you to see if you're still stuck on that tall, dark and handsome fairy-tale stuff."

"Wouldn't life be boring if we didn't have some hope for happy endings?"

Tenderly he traced the outline of her lips with the tip of his forefinger. "You know, Allison," he spoke thoughtfully, "you're beginning to make a believer out of me. Are there any fairy tales that have a prince and a princess who can't ever seem to have any time alone because a dragon keeps popping in?"

Whitney, who had been stalking around the room, growling and menacing Curiosity, stopped in front of her father. "I'm a dinosaur, Daddy, not a dragon."

"I know, honey," Justin said with a smile that was growing less patient by the night. "You're a dinosaur. A cute dinosaur. But definitely not extinct."

Chapter Twelve

"Trick or treat!"

The words echoed throughout the town as ghosts, G.I. Joes, angels and Teenage Mutant Ninja Turtles hurried from house to house. Justin followed Whitney who, with childish energy, could run to the next house, collect her goodies and be back out to the end of the sidewalk by the time Justin arrived at the front gate.

One of the advantages of a small town was that Justin felt it was perfectly safe for Whitney to trick-or-treat even at the houses of people he didn't know, which was nice for Whitney since he didn't know many people in Georgetown, even after living there almost four years.

"There's Miss Greene's house," Whitney announced unnecessarily.

Yes, Justin was well aware of that fact. He had had his eye on the house for the past five minutes. In his opinion it called to him to hurry, hurry... Allison was inside. Only three more houses to go before they reached it.

Finally Whitney opened the picket gate and skipped up the walk. At this one house Justin made an exception and walked to the door with her.

A cowboy, a soldier and the creature from the Black Lagoon were just leaving, so it wasn't necessary for Whitney to ring the bell. But she couldn't resist shouting, "Trick or treat."

"Oh, look. It's a terraverdesaurus. Please, Miss Dinosaur, don't bite me," Allison pleaded.

Whitney gave her best dinosaur roar, then giggled as she held out her almost-full plastic pumpkin. "I promise not to bite you if you give me all your peanut butter cups."

Allison dug through the bowl of candy she held in her arms and dropped several peanut butter cups into the pumpkin.

"Thank you, Miss Greene," Whitney said, then turned. "Daddy, you're standing on my tail *again,*" she exclaimed.

Justin looked down and saw he was, indeed, standing on her tail. He lifted his foot, and, when Whitney scampered inside in search of Curiosity, he stepped forward.

"Now I know why all the dinosaurs died out," he stated with an amused tilt of one dark eyebrow. "They kept stepping on each others' tails and couldn't eat or drink or..." his eyebrows wiggled lecherously "...make love."

"Are you going to write a report about that discovery for *Smithsonian?*"

"Nah, I'll let you do it and get all the credit. I'll bet this is something that has baffled scientists for years, and it's so simple."

Another group of superheroes, freakish monsters and one kid dressed like Ronald Reagan arrived, and Justin stepped aside while Allison dropped candy into their bags and pillowcases. Justin leaned against the wall and took advantage of the interruption to study her.

If he hadn't known who she was, he'd never have recognized her. Dressed in a baggy, ruffled, multicolored clown outfit, her figure was well hidden. A wig of bright red tinsel covered her hair, and a thick layer of white makeup, highlighted with large, smiling red lips, red circles on her cheekbones and a round red nose, completely disguised her face.

"Do you want a peanut butter cup?" she asked when the kids had gone and they were alone again.

"No, because I can't promise not to bite you like my daughter, the dinosaur, did."

He moved closer, his momentum propelling her into the house, and backed her up against the open door. "I've never kissed a clown before. Does that white stuff smear?"

"I don't know," she said with a laugh. "I've never kissed a clown either."

"Then let's add this to our list of things we've never done before we met each other," he said, and proceeded to follow through with a gingerly placed kiss.

"Yes, it smears," she announced when he straightened. "But you look sort of cute with red lips."

"Thanks. Can I borrow your bathroom?"

"Sure. Just don't get your makeup on my towels," she teased. "It's so hard to wash out."

He tried to give her a playful swat on the behind, but he missed as she dodged, his hand brushing harmlessly across the yards of billowy material.

When he returned Allison was, once again, busy handing out treats to more children.

"Whitney, let's go," Justin called. "We have to get you home before the Cretaceous period ends."

"The what?" the little girl asked.

"Your daddy's making a joke, Whitney."

"Was it funny?" Whitney asked, puzzled.

"If there were any paleontologists in this room, they'd be cracking up," Justin answered with a chuckle.

Allison let the screen door ease shut. "It feels like it's getting colder out there. I heard an Arctic Express is going to hit us tonight and you two should head home before it starts snowing.''

"Yes, we'd better go straight back to the car. It's parked several blocks away.''

Whitney yawned but managed to protest, "But, Daddy, my pumpkin's not full yet.''

He glanced down at the mixture of candy. "You have enough treats in there to send our dentist's son to Harvard." A blast of wind buffeted the house and sent a chill pouring through the tiny holes in the screen and into the entry hall. "Let me carry your pumpkin.''

Whitney tried to hide it, but another yawn escaped. She handed him her pumpkin, then held up her arms. "Carry me, Daddy. My feet are tired.''

Justin gathered his daughter into his arms and she promptly rested her head on his shoulder.

"I could drive you to your car," Allison offered.

"It's not that far. Besides, if you got stopped by the police, you wouldn't match the picture on your license and you'd be arrested.''

"I'll bet Mr. Gibson would love that." Allison smiled and stood on her tiptoes to give him another light kiss. "I'm glad you dropped by.''

"I wouldn't have missed your house for the world. What about tomorrow night? Dinner?''

"Let's wait and see how the weather turns out. Maybe we can rent a couple of videos and fix dinner here.''

He couldn't resist giving her one more kiss, knowing he was probably getting a fresh coat of lipstick, before walking out the door. The wind hit him in the face, immediately turning his skin numb. He was always amazed at how quickly the temperature could drop when a cold front rushed through.

All the way to the car, he was walking into the brunt of the storm. He was almost there when he felt the sting of snow against his cheeks, and he was glad Whitney was covered so well by her costume. It was a good thing she wasn't dressed like a ballerina. It was definitely too cold for tutus.

As it turned out, it was also too cold for snow. By morning the ground was covered with a thin sheet of ice but very little snow. Justin was relieved it wasn't Whitney's Friday to go to school, but he was worried about Allison having to drive in such dangerous conditions.

Whitney sat at the dining room table, sorting and resorting her candy as if it were a wonderful treasure. Justin regulated how much she could eat each day, but it didn't seem to be the actual ingestion that interested her. Rather it was the number and variety she had accumulated, as if it were a collection that was of great value.

Justin's own memories of Halloween contained the same ritual. He even found himself picking out a couple of his own childhood favorites, candies he wouldn't think of eating during the rest of the year, but which tasted wonderful when received on Halloween.

He spent all morning at his computer, totally engrossed in a new project. If Whitney hadn't been home, he would have kept working through lunchtime. But the sound of a can opener reminded him of his fatherly duties so he saved the file and stood up.

"So what would you like for lunch?" he asked as he walked into the kitchen. With one hand massaging the stiff muscles at the back of his neck, he leaned against the counter.

"Chili," she answered, dumping the contents of the can into a saucepan. "We *always* have chili when it's snowing hard. It's one of our rules, remember?"

"But it's not snowing...." He lifted his gaze over her and through the dining room window. "Oh, my gosh!" he exclaimed, and crossed the room in several long strides. A thick veil of snow swirled outside the window, blocking everything from view. All he could see was white. The wind had been blowing hard since last night, whistling around the corners of the house and pounding against the windowpanes. But he'd been so preoccupied with his work that he hadn't noticed when the snowstorm hit.

He turned on the radio and listened as a weather report confirmed his worst fears. Already more than eight inches of snow had fallen and another fifteen to twenty inches were expected in the next twenty-four hours. There were school closings all over the area, but the reporter stated the buses were having trouble making it through deep drifts. Snowplows were out in full force, but almost as quickly as they cleared the roads, the wind was dumping more snow on them.

Justin looked up the number and called the Empire school. The line was busy and he had to redial for five minutes before he could get through.

"May I speak to Miss Greene, please?" he asked.

"I'm sorry, but she's with her students right now."

"Are they letting school out early today?"

"Yes, sir, they are. The buses are loading right now."

"Could I leave a message for her?" At the secretary's affirmative answer, he left his name and number and hung up. But, like a caged animal circling a threatening object, he paced around the room, glaring at the telephone as if the very force of his stare would make it ring.

"The chili's ready, Daddy." Whitney set the table and put out a hot pad so her father could bring the pot of chili from the stove. He didn't allow her to carry anything hot.

"Okay, I'll be right there." Casting one last glance at the phone, he walked into the kitchen and picked up the pot. Absently he spooned ladles full of the steaming liquid into the bowls, then sat down. But while Whitney crumbled crackers onto her chili and began to eat, Justin merely stirred his. His gaze flickered from the white world outside his windows to the silent telephone.

When it finally rang, his spoon clattered into his bowl and his chair tipped over backward as he abruptly stood.

"Hello," he practically shouted into the receiver.

"Justin?" a feminine voice answered.

"Allison. I'm glad you got my message."

"I was outside helping my students get on their buses."

"How bad is it there?"

"Pretty bad. I'm about to leave, too."

Justin frowned. "I'm not sure your car will make it."

"Of course it will. It's got front-wheel drive and the snowplows are out there, clearing the highway."

"They are, but I've heard they're fighting a losing battle trying to keep it clear."

"I can't stay here all weekend. Besides, I've driven in snow before. I'll be fine."

Justin wished he felt that positive. "Call me as soon as you get home. Okay?"

"Okay."

"And Allison..." He paused, almost voicing the feeling that was gripping his heart. But afraid that worry felt very much like love and not wanting to say something prematurely, he substituted, "Be careful."

She was silent for a few seconds and he hoped she hadn' guessed the cause of his hesitation.

"I will," she answered at last. "I'd better go."

They said their goodbyes and he hung up the phone.

"Daddy, your chili's getting cold."

Automatically he returned to the table and spooned the still-warm food into his mouth. But now his attention had transferred from the telephone to his wristwatch. It was one-thirty. The trip from Empire to Georgetown in good weather usually took about twenty minutes, in bad weather at least twice that. He told himself he wouldn't start to worry until two-thirty. He'd give her an hour, then . . . he didn't know what he'd do. But he would sure as heck think of something.

Justin tried to keep busy to make the time pass more quickly. He washed the dishes, then tried to concentrate on his work. Usually he could block out all distractions when he was at the computer, but after fifteen minutes, when he found himself staring blankly at the blinking cursor, he shut down the system and returned to the dining room.

"Whitney, pick up that mess. You have candy wrappers all over the place."

At her startled look, Justin realized he'd been unreasonably harsh and he rushed to apologize. "I'm sorry. I didn't mean to snap at you. I'm just thinking about Miss Greene. She's trying to drive home in this storm." He gestured toward the window, where the snow was sticking to the screen, making it even more difficult to see outside.

"Is she going to have a wreck?"

He raked his fingers through his hair. "I hope not."

Whitney's eyes grew even wider. "She could freeze to death. She could slide into a snowbank and no one would find her. She could—"

"That's enough," Justin interrupted, unable to listen to any more grim possibilities. "Miss Greene is a good driver." He peered at his watch. Quarter till three. "She'll be home any minute now."

He must have sounded convincing, because Whitney turned back to her hoard of goodies. But as the minutes

ticked by he felt anything but confident. Three o'clock came
and went. Justin stood at the patio door, glowering at the
deceptively gentle white flakes that plastered against the
glass then slid down until they joined the drift that was
building against the door's frame.

Three-fifteen. He called the school, but there was no answer. He called Allison's house, not expecting an answer and
getting none.

Three-thirty. Justin sat, staring at the television, hoping
for a weather bulletin while the radio blared on the end table beside him. There were no reports of major accidents on
I-70, but in this case, he couldn't accept the old cliché that
no news was good news. No news might mean Allison had
slid off the road and they hadn't found her. Or her car might
have stalled and she was sitting in it, trying to stay warm
until help arrived.

Three forty-five. He called the school again. Still no answer. He paced a few more miles around the house, roam-
ing from room to room restlessly.

Four o'clock. On television, film of the storm that was
battering the entire northern Rockies and the Front Range
highlighted *Good Afternoon Colorado,* the first news show
of the evening. Stories of people being stranded, cars plow-
ing into snowbanks and vehicles sliding through icy inter-
sections were definitely not good news. And Justin decided
he could wait no longer.

"Whitney, put on your boots and get your coat. We're
going to Grandma's." He placed a quick call to his mother
who agreed to watch Whitney although she tried to talk
Justin out of going into the storm. But he couldn't stand to
sit around and wait any longer.

"Miss Greene hasn't called yet?" Whitney asked.

"No, she hasn't."

"Do you think she just forgot to call us when she got home?"

"That could be it," he lied, knowing Allison wouldn't forget. "I'm going to drive over to her house and see if she's there, after I take you next door to Grandma's."

"Why don't you just call?"

"I did, but there was no answer." That response brought the concern back to her expression, so he rushed to add, "Uh...her phone might be out of order. That would explain why she hasn't called us."

"Oh." Whitney nodded, accepting his explanation. "Can I take my candy to Grandma's?"

"Sure. Just hurry." He went into his bedroom, pulled a thick wool sweater over his sweatshirt and stuffed his pockets with several pairs of extra socks. Taking a couple of blankets from the hall closet, he tossed them onto the couch while he put on his snowboots and the warmest coat he could find. After checking that he had a pair of gloves, he picked up the blankets and opened the door that led to the garage.

"Let's go, Whitney."

She carried her pumpkin in one hand and her favorite stuffed rabbit in the other. Justin locked the door behind them. Already it was dark, making it appear several hours later than it actually was.

"Damn, I forgot a flashlight," he muttered, inserting the key and opening the door. A minute later he was back, a flashlight in one pocket of his coat and another flashlight in his hand. He locked the door again, pushed the button that opened the garage door, then picked Whitney up and carried her outside and through the driving snow. It took several minutes to cross the small open area between the buildings.

His mother was waiting at the door, the light spilling out onto the pristine white snow, illuminating the way. Again she tried to dissuade him from going out in the storm, but he wouldn't listen. Allison was out there somewhere, and he was determined to find her. Hopefully she had arrived home in the past few minutes and would be there when he drove over.

Or maybe, she had given up and gone back to the school. But why hadn't anyone answered? Perhaps she was in her classroom and there was no one in the office to hear the phone. If that were the case, then he would go get her and bring her home.

He tossed the blankets into the back seat of his vehicle, got in and shifted it into four-wheel drive. He had no doubt this would be the drive that would test not only his skill but his car's ability to find traction where there wasn't any.

Allison's house was dark and quiet. He couldn't tell if her car was in the garage, so he went to her door and rang the bell just to make sure she wasn't home. He could hear Curiosity's loud, lonely meows through the solid wood plank, but there was no sign of Allison.

On the road out of Georgetown he passed no one. Trying not to consider the possibility that everyone else was smarter than he was, Justin gripped the steering wheel and peered through the gloom, trying to follow tracks of cars that had traveled the road recently. Apparently the snowplows were all busy on the interstate and hadn't ventured onto the side roads yet.

There wasn't any traffic on the highway, either, which was good since it took every ounce of his concentration to try to stay on the road and look for Allison's car on the opposite lanes. He didn't know how he expected to see her when he could barely see ten feet in front of him.

Forty-five minutes later he arrived at the school. The parking lot was empty and the building was dark. He didn't even bother getting out of his car, but made a U-turn and headed toward home. For the first thirty minutes, all the other cars he passed were stalled by the side of the road. He checked each one, but apparently the people had already been rescued by the highway patrol or a passing snowplow. Hopefully Allison too would have been picked up if she had car trouble.

It was getting darker and the snow was falling even more heavily. Visibility had been reduced to practically zero, but he kept straining to see through the gloom. He had begun to think Allison must have made it home, when he caught the glow of her bright yellow car in his headlights. He pulled over, parked behind her and jumped out.

The car sat silently in the storm with no sign of life either inside or out. Snow and ice had built up on the windows, making it impossible to see through them. As Justin hurried forward, he hoped the car would be empty and that Allison had already been rescued and was on her way home.

But what if she hadn't been? He tried to remember what he'd heard about hypothermia. How long did it take for a person to freeze? Obviously, if the car wasn't running, the heater wasn't on.

On the other hand, he knew he would be frantic with worry if he *didn't* find her there. What if she had panicked and decided to try to walk home? With the wind, the snow and the near-zero temperatures, she wouldn't make it far. What if she was lying unconscious in a snowbank? Or what if some maniac had found her and . . . ?

He didn't know what to hope for as he ran the last few steps and yanked open the car door.

Allison was slumped over the steering wheel, her forehead resting on her mitten-covered hands. She didn't seem to be aware of him, then slowly she turned her head.

"Justin?" Her voice was weak. "It's so cold."

He leaned into the car and tenderly gathered her into his arms. With one hand he unbuttoned his coat and wrapped it around her as far as it would go. Burying his face in her hair, he hugged her tightly to him, trying to share his warmth. She felt incredibly small and vulnerable, and his breath caught in his throat at how easily he could have lost her.

"I've got to get you home." He cradled her against him backed out of the car and started to shut her door, but she caught his hand. Her teeth were chattering together so hard she could barely speak.

"Mr. Wiggly Nose and Snow White are in there."

"The rabbits?"

"Yes. I couldn't leave them at school in case the electricity went off. I thought it would be better if I took them home with me. I didn't think we'd all freeze by the side of the road."

Justin carried her to his vehicle and placed her on the front seat. After wrapping a blanket around her shoulders and one around her legs and turning the heater on high, he returned to her car. He took the small animal carriers out of her back seat and loaded them in the rear of his vehicle, then returned to her car to get her purse and briefcase and lock the doors.

"Do you think my car will be okay there?"

"It should be. It's far enough off the road."

She hadn't moved and was still sitting in the middle of the seat where he had set her. Justin wished he didn't have to keep both hands on the steering wheel, because he longed to put his arm around her. The heater was blowing full blast but he couldn't help thinking it was a poor substitute for good old body heat.

"How long were you there?" he asked.

"About an hour."

"But I thought...?"

As she gradually thawed out, she became more talkative. "I wasn't able to leave school until about an hour after I talked to you. Then I got stuck in the school parking lot. I guess I should have taken that as a sign to give up."

"I would have picked you up."

"I didn't want you to have to get out in this." She shivered and gave a mirthless chuckle. "But I guess you did anyway."

"I was worried about you. I had a feeling something was wrong."

"I'm glad you came looking for me. I was driving along when that stupid car just died. No warning. Nothing. It died and wouldn't start again. With the power steering out, I was lucky to get it as far off the road as I did. And no one, not even a snowplow came by."

"I wish you'd called me before you left." His voice was harsh with the anxiety of the past few hours.

She looked up at him and smiled apologetically. "I was trying to hurry. I wanted to get home."

"We'll be there soon," he assured her, flipping the windshield wipers on a higher speed. *I hope we make it,* he thought, not daring to voice his doubts. His headlights barely penetrated the dense snow and, unable to see beyond their weak beam, it was easy to become disoriented. Justin had no idea where they were or how far they had to go before the turnoff to Georgetown.

It seemed like hours, but it was probably only twenty or thirty minutes. Finally the exit appeared and they eased off the highway. The snow was deeper on the roads in town and all tracks had been covered. Justin had to guess where the streets were, trying to center his car between the signs and utility poles. It wasn't until they parked in her driveway that he realized his forehead was drenched with sweat and his hands were clenched so tightly around the steering wheel that his fingers ached.

"We're here," he announced as if it were the greatest achievement in the world. He didn't want Allison to know how difficult the drive had been.

She insisted she could walk, so he took the rabbits and followed her to the back door. When her hands weren't able to stop shaking long enough to get the key into the lock, he handed her the rabbits and took over.

"Gosh, it's cold in here. Where's your thermostat?"

She set the rabbit carriers on the kitchen floor, walked into the living room and pointed to the thermostat on the wall.

He went to it and turned it up to eighty-five degrees. "Okay, now you go take a long, hot bubble bath and I'll see if I can find some chili in your pantry."

"Chili?"

"It's a Sloane Rule," he stated, and gave her a gentle push toward the stairs.

A few minutes later he heard the bathwater running, so he opened the can of chili he'd found and poured it into a pan. Turning the heat on low, he put his coat back on and made several trips outside for some firewood. By the time she came back down the stairs, he had a fire blazing in the fireplace.

"Oh, that feels good," she said, going straight to the fireplace and holding out her hands to the warmth. "My fingers and toes were numb."

"Would you rather eat in here by the fire?" he asked, trying not to think about how good she looked. The emerald-green sweat suit she was wearing clung to her body in ways that would make Jane Fonda jealous. She had left her hair loose, and it fell around her shoulders in a straight pageboy that barely curved under on the ends.

"I'm not really hungry."

"Oh, no, you're not getting by with that. Am I going to have to treat you like I do Whitney?"

Allison didn't turn around but glanced back over her shoulder at him. "I don't need another father."

"That's good, because of all the things I want to be to you, a father isn't one of them." He gave her a wink and returned to the kitchen, where he filled a bowl with chili. He couldn't help but smile at the thought that Whitney had done the same thing for him earlier in the day.

He carried the chili, some crackers and a cup of hot tea to Allison and waited until she sat down on the couch and took a bite.

"What about you? Aren't you going to eat any?" she asked, obediently nibbling a cracker.

"I've had my chili for the day. Now you finish that up while I call my mother to let her know we're all right."

He had been so busy looking after Allison that he hadn't even thought about phoning his mother until now. He knew what her response would be before he dialed the number, but he also knew he'd have to face the music for not being more considerate.

"Hi, Mom."

"Well, I guess now I can call the highway patrol and tell them to call off the search."

"Sorry, but it took longer than I expected. Then when I found Allison, she was almost frozen. I had to take her to her place and thaw her out."

His mother was silent for an eloquent moment. "Thaw her out, huh? Does that mean you're not coming home tonight?'' There was no censure in her words. In fact, Justin thought he detected a hint of enthusiasm in her tone.

He peeked around the corner at Allison, who was sitting, staring into the friendly flames as she automatically spooned chili into her mouth. Curiosity was curled in her lap, keeping a close watch on the bowl in case Allison should abandon it.

"It's not what you think...unfortunately." He chuckled. "But I don't know what time I'll be home. Is everything all right there? Is Whitney asleep?"

"She's watching television with her grandfather. We're all about to go to bed, so don't worry about us. You just take care of your lady. We wouldn't want anything to happen to Whitney's beloved Miss Greene, would we?"

"You have a key to my place, don't you, in case Whitney needs something?"

"Sure do. So don't feel you have to hurry home."

"Mother!" Justin exclaimed, pretending to be shocked. "If I didn't know you better, I'd think you were *encouraging* me to spend the night with Miss Greene."

"Is she a nice woman?"

He glanced at Allison again. She had stretched out on the couch with her head lying on the armrest. Curiosity was on the table, finishing off the chili, and Justin knew Allison must be asleep or she would have been scolding the cat for its audacity.

"She's a *very* nice woman," he answered. "And while I was talking to you, she's fallen asleep."

"Too bad. But she'll wake up sooner or later."

"*Mother!*" he repeated.

"It's time for you to get on with your life, son. And if this Miss Greene is the woman who will make you and Whitney happy, then you have my blessing. Good night."

"Good night, Mom. Kiss Whitney for me."

"I will. Kiss Miss Greene for me."

"You bet." He hung up the phone and turned out the kitchen light. Retrieving the blankets that had fallen onto the floor, he spread one over Allison and wrapped himself in the other. He settled into one of the wing-backed chairs, kicked off his shoes and stretched his sock-covered feet toward the fire, positioning himself so he could keep an eye on her.

Watching her sleep aroused his protective instincts. She looked so sweet and much too young to be a schoolteacher. There was a tiny smile on her lips, and her hair fell across her hand that was pillowed under her cheek.

Yes, she was a very nice woman. And yes, he hoped she would wake up soon. It wasn't only his protective instincts that were aroused when he was with her.

Chapter Thirteen

She woke with a warm body pressed against her. Allison opened her eyes, blinked at the unfamiliar look of her bedroom. There shouldn't be a fireplace there. She flexed her neck, feeling the threat of a crick tightening her muscles. Why was she sleeping on the couch?

Her gaze traveled down to the warm body and saw that Curiosity was tucked snugly into a hollow of Allison's blanket. Well, actually it *wasn't* Allison's blanket. She stared at the off-white velvety covering. Although her linen closet contained a mismatch of her own things in several shades of blue and her aunt's things in yellows and apricot, this blanket definitely wasn't hers.

A shuffling sound from the semidarkness between the couch and the fireplace drew her attention and she saw Justin shifting restlessly in the chair. It was one of the antiques her aunt had collected and it wasn't comfortable even for sitting, much less sleeping. Justin was in an awkward position with his head lying against the wing on one side, his hips pushed against the arm on the other side and his legs stretched out in front of him.

Allison knew she should rescue him by waking him up and sending him home. But, for a moment while she remembered the events of the evening, she enjoyed having the freedom to look at him to her heart's content.

As she studied him, she saw not only the handsome features of his face, but the gentleness and humor etched indelibly on it. His dark hair, which was usually neatly combed, was rumpled and fell across his forehead, making him look sweet and appealingly boyish.

He had risked his own life to come to her rescue. Never had there been a voice so wonderful or a person so welcome as he was when he opened her car door and gathered her into his arms. She remembered feeling his warmth seep through her inadequate clothing and bring her body back to life. She remembered hearing his soft, encouraging words although she couldn't recall anything specific he said. She just knew she felt much better, knowing he cared.

She wished she knew how much he cared. There was a great deal of difference between caring enough to save the life of a friend and caring enough to save the life of a loved one. Allison wanted, more than anything in the world, to be one of the people he loved.

Allison wasn't sure exactly when during the past month, but she had finally accepted as fact that she had fallen in love with Justin. She loved his strength of character as much as the muscular shape of his body. She loved his dry wit and easy laugh as much as his intelligence. And she loved his daughter as much as the affectionate but firmly disciplined way he treated the little girl.

She loved everything about him...except perhaps that he had loved deeply before and might never love that deeply again. He was her first real love and she suspected he would be her last. Was it so selfish of her to wish for the same depth of commitment?

He moved again and the blanket that had been draped across his shoulders fell to the floor. Allison carefully relocated Curiosity to the corner of the couch, then slid her legs over the side and stood up. Walking quietly, she skirted the coffee table and picked up the blanket.

"Justin." She spoke softly as she rested her hand on his shoulder and gave him a gentle shake. "Wake up."

His long, dark eyelashes opened slowly until he was looking up at her with sleepy eyes. A lazy smile stretched across his lips.

"It's after midnight," she continued. "I'm afraid you're going to be sore if you sleep in this chair any longer." She paused, wanting him to stay but knowing it wasn't reasonable. "You can go home now if you want."

She expected him to straighten and push himself out of the chair. Instead he startled her by reaching out, gripping her waist and pulling her onto his lap.

"What would you say if I told you I don't want to go home right now?" he asked, his voice a husky caress.

Allison couldn't answer. It wasn't that she wanted him to leave, but she simply was too surprised to speak.

"You wouldn't believe the dream I just had about you...about us," he murmured, his mouth moving against the side of her neck. "You scared me tonight. I might have lost you forever and it made me realize how important you are to me." His lips found the sensitive area behind her ear. "Let me stay. Let me spend the night with you, keeping you warm and making love with you until the sun comes up."

His hand slid under the ribbed hem of her sweatshirt and over the skin of her rib cage until he reached her breast. Cradling its weight in his palm, his thumb rubbed across the nipple, bringing it instantly awake.

"You're so beautiful," he whispered, his breath brushing across her cheek. "And soft . . . and sexy."

Allison had the sinking feeling that he was still caught in the dream. As her body responded quickly and passionately to his kisses and caresses, her mind cried, *You can't let him do this. He thinks you're his beautiful, sexy Caroline. He doesn't even realize you're plain ol' Allison Greene.*

Still she was tempted. She wanted this one night with him. Briefly she could hold him and pretend he loved her. She could cherish the feel of his lips on her body and the pleasure of having him become part of her and leaving part of himself behind. She might even get pregnant and someday hold their child in her arms.

But her logic and common sense finally kicked into gear. She was a kindergarten teacher. Not only would Mr. Gibson have a coronary, but how would she be able to explain a pregnancy to the children? They greeted her each day with a cheerful, "Good morning, *Miss* Greene." She, as an unmarried mother, would not be a good example to her students. And unless she was ready to move back to Boston and live under her parents' roof, she couldn't afford to give up her career.

Another consideration was tomorrow. Tomorrow she and Justin would both wake up to reality, and he would be disappointed that she was not Caroline. Would her night of happiness be worth the hurt and humiliation of morning? Was she willing to sacrifice her pride and integrity for temporary gratification from the man she loved?

"Justin," she gasped. "Wake up. You don't know what you're saying."

"I *am* awake and I know exactly what I'm saying." He didn't stop kissing her.

Allison wasn't convinced his thoughts weren't still foggy from sleep. It was important that he say her name. She had to hear it spoken from those sensual lips before she would believe him. But as his hands grew bolder and his kisses more persuasive, she was no longer able to resist. Throwing caution to the wind, she wrapped her arms around his neck and let herself give in to the pure sensation of the moment. Soon one of them would wake up from this dream and stop the insanity.

She was ready when his mouth found hers again, and she returned his kiss with all the pent-up passion he had created within her. Their lips pressed together, moving eagerly as if tasting just one spot were not enough. His tongue seductively caressed the inside of her lips before sliding deeper into her mouth. Her tongue met his, intimately performing a preliminary mating dance that increased her urgent need for him.

He moaned and shifted beneath her, bringing her in contact with the swell of his own need. His other hand moved under her sweatshirt, skimming across her skin, leaving behind heated trails of desire. When he began lifting the shirt, she raised her arms and helped him remove it.

His sweater was soft and stimulating against her bare breasts. But the fuzzy friction was soon replaced by the gentle massage of his hands. Again Justin adjusted her on his lap until his lips could reach the hardened peaks. While his tongue stroked one sensitive nipple, his mouth suckled it. The combined stimulus drained away the last of Allison's resistance. She arched her back, encouraging him to continue, to grow even more bold in his lovemaking.

While his mouth moved to the other impatient breast, his hand slipped under the elastic band of her sweatpants and into the sanctity of her panties. A distant part of Allison's very distracted mind registered a regret that she hadn't chosen a pair of those sexy bikinis that were sitting, ignored, next to her sturdier and much less attractive cotton briefs.

Justin didn't seem to notice as his fingers didn't stop to evaluate the type of panties she was wearing. Instead, they moved lower until they stroked the center of her desire. Allison's response was quick and automatic, betraying her physical readiness for him. As if that were the sign he'd been waiting for, he raised her into a sitting position and, after a long, intoxicating kiss on her lips, he stood, pulling her with him.

They were both unsteady on their feet, but he managed to spread one of the blankets on the floor in front of the fireplace and remove her clothing while still showering her face with kisses. He took a pillow from the couch and tossed it onto the blanket, then eased her down.

For a moment he stood looking at her. Allison's heart stopped as she waited for him to realize who she was. Surely he couldn't look at her rather thin, unspectacular body and not come to his senses. By now she not only wanted him, she ached for him. She needed the fulfillment only he could give her. To stop their lovemaking at this point would leave her physically and emotionally devastated.

"You're perfect," he said, not sounding disappointed.

Allison still couldn't believe it. No man had ever called her *beautiful* or *perfect*. She couldn't remember her father even saying she was *cute*. Was it possible that Justin truly did care about her, Allison Greene, the almost old-maid schoolteacher?

He took off his clothes and she watched shamelessly, curiously, her mind memorizing every bulge of muscle, every expanse of taut flesh and the pattern of dark, curly hair that sprinkled lightly across his chest and trickled in a thin, bewitching trail down his flat stomach...and lower. She tried not to let him see her gaze linger there, but his erection was a powerful witness to his arousal. She wanted to remember every detail of the night in case the memory had to last the rest of her life.

With a shaky sigh, he knelt over her, straddling her legs and lowering his torso until his chest barely glazed the swollen tips of her breasts. His kiss captured her lips and set her heart to beating again. More than beating. It was pounding in her chest as her blood raced through her veins.

His knee nudged her legs apart and, because neither Allison nor Justin could survive any more preliminaries, he entered her, slowly and sensually, deeper and deeper. He filled her, fitting perfectly within her.

For a few seconds, he paused, savoring the sensation and allowing her time to accept him. Then he started moving, gently at first, but more quickly and frantically as their passion built. His breath was hot against her neck, and occasionally his teeth would nibble the tender area behind her ear, pushing her, urging her to go further than she had ever gone before.

She wanted to hold on, delaying the satisfaction, anxious to make the moment last as long as possible. But her body had other ideas, moving with his until she felt an explosion deep within her. It radiated from that point, streaking like electrical jolts throughout her with a pleasure that was so intense it was close to pain.

Justin held on until her spasms slowed, then, with one more thrust, he poured his heat into her. At the instant of his release, he cried out and she heard it at last.

"Allison," he breathed raggedly. Then, so quietly she wasn't sure she actually heard it, she thought he added, "My love."

Her heart soared. He *did* know it was she. And he *did* love her—at least a little. It was like a delicious dessert after a satisfying seven-course meal.

Justin rolled to one side but didn't withdraw from her as he held her tightly against him. They didn't speak for several minutes as they allowed their breathing to steady and their heartbeats to regulate.

Finally he said, "To borrow a word from the kids, that was *awesome.*"

She couldn't see his eyes, but she could hear the cheerfulness in his voice, the complete contentment in his tone. "*Totally* awesome," she added, snuggling closer to him, happier than she had ever been in her life.

"Did I pass the test, teacher?"

"With honors," she murmured, breathing in the musky, masculine scent of his skin.

They dozed for a while until the embers in the fireplace burned out, leaving a chill in the air. Allison wasn't totally awake when she felt Justin lift her in his arms and carry her up the stairs to her bedroom. She did wake up, however, when he joined her in the bed. With his nude body next to hers and his hands caressing the curve of her buttocks, she quickly decided she could catch up later on her sleep. The dawn was fast approaching, and she wanted to share her love with him as much as possible in the time they had left.

"GOOD MORNING, MISS GREENE." The voice whispering in her ear was familiar... and definitely not that of her students.

Allison was lying on her side and a warm body was pressed against her back. But even without turning to look at him, she knew *this* warm body wasn't Curiosity.

She shifted, rolling onto her other side so she was facing him. "Good morning, Mr. Sloane. Did you sleep well?"

"Sleep?" He pretended bewilderment. "Did I sleep? That's definitely not the part of last night that I remember the most."

Perhaps it was the morning sun that was peeking in through the lace curtains, illuminating their nudity, or maybe it was the memory of her abandonment the night before, but Allison felt a heated blush color her cheeks.

"You weren't disappointed?" She was horrified the words that were so dominating her thoughts should slip out.

As if sensing her vulnerability, he tenderly brushed her hair back from her face and leaned over for a long, reassuring kiss. "How could I be disappointed with you? You were perfect."

Perfect. There was that word again. Allison had always considered herself to be somewhat flawed. She had never been smart enough, pretty enough, popular enough. The perfection of her brother had been a hard act to follow. His breakdown and suicide had been a major disappointment to her family, and instead of drawing them closer to Allison, it had made them more critical of her imperfections.

Allison wasn't sure how to react to someone who wasn't disappointed in her. The admiration and satisfaction in his eyes went a long way to bolster her confidence. After yet another session where he proved how much she pleased him, she even began to feel a little beautiful.

They were lying in each other's arms, reluctant to get out of bed and rejoin the rest of the world when Allison suddenly sat up.

"Oh, no. Mr. Wiggly!" she exclaimed.

Justin's eyebrows arched wryly as he said in mock horror. "I hope you aren't talking about me."

She gave his bare behind a playful slap. "No, silly. I'm talking about the rabbits. I forgot all about them."

"I don't suppose Curiosity could take care of them for you," he suggested hopefully.

"She shares her litter box and water dish with them. But I think that's about the best I can hope for." She scooted to the edge of the bed. "I've got to let one of them out and put some food and water in the cage of the other one."

"You mean they're litter-box trained? I've never heard of that before."

"Yes, they're good indoor pets. As long as I don't move the litter box, they're very conscientious. They make fewer accidents than most children I know."

"Why not let them both out?"

"You're kidding? Do you know how many rabbits I would have by Thanksgiving?"

"So, let them enjoy themselves." He leaned forward and kissed her bare shoulder. "We did."

Allison glanced back at him, not wanting to get up and leave him but knowing she had shirked her duties long enough. "They'll have their moment—and in the case of rabbits, that's about all it takes—a couple of months before Easter. Until then, they'll have to settle for nose wiggles across a crowded room."

She pulled on a robe and went downstairs. She let Snow White out first for exercise. While she was feeding all of her pets, she heard the shower turn on, which gave her time to have a hearty breakfast almost ready for Justin by the time he came downstairs.

"I seem to have lost my clothes," he said, modeling a pink terry-cloth robe that covered him barely enough to be decent.

Allison had straightened up the living room, hung his clothes over the back of the chair and redressed in her sweat suit. She pointed toward the chair. "They're over there."

"Something smells good." He took a deep breath, then gave her a roguish wink. "I can't imagine why, but I'm starving."

"Hurry and get dressed. Breakfast is almost ready."

Later, as they sat across from each other at the breakfast table, he commented, "It's stopped snowing, but I'll bet we got at least two feet. They probably already have the highway open so we can go out later and see if we can get your car home.''

''I thought a front-wheel drive would get me through the winters here.''

''Usually they're adequate. But that storm last night was a test even for my four-wheel drive.''

''I was going to offer to pick up Whitney, take her to school and bring her home on the days she has class,'' Allison said. ''But now you probably won't trust my driving.''

He reached across the table and caressed her cheek. ''I would trust you with anything I own, including my daughter. Sure, I wouldn't mind if she rides with you. It would be very convenient for me. Usually I'm right in the middle of something when it's time to shut down the system and go pick her up.''

''She could ride the bus, you know. It probably stops right outside your complex.''

''Whitney wants to ride the bus. She thinks it would be fun. But I'm not sure that would be such a good idea.''

''It's a good experience. Besides, she probably wouldn't like it once the newness wore off.''

They finished the meal and he cleaned up the kitchen while Allison took her turn in the shower and changed into her new jeans and a sweater.

Allison dreaded going back out after last night's close brush with death. But as Justin drove through town on the freshly plowed roads, she relaxed as she noticed how beautiful everything looked with its blanket of snow. Already a few conscientious homeowners were shoveling the snow off their driveways and sidewalks, and the park was filled with children, pulling one another on sleds and trying to build perfect snowmen.

The car had barely stopped in Justin's driveway when Whitney burst through the door of her grandparents' house and bounced across the yard, almost foundering in the deep drifts. Justin leaped to her rescue, scooping her into his arms and carrying her the last few feet.

"Grandma said you took care of Miss Greene last night."

Justin and Allison exchanged an intimate glance and smiled before he responded. "Yes, Whitney, I did. Miss Greene's car broke down, and I had to take her home."

"Well, why didn't you bring her here?" the little girl asked with a touch of disappointment. "I could have helped, too."

Again Justin looked at Allison. "Miss Greene went straight to bed, and I stayed..." He hesitated, apparently trying to think of a delicate way to explain the situation.

"Your daddy stayed because he was afraid I would get sick," Allison interjected. "He wanted to be there in case I needed something. And he helped me with Mr. Wiggly Nose and Snow White. They got pretty cold waiting in the car for us to be rescued."

Introducing the rabbits into the conversation succeeded in distracting the child. Allison breathed a sigh of relief. At least for now, Whitney didn't ask any more questions about last night. She didn't realize just how much the whole world had changed in the past twenty-four hours.

THEY FELL INTO a comfortable pattern during the next two weeks. Allison picked up Whitney on the mornings the little girl went to school and when they returned, Justin would either cook dinner for them or take them out. On the other nights, Justin and Whitney would usually come to Allison's house, where they would all pitch in and cook something or call out for pizza.

Although Justin hadn't yet spoken the words *love* or *marriage*, Allison was beginning to feel confident things would work out for them. This was the type of family life she had always wanted. An adorable child, a loving, handsome husband—things were almost perfect.

Perfect. That word kept popping up. Almost perversely, Allison's feelings swung to the opposite end of the spectrum. Instead of worrying that she might never know Justin's love, she began worrying that things were too perfect.

Their love life still left a lot to be desired. Not that it wasn't fantastic—it just wasn't often enough. Without being too obvious, there were very few times, such as the rare nights Whitney spent with her grandparents, when they could have the time and the privacy to make love. Allison felt so much better about her and Justin's chances for a future together that she wouldn't have minded if she had gotten pregnant that first night. She believed he would have been so delighted at the prospect of another child that the subject of marriage would have come up quickly.

However, she wasn't really disappointed when, a few days later, she started her period. Justin made her feel young and beautiful. Before she fell in love with him, she had felt that her prospects of finding a husband and having a child were pretty bleak. But now she felt confident there would be time enough later for babies . . . lots of babies.

They talked often of how much they both loved children and wanted several. But Justin agreed that the time was not right. He had apologized for not being prepared that first night and had been careful to take precautions since then.

As Thanksgiving approached, Allison began planning their dinner. She picked out a turkey and bought all the trimmings to go with it. She decorated the house with arrangements of fall leaves, gourds, baby pumpkins and colorful ears of Indian corn on the mantel and the dining room table. It would be the first time since she moved into the house that she had had an opportunity to serve a special meal in the formal dining room on her aunt's beautiful antique furniture.

And she found herself becoming increasingly involved in Whitney's life. They often went shopping together, without Justin, and the little girl loved to come to Allison's house and make cookies or fudge and play with Curiosity. Allison had also made arrangements with the school's art teacher for Whitney to take private lessons once a week with other gifted children. Allison stayed after school, catching up on lesson plans while waiting for Whitney to learn how to channel her creativity.

It was a wonderful season for Allison—a season of hope and of planning for her future, *their* future. The only way things could get better was if she were to have a wedding ring, or at least an engagement ring from Justin on the third finger of her left hand. But she believed it would happen. There was plenty of time.

Chapter Fourteen

"Of course, we're having Thanksgiving dinner at my parents' house. We *always* do." Justin's statement was matter-of-fact.

"But I already bought everything," Allison explained, positive that once he realized how much trouble she had gone to, he would think her plan was wonderful. "I wanted our first Thanksgiving together to be special."

Justin shook his head. "We can't. My mother would be really disappointed. It's a family tradition. Even when Caroline was alive we'd always go to my parents' for Thanksgiving and her parents' for Christmas."

Allison couldn't understand his stubbornness. "Maybe we could start a new family tradition," she suggested.

"No. This is something we've been doing forever. I couldn't possibly hurt my mother's feelings like that."

"We *have* to go to Grandma's house for Thanksgiving," Whitney chimed in. "It's a rule."

"Like eating chili when it snows?" Allison muttered, surprised that even Whitney was voting against her idea. "I just thought it would be a lot of fun for us to do this together. I've never cooked a turkey dinner before, but we could all pitch in. Then every year, we could get better and better."

"All the more reason to go to Mother's," Justin stated with firm resolve. "She's a terrific cook. Just wait until you taste her turkey and dressing."

"And her punkin pie." Whitney licked her lips at the thought. "With whipped cream and a cherry on top."

"Well, I don't suppose I can compete with that." Allison couldn't keep the sarcasm out of her voice, and Justin's expression was reproachful as if she had blasphemed his mother.

"I'll bet Grandma would let you help her," Whitney added. "She lets me lick the beaters and set the table."

"Well, I guess it's two to one, so we'll go to your mother's." Allison tried not to let them see how devastated she was. She had spent hours planning the meal and had been looking forward to sharing it with her new family. Perhaps, because of the surprise change, she was blowing the whole thing out of proportion. After all, it would be better to spend the holiday with Justin and Whitney at his parents' than to spend it alone.

"Come on over here and watch the movie with us," Justin said, patting the couch next to him. "I haven't seen *Lady and the Tramp* in years."

Allison shrugged, still feeling a little let down that Justin hadn't at least been open-minded about the change, but she was determined not to ruin the evening. She sat where he indicated and was relaxing into the comfortable curve of his arm around her shoulders when Whitney jumped up from where she'd been sitting on the floor and snuggled in between them.

Justin met Allison's gaze over Whitney's dark head and he sighed. At least, in this case, he was as disappointed as Allison was.

She tried to pay attention to the movie, but she'd seen it dozens of times at school. She wished Justin had chosen something else a little more adult. Since she and Justin started dating she'd seen more Disney movies than she'd seen in her whole life outside of school.

Not that she had anything against Disney films. It was just that she felt it wouldn't be a bad idea for her and Justin not to let the world revolve around Whitney as much as they did.

It wasn't that Allison didn't enjoy spending time with the child. Already Allison loved Whitney as if she were her own. But it wasn't healthy to spend every waking moment with the little girl. Allison felt Justin should separate his own life from the life of his daughter.

But she kept silent. It wasn't any of her business. Yet.

When the movie ended, Justin switched the video tape player on rewind and changed channels to the news. During a commercial break, a jewelry store in Denver advertising a sale caught Whitney's attention.

"Daddy, I want to get my ears pierced," she announced.

"We'll talk about it when you're older," Justin responded, distracted by the weather report.

"But lots of other girls my age have their ears pierced," Whitney pointed out. "I want some of those little red earrings."

"Those are rubies and you'd probably lose them the first week you had them," he explained.

She looked up at him with wide blue eyes. "Please," she begged, drawing the one-syllable word out. "Daddy, I *really* want to have my ears pierced. Miss Greene said it was okay."

Justin turned away from watching the television screen and looked at Allison. "You told Whitney it was okay to get her ears pierced?"

"I told her I didn't see any harm in it if you approved."

"Thanks a lot," he muttered to Allison as he stood up and looked at his daughter. "It's getting close to your bed-time, Whitney. Why don't you put your shoes on and tell Curiosity good-night. We'd better get home."

He waited until Whitney had left the room, then he confronted Allison. "Why did you encourage her? She's too young to have her ears pierced."

"I didn't encourage her. She asked if I thought she should have her ears pierced, and I told her I didn't see anything wrong with it, but that it was up to you."

"So I'm the bad guy in this."

"If you think she's too young, then tell her so and stick to your decision."

"Are you trying to say that I don't know how to handle my daughter?" he asked defensively.

Allison couldn't believe how angry he was. Considering their earlier conversation about Thanksgiving, she wasn't feeling very sympathetic about his dilemma. "This has nothing to do with how you handle your daughter. It's about a little girl wanting something and you deciding whether or not she can have it. You're the adult and she's the child."

He stiffened, sucking in his breath at the implication of her words. With forced calm, he walked to the VCR, ejected the tape and inserted it into its plastic case. "In the future, I'd appreciate it if you'd let me make the decisions that concern my child." Without stopping, he passed her on his way to the back door. "Good night." His tone was curt and he didn't wait for her response before he herded Whitney out the door and closed it behind them.

For several minutes Allison didn't move, but sat on the couch and tried to reconstruct the conversation and see where the evening went wrong. She felt bad that he was up-set, but she didn't believe she'd done anything out of line.

He'd been in a strange mood all day. In fact, it almost seemed as if he had been spoiling for a fight.

Regardless of whose fault it was or how silly the whole argument had been, Allison's chest felt tight, as if she were about to cry. She hated confrontations and she didn't like Justin to be mad at her, even if he was being unreasonable. She wished they could start the evening over. Maybe if she had approached the Thanksgiving dinner idea differently, he would have been more receptive. It was just that it meant so much to her and he had dismissed her plan without giving it any consideration at all.

Allison turned off the television and all the downstairs lights except a lamp in the living room and locked the doors before going upstairs. As she took a long, hot shower, all she could think about was Justin. She didn't understand his behavior but guessed he was probably having a problem with the job he was working on. She certainly couldn't imagine what else would have him so on edge. Hopefully a good night's sleep would help him work through the program and restore his good humor.

She dressed in a flannel nightgown and climbed into bed. For half an hour she lay on her back, staring into the semidarkness, watching the shadow of the bare tree limbs outside her window. Backed by a full moon and tossed by a stiff northerly wind, the outlines danced on the ceiling. For no particular reason, she felt very alone. Not even Curiosity had come upstairs with her. Allison's eyes filled with tears—tears of disappointment, tears of frustration, tears of fear that she might lose everything she now held dear. Slowly they leaked out the corners of her eyes and trickled down the sides of her face and into her hair. She loved Justin and she loved Whitney. What would she do without them? It was not something she wanted to find out.

The ring of the telephone was abnormally loud in the quiet room. Allison glanced at the clock and saw it was almost midnight. Who would be calling her at that time of night? She hesitated, not knowing whether to answer the phone. It could be a crank caller or a pervert. It could also be someone calling to tell her that her parents had been in an accident or come down with a serious illness.

Not really wanting to, but afraid not to, she picked up the receiver and answered the call.

"Hello?" It was more of a question than a greeting.

"Allison. It's me, Justin. Were you asleep?"

It wasn't tragic news and yet she didn't relax. They had parted on such unpleasant terms, she wasn't sure what he would have to say.

"No," she answered simply, her nerves on edge as she waited to find out why he had called.

"Me, either." There was a long moment of silence. When he spoke again, his words came out in a rush. "Allison, I didn't mean to jump on you like that. I guess I overreacted a little."

Allison breathed a sigh of relief. He was calling to apologize.

"I couldn't sleep until I talked with you," he continued. "I guess we just had our first fight."

"It had to happen sometime," Allison commented as she relaxed back against the pillows. "At least now it's out of the way."

She heard the sound of the sheets rustling as Justin settled more comfortably on his bed.

"So, what are you wearing?" he asked in an obvious attempt to lighten the tone of their conversation.

Allison looked down at her granny gown and knee-high socks and chuckled. "Nothing but a smile," she teased.

"A big smile or a little smile?"

"A lonely smile. I wish you were here."

They talked for an hour, sweet, sexy pillow talk that made them forget their argument and count the hours until they would be together again. They had survived their first major quarrel and Allison felt more positive than ever about their relationship.

THE NEXT DAY Allison picked Whitney up for school as usual. Thanksgiving was only a week away, and the kindergarten class was very busy working on their Indian and Pilgrim costumes for the reenactment of the first Thanksgiving dinner. Allison was busy supervising her students as they cut grocery bags so there were armholes and a split up the front to make them resemble Indian vests. The children then drew colorful Indian-styled symbols and designs all over the vests.

At the same time, Allison was overseeing the making of Pilgrim hats and collars out of construction paper. The children who were designated as Pilgrims were also responsible for building the village, so they were busy coloring a mural that had log cabins, trees and animals on it.

There was quite a mess when the bell rang at the end of the school day. The children had put up their supplies, but they hadn't had time to put their projects away or to pick up all the scraps.

As usual, Allison escorted her class to the bus-loading and parent-pickup areas. Whitney tagged along even though she would be riding home with Allison.

"Can I ride the bus today, Miss Greene?" the little girl asked as she watched her friends board the big yellow vehicle. "Please?"

"Your father said he didn't want you to ride the bus," Allison answered. "Come on, let's go back and clean up the classroom."

"If I could ride the bus just *once,* I would never ever ask to ride it again. Please, Miss Greene. I could sit with Jennifer. Daddy won't mind."

Allison wasn't so sure. She knew Justin's original decision had been against it, but they hadn't discussed the matter for quite a while. Perhaps this would be a good time to let Whitney try riding the bus to see if she really liked it and to prove to Justin that there was no danger involved. Besides, Whitney would probably get home sooner if she rode the bus than if she waited for Allison to finish cleaning the classroom.

"Okay, Whitney, but you have to remember the bus rules. Stay in your seat, don't throw things out the windows, don't stick your hands or head out the windows and no screaming."

The little girl bobbed up and down, sending her ponytail dancing wildly. "I'll be *very* good. I promise."

"Tell your daddy I'll be by as soon as I finish here," Allison added as she ushered Whitney onto the bus. After telling the bus driver where Whitney lived, she stepped back. Whitney's small face beamed back at her through the window as she waved.

Allison watched until the bus turned onto the main road and disappeared around a curve.

"Hey, Ali, wait up." Chris caught up with her and they walked into the building together. "So, how's the romance going? Should I be shopping for a maternity dress to wear to a wedding?"

"I hope so. I think we're getting close to discussing a future," Allison said, knowing her smile was as bright as Whitney's had been. That was how she felt, like a child who has just been granted her dearest wish. "I already feel like Whitney's my daughter."

"That's terrific. Maybe we'll both become mothers at about the same time."

"Speaking of which, how've you been feeling? Any morning sickness? Can you feel the baby kicking yet?"

"I've had a little nausea, but nothing to get me down. Sometimes I think I feel a little flutter, but it could be my imagination."

"Have you and Jared decided on any names?"

Chris rolled her eyes. "We've run the gamut from exotic to traditional, but I think when it comes right down to it, it'll be Raymond after Jared's dad if it's a boy and Crystal if it's a girl."

"Those are both nice. It must be so much fun to pick out names for a baby."

"It is. To think you have a child's whole life in your hands is sort of scary, but it makes you see everything in a whole new perspective." Impulsively Chris reached out and gripped Allison's arm. "I hope you get pregnant soon. It's an incredible experience. And you'll make a terrific mom."

Allison's heart felt as if it would burst from the intense happiness and excitement about her future as a wife and a mother. She couldn't wait until a child was growing in her womb...Justin's child. She would probably wear maternity clothes from the very first day she found out she was pregnant, because she wanted the world to know and share in her joy. If Mr. Gibson hadn't chosen that moment to emerge from the depths of his office, Allison would have probably broken into a very undignified skip.

He nodded in the direction of the two women but didn't speak as he hurried to the parking lot.

"Anxious to get away, isn't he?" Chris whispered. "Maybe he's on his way to an illicit assignation."

"Lord, I doubt that. No woman could be that desperate."

The two friends were laughing as they parted at the doorway to Allison's classroom.

"See you at recess tomorrow," Chris called.

"If it doesn't snow and the Pilgrims finish their village," Allison replied cryptically.

Since both classes were going to work on the mural, she could leave it out. But all of the vests and Pilgrim accessories had to be put away. First, Allison checked to see if there were names on the items, then she stacked them on a shelf. On the tables, there were still a few pairs of scissors and some crayons that the children had forgotten to put away. Tomorrow the other class would work on the same projects, plus the Indian headbands and place mats Whitney's class would make on Friday.

As Allison drove to Justin's house, she was still thinking about her conversation with Chris. Justin had shown her Whitney's baby pictures, so it was easy to imagine what Allison and Justin's baby would look like. Allison hoped it would have his dark hair and bright blue eyes, just as Whitney did.

The one thing Allison knew for sure was that she would raise her child much differently than she had been raised. There would be no nannies or housekeepers watching over her baby. With Justin at home during the day and Allison off all summer, it would be an ideal situation for taking care of their children.

She wished she could talk with Justin about having a baby. But she didn't want him to feel pressured. He *still* hadn't told her he loved her in so many words. Anyway, she had decided that even if he was never able to love her as much as he had loved Caroline, Allison loved him enough for both of them.

Without stopping at her house first, she went directly to Justin's. She parked in his driveway and hurried to the door.

He answered the bell and pulled her into his arms for a welcoming kiss.

"How was school today?" he asked.

"Wild and crazy as usual. We're making corn bread next Tuesday and Wednesday and everyone is going to dress up like either an Indian or a Pilgrim. Today we had to costume the entire settlement." She stepped inside, took off her coat and hung it on the coatrack in the hall. When Justin didn't follow her, she stopped. He still stood in the doorway, looking outside.

"So how did Whitney like her bus ride?" she asked.

He looked at her sharply. "What do you mean? Isn't she with you?"

"No, I had to stay after school, and Whitney pleaded with me to let her ride the bus home. So I let her."

He glanced outside again as if he didn't believe what he was hearing. He even stepped onto the porch and peered around the corner to see if she was playing a joke on him.

"She's really not with you?" He returned to the entry hall and confronted Allison.

"No, I told you, she rode the school bus."

"Then where is she?" He was practically shouting.

"I thought she would beat me home. But that bus has a long route, so I'm sure she'll be here any minute."

"You *knew* I didn't want her riding that bus. What gave you the right to let her do it?" he demanded.

Allison recoiled as if she had been struck. *What gave her the right?* He made it sound as if she were a stranger, not someone who was hoping to become Whitney's stepmother soon.

"It's not like I let her go to a bar and get drunk. She's just riding a school bus home, like millions of other students, for goodness' sakes."

He heaved an angry sigh and dragged his fingers through his hair in frustration. "I can't believe you went against my wishes like that. Whitney is *my* daughter, not yours."

"Thank you for pointing that out to me." Allison responded with a hint of sarcasm to hide the pain his words had caused.

"I think I've done a damn good job of raising her, and I don't want outside interference at this stage of the game. I realize you're a teacher and think you know a lot about kids, but you don't know anything about the actual day-to-day responsibilities of being a parent."

This time the hurt was too deep for her not to lash back. "Maybe not, but I know that a child should be allowed to be a child and not be stuffed into the mold of a miniature adult."

"What's that supposed to mean?"

"Poor little Whitney has never had a childhood. She never goes to a friend's house to play. You won't let her ride the bus. She has no pets, and until her art lessons started, no outside interests. Yes, you've done a wonderful job with her. She's remarkably unspoiled, especially for someone who is the focus of two sets of grandparents and a doting father. But she looks after you and worries about you as if she were your wife rather than your daughter. Instead of cooking your dinner, she should be outside building a snowman or playing in the leaves."

"I think Caroline would be pleased with the way I've handled Whitney," he stated defensively.

"I'm sure she would," Allison retorted. "There's every possibility that Whitney could turn out just like Caroline's mother. What a warm, spontaneous person that woman is!" Allison knew that was a low blow, but she understood enough about juvenile psychology to recognize the results of a warped childhood.

"Unintentionally you've pushed Whitney into missing an important step in her growing process," Allison continued. "First she needs to be a child. Sure, she's going to fall and scrape her knees, but that happens to all of us. That's how we learn."

"You don't know what you're talking about."

"I know more about it than you can imagine." She didn't go on to explain that her own childhood had been so sheltered she'd had to run away to be able to breathe and find herself as a person. The only difference between her and Whitney was that Whitney was growing up surrounded by love. Allison had been merely surrounded by money and two strangers she called her parents.

"Whitney's doing fine. She's intelligent, mature and very well adjusted. She and I don't need anyone else to be happy. I'm not just her father, I'm her best friend."

Allison bit her lower lip to keep the tears from rushing out. "That's the main problem. You've made yourself her whole world. That's not good for her. And it's not good for you. Now that she's seen there's life outside these walls, you're suddenly scared to death that you're going to lose her. That's why you won't let her stretch her wings and try to fly on her own, even with such simple things like riding the school bus or spending the night with a friend."

"I've never told her she couldn't spend the night with a friend," he stated. "She's never asked."

Allison shook her head sadly. "I think you should know that she's very popular at school. But every time one of the other girls asks her over to play or to a birthday party, I've overheard Whitney turn down the invitations. She says you need her at home and she can't leave you alone that long. Well, that's a pretty heavy load for a little girl."

She took her coat off the rack and headed for the door. "Frankly, I think it's time you grew up, and, at the same time, it's time you let her stop being so grown-up. She's not a short adult. She's a child.''

"And I think she's very happy with the way things are.'' He straightened to his full height and looked down at her as if they were only casual acquaintances. "There for a while, I thought it might be good for her to have someone for a mother figure. But now I believe she and I are better off looking after each other.''

He took off the glasses he had been wearing while working at the computer before she arrived, carefully cleaned them with the bottom of his shirt and put them back on. It was more of a gesture to give himself time to collect his thoughts than because the lens were dirty. As he continued, his voice was totally lacking in emotion.

"Just look at how confusing it's been these last few weeks with all the weird clothes you've been buying for her. You tell her it's okay to have her ears pierced, you make plans for Thanksgiving without discussing them with me first, and now this school bus incident. She hasn't been home very much lately and I've been neglecting her because of all our dating. I can see now that having another person involved in our lives just wouldn't work out.''

Allison didn't bother putting on her coat, but yanked open the door that had been standing partially ajar. She struggled for a brilliant parting response, some perfectly chosen words of wisdom that he would remember forever. But her mind was blank. All she could manage was, "Goodbye, Justin. I won't be butting into your perfect little family anymore.''

She didn't care who saw her as she ran to her car. Allison simply had to get away as quickly as possible before he saw how deeply he'd wounded her. In mere moments, her whole world had come crashing down. Her hopes, her dreams, her plans to have a baby and to be a mother to Whitney were all gone. Her thoughts and emotions were in a turmoil, and there was an ache inside her that felt as if she'd been stabbed with a dull knife over and over until all her blood drained out and there was nothing left. Like an injured animal, her instincts told her she had to get home. She would be safe there. She could cry and hide in the dark and lick her wounds.

As she rushed past the hedge of evergreens near the front door, she didn't notice the child who crouched there. Allison would have been able to sympathize with the tears on the girl's cheeks. They reflected the pain and disappointment that nothing, no matter how hard you try or how much you want it, is perfect.

THAT EVENING she decided not to answer the phone if it rang. If Justin wanted to call to apologize, she would play hard to get for a few days until she was able to calm down enough to talk to him and tell him how very much he had hurt her.

But as she lay in bed, the tears still streaming down her cheeks several hours later, she leaped for the phone, picking it up on the first ring.

"Hello," she sniffled.

"Allison?"

She'd been so positive it was Justin that, at first, she didn't recognize the voice. "Yes."

"This is Angela."

"Oh, hi, Angela." Allison tossed another soggy tissue into a trash can and pulled a fresh one from the box.

"Do you have a cold? You sound sort of stuffed up."

Allison considered lying. But she and her sister-in-law had always gotten along well. They had become close friends, especially after Craig died. Allison thought when Angela married Jeff Hawkins and moved to Colorado a little over a year ago that she and Allison would lose touch. But fate had intervened, bringing Allison to Colorado also, although they hadn't had a chance to get together for a visit yet. Jeff's ranch was on the other side of the mountains from Georgetown, not far as the crow flies, but traveling across the passes and along the curving highway, it was a trip that would take several hours.

It was because they had always been honest with each other that Allison felt compelled to tell Angela what had happened.

"I fell in love."

"Terrific!" Angela exclaimed.

"Not so terrific. It's over. He told me today that he and his daughter don't need anyone else in their lives."

"Oh. Good."

"Good?"

"Not good that the guy is so stupid he doesn't know a good thing when he sees it. But good that this probably means you don't have plans for Thanksgiving."

Allison had completely forgotten about her now infamous Thanksgiving plans. The last place she would want to be on Thanksgiving day would be Justin's parents' house. But the second-to-last place she'd want to be on Thanksgiving day would be home alone.

"I hope you haven't decided to go to your parents' for Thanksgiving, because Jeff and I would love to have you come to our house for the holiday."

Allison made a correction in her list making. The second to the the last place would be her parents' with the third-to-last to be home alone. But still she hesitated, not wanting to be a wet blanket on someone else's festivities.

"I doubt that I'd be good company," she replied.

"The best thing you could do is to get out of town and do something totally different. Besides, I can't wait for you to meet Randy. He's growing so fast."

Allison knew that Randy was the son Angela and Jeff had adopted during a trip to Vietnam. Angela had assisted in the baby's birth and when the mother abandoned the newborn, Angela had talked the doctor into listing her and Jeff as the parents on the child's birth certificate and they had brought Randy home. As much as she wanted to see the boy, Allison wasn't sure it wouldn't make her feel even worse about not being able to have her own baby anytime soon.

On the other hand, Angela did have a good point. It would be nice to be somewhere other than Georgetown or Boston on Thanksgiving. If she stayed home all she would think about was what Justin and Whitney were doing, and she would be miserable.

"I can't guarantee I'll be the best company," Allison said, "but, yes, I'd like to spend Thanksgiving with your family."

"That's terrific. It's about a four-hour drive from Georgetown so you could either come out on Wednesday evening if the weather's good or Thursday morning. And we want you to stay as long as you can."

"I'll call you next week after I've heard the weather report and let you know. What can I bring?"

"Oh, don't worry about that. I'll take care of everything."

"If you haven't already bought a turkey, I've got one that's taking up every inch of space in my freezer. Why don't I bring that?"

Angela laughed. "Sure, bring it. I haven't done any shopping yet."

"Thanks, Angela, for inviting me. I don't know how I would have handled the holiday alone."

"Don't ever forget that we're still family," Angela reminded her gently, then added with genuine enthusiasm. "It's going to be so much fun having you here."

Chapter Fifteen

"Don't you like me anymore, Miss Greene?" The little girl's eyes were filled with tears, and her voice quivered with emotion that ran deeper than the simple question.

Actually the question wasn't as simple as it sounded. Allison could see that the child's hurt and confusion were as deep as her own. How could Allison explain why everything had changed when she didn't understand it herself? Allison had no idea what Justin had told his daughter about why they no longer went to dinner together or why Justin had resumed chauffeuring Whitney to school and back. Did the little girl think it was Allison's idea? Did she think Allison didn't want to spend time with her and Justin anymore?

It had been nearly a week since Allison left Justin's house after their final argument. She'd seen Whitney only at school and had tried, as much as possible, to treat the little girl the same as before. But, of course, there were differences. With Justin dropping her off a few minutes before the bell rang in the morning and waiting to pick her up as soon as the bell rang in the afternoon, Whitney and Allison were able to spend no time alone.

Allison sat down on the bench at the edge of the playground and patted the place next to her. It was almost time for recess to be over, and then the students would return to the classroom, dress in their costumes and eat the corn bread they had made earlier in the morning.

Whitney, perched on the edge of the bench, turned so she could look into Allison's face as they talked.

"Of course, I still like you," Allison replied. "I like you very, very much."

"Then why don't you come over?"

"Did you ask your father about this?"

"Yes, and he said it would be better if just him and me did things together. But I liked it better when you went with us."

"We had a lot of fun together, but I won't be seeing your father after school anymore."

"Don't you like my daddy?"

I love your daddy, Allison's heart cried, but aloud she said, "Your father and I had a little disagreement and we decided we should stop spending so much time together."

"But when are you coming back to our house?"

Allison reached out and, in the guise of smoothing back loose tendrils, caressed the little girl's dark hair—hair that was so like her father's. In fact, Allison felt as if she were looking down at a miniature feminine version of Justin and it broke her heart. She didn't just like this child...she *loved* her. She didn't want to hurt Whitney, but Allison believed it was important to be totally honest with the girl.

"I won't be coming back to your house, Whitney."

"Never?" The question was asked weakly...anxiously.

Allison shook her head. "Never," she confirmed.

"Not even for Thanksgiving?"

"No, I'm going out of town for Thanksgiving."

"I'll come to your house if you'll stay," Whitney offered in desperation. "Me and you can cook the turkey and the punkin pies."

For the first time during the conversation, Allison smiled. It was not a smile of joy, but a wistful smile, sorry that she would never share a Thanksgiving or a Christmas with this child. "Thanks, Whitney. But your grandparents would miss sharing their holiday with you. It's a Sloane Rule, you know."

Whitney's frown was thoughtful. "I think that rule should be changed."

The bell marking the end of recess rang, and the children reluctantly left the swings and monkey bars and lined up in front of Allison. They'd been granted two weeks of beautiful weather that had melted all but the most stubborn patches of snow. Allison found it ironic that all evidence of the big storm, from the snowdrifts to the relationships were almost gone.

Back in the classroom, the students couldn't settle down, especially once they were dressed in their feathers and Pilgrims' hats. They were too excited about the roles they were playing and the upcoming long holiday weekend. The mural stretched across the back wall, and a long table had been set where the Pilgrims and Indians would sit down together and eat their meal of corn bread and cherry Kool-Aid.

After reading the children a story about the first Thanksgiving, Allison watched as the students served one another, then gobbled down their corn-bread muffins as if they were chocolate cake. After most of the mess was cleaned up, Allison knew the children were beyond concentration on schoolwork, so she let them have the rest of the afternoon as free time. They split into small groups and went to the play kitchen, the computer center, the book corner or the game area. With Whitney's help Allison had managed to put together more than half of the puzzles and they were back in place on the shelves.

Allison sat at her desk and took advantage of the children's involvement in their chosen activities to clean up a little paperwork. There were only about thirty minutes left in the school day and Allison didn't plan on staying any longer than it took to load the children into the cars and buses. She had left plenty of dry cat food and water for Curiosity, and Allison's suitcase was waiting in the car, because she had decided to drive to Angela's house tonight. Since she would arrive there after dark, she'd made arrangements to meet Angela and her husband in Montrose at a restaurant that was on the main street.

The day after Angela called, Allison had regretted accepting the invitation. As much as she wanted to see the Hawkins family, she wasn't enthusiastic about the drive or the thought of having to smile and be cheerful for four days.

But after spending last weekend alone with only Curiosity for company, Allison had begun to look forward to the holiday. Before Justin and Whitney became such an integral part of her everyday life, Allison hadn't been lonely. Now the silence throbbed like a heartbeat inside the house.

Allison understood why her Aunt Millie had invited her back each summer. The house needed to have a child's laughter echo throughout its hallways. Aunt Millie must have spent thousands of long, lonely evenings in front of the fireplace after Uncle Bob died. She was with children all day, just like Allison was, which would make it logical to conclude that an evening of quiet would be welcome. But Allison knew it only served to emphasize that there was something lacking in her personal life.

"He's hurting her."

"No, they're just playing."

The voices of the children drifted into Allison's thoughts. She glanced up and saw they were clustered in a group near the rabbits' cages, but she didn't hear any sounds that would make her believe they were fighting. In fact, they seemed calmer and more quiet than usual.

"They're not playing, silly," Sean's voice separated from the rest. "They're doing it."

"It?" one of the girls asked.

"*It!*" Sean repeated knowingly.

"What's it?"

"They're making babies," one of the other girls explained.

Allison's head jerked up. Had she heard what she thought she heard?

Sean added with great authority, "That's what I meant. They're having sex."

That brought Allison abruptly to her feet. She crossed the room and watched in horror as Mr. Wiggly Nose finished mounting Snow White and fell off onto his side on the cage's floor.

"Is he dead?" Rosa asked, her dark eyes widened with shock.

"No, he's just happy," Sean informed her, nodding sagely as Mr. Wiggly Nose recovered his poise, got up and immediately began chasing Snow White again.

"What's going on here?" Allison asked in her most stern voice.

"They're having s—"

"Thank you, Sean, but I know what the rabbits are doing. What I want to know is how Mr. Wiggly Nose got into Snow White's cage."

There must have been a convincing note of authority in her voice, because the children's code of honor was broken as everyone pointed at Whitney simultaneously.

"Somehow this shouldn't surprise me."

"Look, they're doing *it* again," Meagan pointed out, and Allison threw her body in front of the cage, trying, in vain, to shield the sight.

"Everyone, return to your tables immediately and get your things together. The bell is about to ring."

Still trying to sneak a peek at the rabbits, the children shuffled away.

"Except for you, Whitney Sloane," Allison added, halting the girl in her tracks.

Before continuing, Allison retrieved a very tired but satisfied Mr. Wiggly Nose from Snow White's cage and returned him to his own. While the other students tried to overhear the conversation, Allison led Whitney to the computer center and sat her down in a chair. After pulling up a chair for herself, Allison sat across from Whitney and tried to calm down enough to speak in a tone that wouldn't terrify the child.

"Whitney," she finally began, "you, more than any other student in this room, know that Mr. Wiggly Nose and Snow White should not have been put in the same cage. What you did was wrong. Very wrong. I'm disappointed in you. I had hoped you would stop being naughty just to get your own way."

Allison could see that, while Whitney was listening, the girl didn't seem to be too upset.

"So I guess you'll have to call my daddy, huh?" she asked, looking at Allison with hopeful eyes that struggled to look innocent.

"No, I'm not going to call your father." Allison ignored the child's crestfallen expression. "I realize that's why you did it, but this time it's not going to work. You've got to learn that the whole world does not revolve around your wishes. You simply cannot manipulate other people's lives. Your father and I are not going to get back together. But you, on the other hand, are going to be punished. From now until we come back from the Christmas break, you're going to spend every recess in the library. And you will not be eligible to be the class helper during that time.''

The first punishment hadn't phased Whitney, but the second brought a cry of protest. ''Oh, please, Miss Greene, don't take my stick out of the cup. I'll be good. I *really* like to be your helper. I won't *ever* do anything bad again. I'll just sit in my chair and be so quiet. Please . . . please.''

Allison had to steel herself not to give in. She knew how much it meant to Whitney to be the helper. ''I'm sorry, Whitney, but that's the punishment. You have no idea how much trouble this latest mischief might cause.'' Although these children lived in a rural area it didn't mean they were familiar with the mating rituals of nature. Most of them, like Whitney, didn't even own pets and had never witnessed anything so provocative, and Allison was sure some of the parents would not be too happy about their children learning about sex so early.

The bell rang and Allison escorted the children outside. She heard their murmurings, not about the Pilgrims and the Indians, but about Mr. Wiggly Nose and Snow White, and she wondered how long it would take Mr. Gibson to hear about the incident. She probably wouldn't have to bother unpacking her suitcase when she returned.

''LOOKING BACK, I know I was wrong to let Whitney ride that bus when I knew Justin didn't want her to,'' Allison admitted. She was sitting at the kitchen table, watching Angela try to coax the baby into eating his green beans instead of throwing them on the floor. ''I guess I was too deep into my self-cast role as stepmother-to-be and didn't think that Justin would get upset.''

"Men get very set in their ways," Angela commented. "Jeff and I had to make huge adjustments when we got married. He'd been single, taking care of himself for more than twenty years and it was hard for him to have another person to consider on even the most inconsequential everyday decisions."

"I suppose I stepped on his toes, but it was so wonderful to feel like I had a real family," Allison remarked with great sadness. "I guess I went a little crazy, sewing her a Halloween costume, shopping for new clothes and helping her with her art lessons. But I still don't understand why he completely called it off. That whole last week he'd been looking for reasons to pick fights. I think if it hadn't been the school bus thing, it would have been something else." It hurt even worse knowing that Justin's argument hadn't been completely spontaneous. She now believed he'd been planning the breakup and just waited for a good excuse to initiate it.

"It sounds to me like Justin was suffering from cold feet. I think he saw you as a threat to the predictability of his life." Angela walked to the oven and checked on the turkey. "With Whitney going off to school and then latching on to you, he probably felt he was losing her. Men, usually, don't like change and there was no way he could add you permanently to his life without making some major changes."

Allison considered that explanation and knew Angela had wisely discovered the core of the matter. But knowing what the problem was and knowing how to deal with it were two different things. As long as Justin was determined the relationship wouldn't work, then there was nothing she could do.

"Enough about me and my problems. Your baby is adorable. I'm so glad I finally got to see him."

"Jeff and I think Randy is about as perfect as a child could be." She smiled at the small boy, her gaze filled with pride. Her fingers tidied his straight black hair and wiped a piece of green bean from his tiny chin. "We're hoping to adopt another baby, but it'll be more difficult next time. Randall was our gift from God."

"I'm glad you're so happy. I always thought you did everything you could to help Craig. But he never was the same after he came back."

"It's funny how things work out, isn't it?" Angela mused. "I married Craig because I thought Jeff took too many chances and would never settle down. I wanted security and safety. See, even women shy away from change."

"And Jeff waited for you all these years. I think that is so sweet."

"He didn't exactly wait for me. I was just lucky he didn't find someone else to fall in love with until our paths happened to cross again."

The back door opened and Jeff walked in. He draped his jacket on the back of a chair and leaned over to rescue Randy from his highchair. The boy had started shouting, "Daddy, Daddy" and holding his arms up as soon as he saw Jeff.

"Hi, partner. How's Daddy's boy been today? Are you helping Mommy with the turkey?"

"Turkey," Randy echoed.

Jeff dropped an affectionate kiss on his wife's neck and hugged her with his free arm. The baby reached up and tangled his short, plump fingers in Angela's smooth, dark hair.

Allison watched with envy. She was touched by the warm, loving picture they presented—a happy family united by their devotion to each other. It wasn't that she begrudged them a second of their happiness. But she longed for a family of her own. She hadn't known what she was missing until she was with Justin and Whitney. Now Jeff, Angela and tiny Randall were additional proof that the fairy tale was possible.

They had been through so much during the Vietnam War when Angela and Jeff met and fell in love. But circumstances kept them apart for almost eighteen years until they met at a Vietnam veterans reunion. Jeff, who had been known by the nickname "Hawk" because of his bravery and cunning in battle, owned a sheep ranch in Montrose, and Angela had spent her vacation helping him with the lambing. There were old hurts to heal and memories to deal with, but this time they realized how important and eternal their love for each other was. If ever anyone was living a happily-ever-after life, they were.

Allison spent the rest of the weekend playing with the baby as she and Angela sat around, catching up on New England. They had come from similar backgrounds and, although they hadn't met until Angela's marriage to Craig, they'd grown up only miles apart. And they talked about men and love... and about rabbits.

"I expect the worst when I get back," Angela admitted. "Mr. Gibson will definitely not approve of my kindergarten class having an impromptu sex education lesson. If I get fired, I have no idea what I'll do. The next closest school district is probably an hour's commute, and with the weather we get in the mountains, I wouldn't want to risk it." She buried her face in the softness of Randy's fine hair and breathed in his sweet baby scent. "I don't want to leave Georgetown. I love Aunt Millie's house and I would hate to think I'd never see Whitney... and Justin again."

"Well, maybe you're worrying about nothing," Angela said. "Mr. Gibson might think the whole rabbit show is funny."

Allison shook her head doubtfully. "I don't think Mr. Gibson has a sense of humor. I'm really afraid of what he might put on my permanent record. It could affect my résumé wherever else I should apply. I just don't want to have to go back to Boston with my tail between my legs."

"We won't let that happen," Angela assured her. "Jeff knows the school superintendent in Montrose. I'm sure he could help you get a job. And I could find you a nice house. The prices aren't bad here. It would be fun to have you living so near."

It was one of the better options she had. Her heart skipped a beat as she dreaded going to school on Monday. If she had to leave Georgetown, all chance of ever working things out with Justin would be over. Deep inside, she still clung to the hope that a miracle would happen and Justin would show up on her doorstep with dozens of roses and an engagement ring. He would tell her he loved her and promise to be more open-minded about his daughter.

Snap out of it, she reprimanded herself. None of those things were going to happen. And if she persisted in thinking they would, then it proved she believed in fairy tales.

"HELP ME WITH this VCR, son. I'm having trouble fixing it."

Justin looked up from the magazine he'd been reading to see his father peering nearsightedly into the open body of a video recorder. His father, who had retired a couple of years before, repaired appliances in his basement to earn extra money. He loved tinkering with things so much that he couldn't even let a holiday pass without working on something.

"Sure, Dad. What's wrong with it?"

The two men studied the machine, adjusting and checking different circuits and wires until they heard the call that dinner was ready.

"Everything looks good, Mom," Justin said as he sat down across the table from Whitney. "Did you help Grandma, Whitney?"

"I don't think she feels well, Justin," his mother responded. "She didn't even want to lick the whipped cream bowl."

Justin looked over at his daughter and thought she did look a little flushed. "Do you feel bad, Whitney?"

The girl nodded. "I think I have the weasels."

"You mean the measles," Justin corrected automatically.

"Matthew has the weasels," Whitney added. "He had red spots all over his face and he had to go home from school early and missed being an Indian."

Justin's mother leaned over and placed her fingers on Whitney's forehead. "She feels like she has fever. Let me get the thermometer."

Three hours later, Justin sat in his own kitchen, eating a cold turkey sandwich. Whitney lay sleeping on the couch, a blanket tucked around her feverish form. Already tiny red blisters had popped out all over her body. Because it was a holiday, it had been difficult to get in touch with her doctor, but the final diagnosis wasn't measles, but chicken pox.

She stirred fitfully and Justin went over to check on her. It always terrified him whenever she was sick. No matter how much the doctor tried to assure him that she would be okay, Justin always feared the worst. Caroline had died from an illness from which people usually recovered.

Maybe he was overprotective of Whitney. But surely that was understandable. What would life be without her?

He walked across the room and picked up Caroline's photograph. She smiled back at him, so confident, so beautiful. Why had she fallen in love with him? What had she seen in him that no one else had?

They hadn't had that much in common. Their backgrounds, temperaments, interests and even their goals were different. But their relationship had worked because she loved him and he worshipped her. They could probably have gone through life quite well together.

The image of Allison lying in the leaves came unexpectedly to his thoughts. He could still hear the sound of her laughter. In one of the imponderables of life, he and Allison had had a lot of things in common, yet they hadn't made it through the winter.

He was glad things were over between them. He had so much more time for Whitney and for his work. His life had quickly fallen back into the old routine and that's how he liked it.

Then why was he so unhappy? He replaced Caroline's picture on the mantel and walked to the French door that led to the patio. Standing on the balcony, he leaned on the railing and looked out into the night. A full moon spread its light over the landscape, spotlighting the bare rocks on the mountainsides and polishing the surface of the lake to an ebony glow.

It was a beautiful view, but tonight it only served to remind him how lonely he was. A steady stream of traffic passed on the distant highway, people returning home after a day of celebrating Thanksgiving with their family and friends. Justin sighed. Even the traditional dinner at his parents' house had been flat. Had it always been so boring, just sitting around reading or sometimes watching a football game, then eating a big meal and going home?

Granted, Whitney's illness had cut short the afternoon. But, other than that, things had been pretty much the same as they had been since he was a child.

Once again the thought of Allison popped into his mind. She'd had her heart set on making dinner for him and Whitney. He knew he'd hurt her feelings by refusing her offer. But she should understand that families have traditions.

Actually, to be more accurate, his parents had traditions, Caroline's parents had traditions, and Justin had always followed along with their traditions without ever having to bother to make new ones for him and Whitney. Their only personal Sloane Rule was the chili-when-it-snowed rule.

When he considered it, he and Whitney weren't really a family of their own but an extension of the two sets of grandparents. Even when Caroline was alive, she and Justin had arranged their plans around those of their parents.

Was Allison so out of line for trying to create a family for them? He realized he knew nothing about Allison's family except that they lived in the East and that her brother had been wounded in Vietnam. For all he had seen of her relatives, she seemed to be totally alone.

He recognized in her the same lack of self-confidence that he'd had before Caroline's love convinced him he was a worthwhile, attractive human being. Just as Caroline had seen beneath his nerdy surface, he had seen beneath Allison's intellectual front to the sensitive, warm, beautiful person beneath.

Oddly enough, the kids were more perceptive than adults in this matter. It didn't take them long to see the real Miss Greene. Around them, she was wonderful—relaxed, firm yet compassionate, supportive, interesting—the consummate teacher. He had always admired the way she handled her students. And he couldn't help but notice that they adored her. He still heard Miss Greene's name from Whitney's lips at least a dozen times a day.

Allison had blossomed while they were dating. He wondered what sort of childhood she could have had that would leave her so vulnerable. Had no one ever told her how beautiful she was? Had no one ever told her they loved her?

It occurred to Justin that he hadn't, even though his feelings for her had been powerful ... feelings that even anger hadn't completely dissolved. Actually, anger was merely the surface response to a deeper emotion ... fear.

As much as he hated to admit it, Allison was right about several things. His and Whitney's lives had been very self-contained before his daughter started school. He'd enjoyed his role as Whitney's father, mother and best friend. Now she had new friends and interests. Then when Allison and Whitney grew so close, the teacher had also taken over the mother role.

Whitney was all he had. And as selfish as it seemed, Justin knew he was holding on so tightly because he simply couldn't stand the thought of losing her either physically or emotionally. As Miss Greene became more of a fixture in their everyday lives, Justin felt his influence on Whitney slip. No longer did the child automatically run to him when she had a question or a problem.

He walked back into the house, shivering as the chill of the evening penetrated through his clothes. He looked down at the stone-washed jeans and the pink shirt. Every time he wore them, he couldn't keep from thinking of that day they had all gone shopping. Usually he hated shopping, but he had enjoyed that trip. In fact, he'd enjoyed almost every moment he'd spent with Allison—except the last ten. But those were the ones that counted.

By Saturday, Whitney was feeling much better but looking much worse. No part of her body was spared from the

ugly red sores and it took constant baths in an oatmeal so-
lution followed by a layer of lotion to keep her from
scratching them. But she was well enough to be disappointed that she had to miss the whole week of school.

WHEN WHITNEY RETURNED from school on the following
Monday, her spirits were so low she went straight to her
room without stopping to chatter about the events of the day
as she usually did. Justin exchanged glances with his mother,
who had picked Whitney up, but the older woman lifted her
shoulders to say she had no idea what was wrong. After she
left, he followed his daughter and knocked on the door.

"Come in," she said unenthusiastically.

He walked in and looked down at Whitney, who was lying flat on her back on the bed, staring up at the ceiling.

"What's wrong, Whitney? Did you have a bad day?"

"Miss Greene is leaving," she stated, her chin quivering.

He was shocked. Of all the things he'd expected, that was
certainly not one of them. He felt an unexplained catch in
his chest as if his heart had suddenly stopped. "She's leaving? Why?"

"She was fired."

If he thought he was shocked before, now he was stunned.
"How do you know?"

He thought he detected a guilty look as she replied, "I
think it was probably the rabbits. The prince didn't like it
that they did it."

"The prince? Did it?" Justin frowned, trying to trans-
late. "Oh, you mean the principal. But what did the rabbits do?"

"*It,*" she repeated as if he were hard of hearing. "They
had sex while everyone was watching."

Justin felt the sudden need to sit down. "How did the rabbits happen to get together? I know Alli... Miss Greene is very careful to keep them apart."

Whitney shifted uncomfortably. "Uh... I suppose I sort of put them together."

With much prompting, the whole story finally spilled out. Justin gave her a long lecture and grounded her to her room for the rest of the day. He couldn't help thinking that interfering was a feminine trait of young and old alike. But as he was leaving, he was compelled to ask, "Do you know how much longer she'll be at school?"

"Miss Greene hasn't told us anything, but Meagan said her mommy said Miss Greene wouldn't be coming back to teach us after Christmas vacation."

"And Meagan's mother probably knows," Justin muttered.

"What can we do to get her to stay?" Whitney cried. "We don't want Miss Greene to leave us like Mommy did."

Justin started to protest that it wasn't the same thing, but he realized that, to Whitney, it was. She had never known her mother, but she did know Allison. And Allison's disappearance would hurt the child much more than her own mother's had. Whether he liked it or not, Miss Greene had become very important to his daughter.

For the first time, he saw that his decision to not date Allison anymore didn't just affect him. Equally surprising, he realized the thought of Allison disappearing forever from his life didn't hold the appeal he had thought it would. It made everything so final.

"No, we don't want to lose Miss Greene," he agreed. "I'll see what I can do."

He found out he couldn't do much. Miss Greene's days were indeed numbered. Apparently, a parent, who the principal insisted would remain nameless but whose identity Justin could easily guess, had filed an official complaint, and Mr. Gibson felt he could no longer ignore Miss Greene's incompetence.

Justin's hackles rose at the term "incompetence." As angry as he was with Allison, he knew that charge was absolutely unjustified. He had never known a person more qualified to teach. But even though he rose to her defense, Mr. Gibson was adamant. Justin followed up with a call to the school board, but they said they would back the decision of the principal.

When practice for the Christmas play began, Whitney had to stay after school every class day. Justin, whose feelings about Allison were still very confused, stayed away. Somehow every time he saw her, he thought less about how wrong she was for him and Whitney and more about how much he missed her.

It didn't help when he bumped into her at the grocery store. They both muttered a few awkward words of greeting, then hurried off in opposite directions. He wanted to ask her what she was going to do about a job, but he figured she'd interpret it to mean that he cared. Which he didn't.

So why did his throat tighten when he drove past her house and saw a For Sale sign in her yard? He knew how much she loved that old house. He, himself, had grown pretty attached to the place. He and Allison had made some pretty special memories there. And, of course, Whitney thought Miss Greene's house was some sort of enchanted cottage.

And it hadn't mattered at all when he saw her with another man at the Christmas Market. Every year the residents and merchants of Georgetown decorated their homes and stores with wreaths and garlands of evergreens. Capitalizing on the town's Victorian charm, they held a special event on the first two weekends of December with sleigh rides, choirs and other entertainment, food booths and a thirty-five-foot-tall Christmas tree downtown.

Usually Justin, like most of the locals, tried to avoid the downtown area during those days, because of all the traffic. But he had to go to the computer store for ribbons for his printer and didn't want to wait until Monday. As he made his way through the crowds on the sidewalk, he glanced up in time to see Allison standing outside a store with an attractive man with dark, curly hair. They were looking in the window and laughing. A wave of people passed in front of Justin and when the path cleared again, Allison and the man were gone.

Of course, he didn't care that she was dating someone else. It didn't bother him one bit that this man might be holding her in his arms and kissing those soft, delicious lips. Allison was a grown woman and she could do whatever she wanted. What he couldn't explain was why he hadn't been able to concentrate for the rest of the evening. Even Whitney had noticed his foul mood, accusing him of being cranky and threatening to ground him to his room.

As the day of the school play approached, Whitney became more and more depressed and Justin became increasingly edgy. It would be the last time either of them would ever see Miss Greene.

Chapter Sixteen

Allison moved among the kids, positioning them where they should be and prompting them on their lines. They were excited, bouncing around the stage behind the closed curtain as if they had swallowed a handful of pep pills. On the other side of the curtain was the noise of parents shuffling among the rows and sitting on the squeaky metal folding chairs.

"Miss Greene, will you still be here when our play is over?"

Allison looked down at Rosa's huge dark eyes. "Yes, I'll still be here," she assured her, and straightened the girl's halo. She was touched that Rosa should be more worried about Allison than the lines the girl was about to speak in the play. Allison had been working with Rosa to help her overcome her shyness. "Now go wait with the other angels. And remember, I'll be standing right offstage, sharing my courage with you. You're going to do just fine."

She wasn't sure how the children had heard about her firing. But within days after her third and final talk with Mr. Gibson, the word had spread all over the school. Her students had clung to her, begging her to stay, not understanding that it wasn't her decision to leave. Every day before leaving, they would solemnly ask if she would be back the

next day and she would assure them she would. But toda
when they asked her that same question after the play, he
answer would have to be different. She would have to te
them goodbye.

It was the last day before Christmas vacation. With th
play rehearsals and all the last-minute paperwork and les
son plans she had worked up for the teacher who would b
replacing her, Allison hadn't had time to start packing. A
least the people who had bought her house weren't requir
ing her to be out until the first of the year.

"Five minutes till show time." Chris brushed the jing
bell that hung from the end of her green hat out of her eye
"I'm glad Christmas isn't a month later or I wouldn't hav
fit into this elf costume."

Allison looked down at her own green-clad body an
groaned. "Whose idea was this, anyway?"

"Probably Mr. Gibson's," Chris snorted.

"And to think, I accused him of not having a sense c
humor."

Chris laughed. "Jared said to tell you thanks for goin
shopping with him last weekend. He hates to go alone."

"No problem. I enjoyed it. Besides, it gave me a chanc
to buy a few things for my parents so I won't have to worr
about that later."

Chris frowned. "I wish you weren't..." She didn't fir
ish the sentence, because they both knew it was somethin
they didn't want but couldn't change. "Oh, by the way, w
found a man to play Santa Claus."

"Great. What a bad time for Pete to come down with th
flu," Allison said. "At least he didn't get the chicken po
like half the school."

Mrs. Armstrong, the music teacher, started the tape re
corder, the opening notes of "Jingle Bells" marking the cu
for the play to begin. Allison did a last-minute check of he

students while the other teachers did the same, then stood on the edge of the stage, out of sight from the audience but where her students could see her.

There were the usual glitches with two of the trees getting into a scuffle and one of the angels' halos getting caught on a reindeer's antler. But those were the kinds of things that made the parents laugh and made them treasure their videotapes for years to come.

As the curtain went down and Santa Claus began circulating among the children in the audience, Mr. Gibson stood up and came onstage. Allison was off to the side, getting the stockings filled with treats she had prepared to give to her students. When Mr. Gibson took the microphone, she barely paid attention until she saw Whitney, Rosa, Meagan, Sean and all the other children in her class gather in a group and walk up to Mr. Gibson.

"Mr. Principal, sir, we want to talk to you," Whitney said, her solemn blue eyes looking up at the older man.

With a smile that said he thought she was about to give him a Christmas gift, he bent down and answered, "Of course, dear. What is your name?"

"My name's Whitney Sloane and I wanted to give you this." Instead of a wrapped package, she handed him a piece of paper. The other children in the group took other copies of the paper and began handing them out to the audience. As Rosa neared Allison, she smiled shyly and handed her a copy.

"Thank you, Rosa," Allison said. "What is this?"

"It was Whitney's idea. We want the school to let you stay."

Allison read the letter with everyone else, including Mr. Gibson. It looked as if it had been printed on a computer, and it was signed in large, crooked letters by everyone in her class.

Dear Mistr Prinsipol

plese do not fire Miss Green. She is a verey good teecher. We reely love her. If you let her stae here we promis to be good.

A murmur rose from the audience as everyone began commenting on the letter.

Looking flustered, Mr. Gibson straightened. "Everyone, please disregard this. We've had a little trouble with Miss Greene and that is why she'll be leaving us."

The murmuring grew louder until Santa Claus stepped forward.

"Mr. Gibson, we don't want to disregard this letter. We prefer to address this issue here and now."

Mr. Gibson peered over his glasses at the man with the fluffy white beard and well-padded red suit. "I beg your pardon, sir. What is your name?"

The man was grinning as he answered. "Ask anyone in this room. I'm Santa Claus."

Mr. Gibson's sputtering blasted through the microphone like machine-gun fire.

"I've checked my list and Miss Greene has been good all year," Santa continued. "I understand a few of her students did some mischievous things, but kids will be kids. Frankly, Mr. Gibson, if *I* can forgive them for their naughtiness, surely you can. And, of course, you shouldn't hold Miss Greene responsible for the active imagination of five-year-olds."

"But I...they...she..." Mr. Gibson was totally flustered.

"I'm sure these parents will agree with me that we can't afford to lose such a fine teacher as Miss Greene and that you should ask her to stay for as long as she wants. The kids do love her...and need her. Right?" He turned to the au-

dience, and they all stood to their feet and clapped their
agreement.

"But we got complaints about the rabbits," Mr. Gibson
said, looking out at Meagan's parents, who were the only
people still sitting.

"What better illustration of the Christmas story than for
those rabbits to create new life," Santa went on. "When the
kids return from their vacation, there will be baby bunnies
to watch and learn from. What those rabbits did was not
obscene, but an instinctive act of nature. Perhaps some of
the kids were a little young to learn about the physical act of
love. But it shouldn't be treated as if it were a dirty, dis-
gusting thing." Santa leveled a look across the room, directly at Miss Greene. "Love is a beautiful thing. It should
be cherished and nurtured. Sometimes people make mistakes and think other things are more important than love.
But when it comes right down to it, that's all that really
matters."

He turned back to Mr. Gibson. "And Mr. Wiggly Nose
and Snow White are obviously in love, so it was perfectly
natural for them to want to make babies. Now unless you
want your stocking filled with coal for the rest of your life,
you'll reconsider your decision about letting Miss Greene
go."

Mr. Gibson scanned the audience, apparently trying to
decide whether he should go with the majority or stick to his
decision. All of the children in the school had gathered
around Santa and were glaring at the principal as if he were
the Grinch. "Uh...Santa...it appears you've made a good
point," Mr. Gibson said, wisely choosing not to side against
Santa Claus, especially since he wanted to keep his job at the
elementary school and would be dealing with these kids and
their parents for years to come. Stiffly he looked at Miss

Greene and said, "Miss Greene, would you like to retain your job?"

At her enthusiastic nod, he added, "Then consider this an offer for you to rejoin our staff."

"Say please," Santa prompted.

"What?" Mr. Gibson gasped.

"Mr. Gibson, you should be a good example for these wonderful kids and show them that it's nice to be polite."

Mr. Gibson gritted his teeth. "Please," he grunted.

"And I'm sure you'd like to include a raise with Miss Greene's new five-year contract, wouldn't you?" Santa suggested.

"Look, Santa, don't press your luck," Mr. Gibson growled. But at the shocked expressions on the students' faces, he conceded. "I suppose a small raise and a three-year contract isn't out of the question."

"Thank you," Santa said politely. "Now, remember, boys and girls, you promised to be good." He waved. "See you all on Christmas Eve. Don't forget the cookies and milk. Ho! Ho! Ho!" he exclaimed as he left the room.

The parents were smiling at the impromptu show as they gathered their children and followed Santa out the door.

Allison, still shocked at the unexpected turn of events, quickly passed out her treats and wished her students a Merry Christmas. She then escorted to the bus the children whose parents hadn't been able to come to the play. When she returned to her classroom, she was still musing over how Santa Claus had come to her rescue.

Slipping her glasses on, she shuffled through the pile of Christmas gifts and cards that had been given to her by her students. They were the usual—cut-glass vases, apple-shaped plaques, ceramic animals, especially rabbits, and other inexpensive gifts that would catch a child's fancy.

A knock on the door made her look up.

"Ho! Ho! Ho! Do you have a few minutes to talk to Santa?" he asked, hesitating in the doorway.

"Sure, come on in." She stood and walked toward him, her hand outstretched. "I wanted to thank you for what you did, Mr...?"

"Claus," he supplied, his blue eyes twinkling. He reached into one of his deep pockets and pulled out a small wrapped gift. "Here, I found this in my sleigh. It has your name on it."

Allison blinked in surprise, but she took the gift from his outstretched glove-covered hand. "Do I open it now or wait until Christmas?"

"Now."

She carefully removed the bow and tried to get the paper off in one piece. She had never been a paper ripper like her brother, who could open all his gifts in half the time it took her. It looked very much like a box jewelry came in and, still expecting some sort of joke, she gingerly lifted the top.

"Oh, my gosh. It's an engagement ring!" she exclaimed.

Santa dropped down on one knee in front of her. "Allison," he stated, shifting to a serious tone, "I'm sorry for being such a jerk. It took me almost losing you to realize how much I love you. Can you ever forgive me? And if you can forgive me, will you marry me?"

"Justin?" Her expression was incredulous. Under the makeup and the padding, she honestly hadn't recognized him.

"Who else were you expecting?" he asked, his voice a little perturbed that she had to ask. After all, how many men were there who might be proposing to her?

She took his gloved hand in hers. "Of course, I forgive you. I'm sorry, too. I shouldn't have been so presumptuous with Whitney. She's your daughter and I won't interfere in how you choose to raise her."

"No, I've been thinking about what you said, and yo
were right. I *have* been overprotective of Whitney. I wa
your help. Whitney needs a mother."

"Are you saying you're marrying me just to give Whi
ney a mother?"

Santa reached out and gathered Allison into his arms a
he stood up. "No, that's merely a fringe benefit. I'm ask
ing you to marry me because I love you and have realized
don't want to live without you."

"In that case, then, how could I say no? I sure wouldn
want my stocking filled with coal for the rest of my life."

"No chance of that," he murmured as he leaned towar
her. "You've been a *very* good girl, and Santa plans t
spend all of Christmas Eve at your house."

"Oh, no!" Her eyes widened as she suddenly remem
bered the contract on her house. "My house has been sold
I've got to move before January 1."

"Oh, I just happen to know the new owners, and if w
can arrange a marriage between now and January 1, yo
won't have to leave . . . Whitney and I will just move in."

"You bought my house?" She was completely flabber
gasted. "That's why the real estate agent wouldn't tell m
who was the purchaser. I was surprised at how fast the hous
sold the way the market is right now." She looked at hi
with suspicious eyes. "So you had this all planned."

"Whitney and I had to do something to keep you fro
leaving. It was her idea to write the letter and I ran off th
copies. Then the rest of the class volunteered to hand the
out. We figured we had to get your job back first, espe
cially since Whitney was more than a little responsible fo
you losing it."

"What would you have done if Mr. Gibson hadn't give
me my job back?"

"I'd have parked my reindeer in his front yard and let them poop on his porch."

"And what if I hadn't accepted your proposal?"

"I'd have moved in, anyway. Sooner or later you'd get embarrassed by having to share a bed and a shower with me and you'd have to give in."

Allison swallowed around the lump in her throat. "Whose picture will be on our mantel?" she asked, knowing she couldn't bear having Caroline in her house.

Justin didn't pretend to misunderstand. "I've packed Caroline's things away in case Whitney ever wants to see them. But Caroline's part of my past and you're my future. There'll be no ghosts in our marriage...unless that old house has some of its own."

"You're pretty sure of yourself, aren't you?" she teased after breathing a sigh of pure joy.

"Of course, I am. I'm the most beloved man in the whole world."

"You are while you're dressed in that red suit," she pointed out. "But what about when you take it off?"

He chuckled and his fluffy cotton eyebrows lifted roguishly. "That's all you think about...taking my clothes off. But don't get me wrong. I like that in a woman. Now, take off your glasses and kiss me."

"I've never kissed Santa Claus before. Does your beard tickle?"

"I've never kissed Santa Claus either, so I don't know. Kiss me and see."

"Does this mean I'm going to get a baby sister for Christmas?" a happy voice asked.

Allison and Justin turned toward the door, where Whitney was peering around the frame.

"Not this year, Whitney," Justin answered. "But I would say a baby by next Christmas isn't out of the question.

However, you're going to have to start knocking before you enter a room, *and* you're going to start making friends and spending nights at their houses every once in a while. Miss Greene and I have a lot of things to *discuss*. . . alone.''

Whitney nodded. ''Can I be your best woman?''

Allison and Justin exchanged a puzzled look. ''You mean my maid of honor?'' Allison asked.

Whitney walked into the room and stopped next to them. ''Yes, can I come to your wedding and be your maid of honor?''

Justin reached down and gathered her into one arm while he kept the other arm wrapped around Allison. ''Yes, Whitney, you can come to our wedding. Now that we're a real family, we're going to go everywhere together.''

''Everywhere?'' Allison asked.

Justin leaned over and gave Allison a belated kiss. ''Everywhere *except* on our honeymoon. How do you feel about Hawaii?''

''It sounds wonderful. And I just happen to have a couple of weeks off.''

''Hey,'' Whitney stated with a big smile, ''does that mean that when school starts again we'll have to call you Miss Sloane?''

Allison looked at Justin and saw the love and laughter in his eyes that she so longed to see. She had no doubt there would be a few bumps on their road to happily ever after, but it would be worth the trip. ''It will be *Mrs.* Sloane,'' she confirmed, correcting the title.

Justin hugged her closer and leaned down so only Allison could hear. ''And every day for the rest of our lives, you'll wake up in my arms so I can say, 'Good morning, Mrs. Sloane.' ''

''And you didn't believe in fairy tales,'' she scoffed, so happy she thought she must be dreaming.

"What more could you want, but your very own Prince Charming and your very own dragon?" he asked, nuzzling his beard-covered cheek against her head.

"Nothing. I couldn't ask for anything more," she murmured, "except maybe a baby dragon."

"Then we'd better get started with those wedding plans," Justin declared. "Let's go home. We have a happy ending to make."

HARLEQUIN
PROUDLY PRESENTS
A DAZZLING NEW CONCEPT IN ROMANCE FICTION

One small town—twelve terrific love stories

Welcome to Tyler, Wisconsin—a town full of people
you'll enjoy getting to know, memorable friends and
unforgettable lovers, and a long-buried secret that
lurks beneath its serene surface....

JOIN US FOR A YEAR IN THE LIFE OF TYLER

Each book set in Tyler is a self-contained love story;
together, the twelve novels stitch the fabric of a
community.

LOSE YOUR HEART TO TYLER!

The excitement begins in March 1992, with
WHIRLWIND, by Nancy Martin. When lively, brash
Liza Baron arrives home unexpectedly, she moves
into the old family lodge, where the silent and
mysterious Cliff Forrester has been living in seclusion
for years....

WATCH FOR ALL TWELVE BOOKS
OF THE TYLER SERIES
Available wherever Harlequin books are sold